Under an English Heaven
(An Ellie Kent Mystery)

by

Alice K. Boatwright

For information, email **Cozy Cat Press**, cozycatpress@aol.com or visit our website at: www.cozycatpress.com

COZY CAT
PRESS

ISBN: 978-1-939816-36-8

Printed in the United States of America

Cover design by Keri Knutson
http://www.alchemybookcovers.com/

1 2 3 4 5 6 7 8 9 10

For Jim Mullins, with love

Acknowledgements

My love affair with England goes back to my early childhood, so it would be impossible to name all the people and writers who inspired this book. I will settle for naming two: my father, Howard Boatwright, and my husband, Jim Mullins. I would also like to thank those who read drafts and encouraged me: Janet Basu, Kathy Chetkovich, Martha Conway, Michelle Dionetti, Marianne Faithfull, Mark Fishman, Marion Gibbons, Seamus O'Connor, Carol Sanford, and Victoria Schultz. Very special thanks also go to my editorial advisors: Ann Mansbridge, Rev. John Dane, and Jennifer Noon Hess.

Alice K. Boatwright
Paris, February 2014

Sunday, October 30

Chapter 1

"No matter what I wear, I'll never be Mrs. Vicar in Little Beecham," said Ellie Kent, as she wriggled the skirt of her new tweed suit down onto her hips. "People here will always think of me as the young wife who snared you on that unfortunate sabbatical in California."

Graham Kent lay propped against the pillows on their brass bed, with one long ropy arm flung behind his head. His gingery hair was tousled, and his eyebrows were twisted into wild curlicues that suggested he had spent an active night.

"You look happy," said Ellie, pulling up her skirt to show him a bit of nyloned thigh. "Is this how the English cleric gets off? Watching his lady put on her tweeds?"

He laughed his unexpectedly warm hearty laugh. "It is. And you vastly underestimate your powers, Mrs. Kent. I'm sure everyone will come to love you."

"But you're paid to be an optimist, and I'm not," she said, as she put on the suit jacket and studied herself in the mirror over the dressing table. The color of the tweed picked up her gray-blue eyes, but they looked back at her now, alarmed by the unfamiliar person who appeared in the glass. The Ellie they knew wore black and more black, and then to relax, jeans. In search of her former self, she ruffled up her short dark hair.

"Come here," said Graham, reaching out for her.

"I can't. I'm late for church."

"No, you're not, and no one knows better than I do how long takes to get there."

"All right," she said, going to the bed. She perched herself on the edge, but Graham pulled her down beside him so their faces were close.

"Listen. I'm not denying that people will take time to adjust, but what kind of example would I be if I couldn't show them that renewal in life is possible, as well as life after death?"

Ellie smiled. He looked so vulnerable and wise, a combination she found utterly irresistible. "Not the one I married," she said, giving him a long kiss.

From the church next door, they could hear the first bells begin to ring: Ding, dong, ding-ity, dong, ding, dong, ding, dong, ding-ity, dong.

Ellie pulled herself out of his embrace, stood up and straightened her clothes. "You now have exactly twenty minutes to shower, dress, and get to church."

"Watch me work a miracle," he said, as he threw off the covers and disappeared, naked, into the bathroom.

A few minutes later, when he came down to the Vicarage's stone-floored kitchen, his hair was damp from the shower, but he had been transformed from Ellie's Graham into that other person, the man in Holy Orders, a black-robed priest.

"Drink this," said Ellie, handing him a mug of sweet milky tea and a piece of toast smeared with Marmite. His favorite—and to her, uneatable—breakfast. "My reputation really will be ruined if you collapse from fatigue and hunger during the service."

"I promise I won't," he said, alternately taking bites of toast and swallows of tea, as he pulled on his overcoat. "By the way, I have a present for you." He took a red paper poppy out of his pocket and pinned it to the lapel of Ellie's coat.

"What's this for?" she asked, angling her head so she could see the little flower.

"Remembrance Day. It's like your Veterans' Day."

"I thought we were celebrating saints and souls this week."

"We are, but every proper English person wears a poppy in the run-up to Remembrance Day."

"You think this will persuade anyone that I'm a proper English person?"

"It will help."

"'If ye break faith with us who die, we shall not sleep, though poppies grow in Flanders fields',"she intoned, quoting the famous World War I poem.

"Exactly." He glanced at his watch. "Now we really do have to go."

The second round of bells had begun. Ding, ding ding-ity, dong, dong, dong, dingity-dong.

He opened the back door, snapped open a large umbrella to protect them from the pelting rain, and, arm in arm, they hurried down the pebbled path from the Vicarage through the graveyard to the church.

Ellie Kent had never met a vicar's wife in person before she moved to England, but she knew plenty of them from her years of teaching literature. This was the destiny of Eleanor, the "Sense" of *Sense and Sensibility*; the fate of the pragmatic spinster Charlotte in *Pride and Prejudice*; the doom of Charlotte Brontë, who damped her outspoken writer self to fit the needs of her curate husband and died soon thereafter.

Times had changed though, hadn't they? Surely, they must have.

She braced herself with that thought as she said goodbye to Graham in the vestry and entered the church, where Mr. Dunn, the volunteer organist, launched into his prelude with a clumsy flourish.

The church was only sparsely filled, with people sitting in ones and twos, bundled up in heavy coats dotted with paper poppies. A damp chill pervaded the stone building, and Ellie was glad of her warm tweed suit as she slipped quickly into a pew. A moment later, Graham entered the chancel in his full vestments to open the service. Mr. Dunn played the intro to the first hymn, and everyone stood to sing in wavering voices "For all the saints, who from their labors rest."

"Bring the body and the mind will follow," Graham had said when he explained the rituals of the Church of England, and Ellie hoped he was right. So far she still found it tricky to remember when to sit, stand, and kneel and how to navigate the various books, especially since she imagined the eyes of the congregation's white-haired ladies and pink-cheeked gentlemen were on her every moment, watching for mistakes. She hadn't even begun to tackle her theological doubts.

Nevertheless she had already come to love St. Michael and All Angels—a small stone church with an imposing air and a square Norman tower dating back 800 years. Sitting quietly under its vaulted roof, she felt both timelessness and the passage of those centuries.

While the prayers and readings droned on around her, she contemplated the faint traces of medieval decorative painting, the carved angels on the stone pillars that had been beheaded during the Reformation, and the Victorian stained glass windows depicting the life of Christ.

The lone contemporary feature was a stained glass window dedicated to Henry and George Rutherford, local men who had died during World War II. In vivid colors and sharp angular shapes it depicted them clutching the Union Jack as the light of God illuminated their path to heaven. "We will never forget them," it said, and every week, their sister, who still lived in the village, proved it by placing a posy of fresh flowers on the windowsill.

But the memorial that most often drew Ellie's gaze was one that a casual visitor would not even notice. It was a small bronze plaque that read: "In memory of Louise Greenhall Kent, Beloved wife of Graham and mother of Isabelle, Faithful and loved servant of this parish." In case she ever happened to forget that there had been another Mrs. Kent before her, it was always there to remind her. She found it hard to imagine that any such plaque would ever be mounted in her memory, but maybe, as Graham suggested, she underestimated her gifts.

When he stepped up to the pulpit, she turned her attention to what he had to say about the commitment and sacrifices of the Christian saints. Personally, she had no interest in achieving sainthood, or anything like it, but if there were a God, she hoped he would help her find a way to be herself and succeed in her new life too.

Chapter 2

She soon found out what a challenge succeeding as a vicar's wife might be.

"Mrs. Kent, a word, if you will," Ellie heard a voice say, as she stood in line for a cup of tea. The service was over, but it was the custom for everyone to gather at the back of the church for refreshments. She turned to face the daunting figure of Mrs. Emily Rutherford Hughes, window donor, posy maker, and last survivor of what had once been Little Beecham's leading family.

Ellie was tall, but Mrs. Rutherford Hughes was taller, and the charcoal-grey suit she wore accentuated her bony severity. Her hawk-like expression looked like it had been honed by generations of making a meal of others, and at the moment her pale eyes were fixed on Ellie, who unconsciously straightened up and greeted her with what she hoped was a confident smile.

"I'm forming up the committee for the Christmas coffee morning," announced Mrs. Rutherford Hughes, "and I think it's a good opportunity for you to begin learning how we do things here."

"OK, that sounds great," said Ellie, suddenly hyperconscious of her American accent and way of speaking. "I've really been looking forward to getting involved in church activities," she added.

"Have you?" said the older woman, her voice heavy with what? Doubt? Disbelief? Disdain? Ellie was impressed by how much subtext she could squeeze into two short syllables. "That's settled then. The first meeting will be at Castor House on Friday at two," but she turned and left before Ellie could even ask where Castor House was.

"Tea or coffee, Mrs. Kent?" asked Miss Priscilla Worthy, who was serving that morning. She was a plump little woman who looked like a fluffy bird with her cap of white hair, bright dark eyes, and layers of grey sweaters.

"Thank you, Miss Worthy. Tea, please, with milk and no sugar."

"I didn't mean to eavesdrop," said Miss Worthy, as she handed her a cup of tea that steamed in the chilly air, "but I couldn't avoid overhearing that you're going to help us with the coffee morning."

Ellie nodded and took a thick finger of homemade shortbread.

"That's brilliant, because, to be honest, we've made rather a hash of it since Emily took over. Those of us who've lived here forever are used to her ways, but the younger people won't be bothered."

"She is rude, isn't she," said Ellie, who quickly realized from Miss Worthy's expression that there were limits governing 'to be honest.' "I'm happy to help, of course," she continued quickly, "but I really have no idea what it's all about. Other than the obvious. Coffee and morning."

"Oh, it's much more than that. Everyone contributes home produce like jams and marmalade, and there's a tombola, and lovely biscuits and cakes. At least, that's the way it used to be when..." Miss Worthy's cheeks pinkened. "Well, that is, when the first Mrs. Kent ran it. She was a marvelous baker and wonderful at so many other things too."

Ah. Ellie hoped her dismay at this news did not show. She hadn't baked a cake since she was nine years old and turned a Duncan Hines mix into a flat chocolate cinder because she was reading *David Copperfield* and forgot the thing was in the oven.

"What are you saying about the coffee morning?" asked Mrs. Bell, a petite, elderly woman dressed in an immaculate cream-colored suit. She held her heavy porcelain teacup as if it were fine bone china.

"I'm afraid I've been prattling on about what a nice event it was when Louise ran it."

Mrs. Bell sipped her tea and regarded Ellie as if she were the wolf in sheep's clothing. "It's true. Louise had a real gift for bringing the community together."

"That's right," said Miss Worthy. "People would do anything for Louise."

"Not quite anything," announced Mrs. Geraldine Bigelow, as she scooped up the last two shortbreads. "She asked me a number of times to do a benefit concert for the church, and I'm afraid I had to say no."

They all stared at her. A large pillar of a woman with purple hennaed hair, Geraldine Bigelow claimed to be a retired opera singer, but Ellie had already discovered that these days she made a full-time job of looking out the windows of her house, which was, unfortunately, directly across from the Vicarage.

"I thought her true gift was in gaining people's confidence. I'd even venture to say that her influence was rather too much for the vicar at times," she went on.

"What *can* you mean by that?" asked Mrs. Bell with a frown.

"One flock with two shepherds? It's not a strategy for success."

"But everyone loves Graham. He's done a brilliant job all these years," said Miss Worthy.

"Nevertheless, Louise was the one to go to if you had something to confess, and I'm sure it became quite a burden for her."

"Nonsense. I don't know where you ever got such an idea," said Mrs. Bell.

"I never felt Louise was burdened," said Miss Worthy. "I thought she thoroughly enjoyed her life. That's what made it so terrible. When she died so suddenly."

Ellie coughed as her tea went down the wrong way.

"For heaven's sake, Priscilla." Mrs. Bell set her teacup down with a clatter, and Mrs. Bigelow looked thoroughly pleased by the dust up she'd created. "I hope you'll forgive us, Mrs. Kent, but it's true that Louise's death was a huge loss for the whole parish, and it would be a disservice to you if you were not aware of that."

"But that's why we're so glad you've come," said Miss Worthy anxiously. "We've had such a need for a fresh face in our midst."

"Indeed. I'm sure we all agree," said Mrs. Bell, smiling thinly. "Until Friday then."

"What's on Friday?" asked Mrs. Bigelow, but no one replied.

Chapter 3

That afternoon, after Sunday lunch, Ellie and Graham ensconced themselves by the fire in what she called the living room, and he called the sitting room. It was a comfortable room at the back of the sprawling Georgian vicarage, separate from the study/sitting room where Graham worked and met with parishioners. This was a family room with comfortable old furniture, and the bookcases were crammed with everything from children's books, photo albums, and jigsaw puzzles to Graham's complete set of the 47 novels of Anthony Trollope.

Ellie had taken off her tweeds and put on jeans, an Irish sweater, and slippers. She lay on the sofa while Graham took his leather armchair near the fire. The thick Saturday and Sunday newspapers were scattered across the floor between them like shed clothing; and Hector, Graham's rough-coated Jack Russell terrier, lay on his back on the hearth, snorting with pleasure in his sleep. The rain continued to clatter against the windows.

Ellie set down the book section after reading the review of yet another book questioning the identity of Shakespeare and said, "You know what? I said a prayer today, and it has already been answered."

"Really?" Graham glanced up from the crossword puzzle that he was filling in with a pen. "It's nice when it happens that way, isn't it."

"You mean it's no guarantee that I've tapped into a direct line."

"Unfortunately not."

"Aren't you going to ask me what I prayed about?"

"No, but you can tell me if you want to."

"I do. It happened at church. I was wondering about what contribution I will ever be able to make here and not ten minutes later Mrs. Rutherford Hughes asked me to join a committee. For the Christmas coffee morning."

Graham looked at her over his tortoiseshell glasses and smiled. "I see. And you are already sensing that this is a mixed blessing?"

"Exactly." Ellie got up from the sofa and squeezed in next to him in his chair.

"Not quite like developing a new course on Jane Austen, is it?" he said, putting his arm around her.

"No." She rested her chin on his shoulder. "In fact, I think I might have to bake a cake that everyone will judge, which is a horrible prospect to contemplate."

"Isabelle could help with that bit. She loves to bake, and I'm sure she'd welcome the excuse to come down from Cambridge."

"Hmm. That would be fun." Ellie fell silent. She was not sure that baking with her new stepdaughter would be any less stressful than displaying the results at the coffee morning.

"Is there something else?" he asked, edging over to make more room for her.

She hesitated, then said, "Yes. I know it's bound to happen, but at tea everyone was talking about Louise. How great she was at everything, and how much they missed her."

"I'm surprised they would be so tactless."

Ellie shrugged. "I don't think it was meant that way. One thing just led to another. But I was taken aback by their saying how sudden her death was. I thought she died in the hospital."

Graham took off his glasses and rubbed his eyes until his eyebrows stood up like exclamation points. Ellie shifted in the chair to get a better view of his face.

"Is this a bad topic to bring up?" she asked.

"No, not at all. It's my fault really. I should have told you more, but, when we met, I was trying to move on a bit. Not dwell on it."

"So what did happen?"

"She had a cyst on her ovaries, and we were assured that removing it would be one of those totally 'safe' operations.

In fact, the surgery went off very well, but she developed an infection. A high fever they couldn't seem to control. And then, without any warning at all, her heart stopped." As he spoke, Ellie could see shadows of loss cross his face.

"Just like that?"

"Just like that. She died, and our whole life ended, as if in mid-sentence."

"And they never explained why?"

He looked away through the window, as if the answer could be found among the gravestones. "They told us it happens sometimes. Not that more of an explanation would have altered the facts."

"Of course not. But, I mean, wasn't there a post-mortem?"

Graham shook his head. "No, I wouldn't allow it. It was enough to deal with the fact that she was gone."

"Oh," said Ellie, surprised. "I guess it's just that in my family we are great ones for knowing why. About anything and everything. That's always the question."

"In my line of work that's exactly the question that gets you nowhere. Anyway, it was quite a shock for the whole parish. You'd think I at least would be used to the fact that people die in every kind of unexpected way, but I was utterly unprepared for it in my own case, and that made it all the more shattering. I'm afraid I wasn't much help to Isabelle or anyone else during that time."

"You carried on though. Isn't that the most anyone can expect?"

"Form without substance?"

"You told me yourself that sometimes we all have to go with that."

"Did I? Well, then it must be right," he said with a wan smile.

After that, for a time, the only sounds were the rain and the soft crumbling of the logs on the fire as they settled into ash. Then Graham began to unravel himself from Ellie's embrace.

"You know I promised to visit Jim Finch this afternoon. Do you want to advance your new program of good works by coming along?"

Jim Finch and his wife Gladys did the gardening and cleaning for the Vicarage, church, and cemetery and seemed to Ellie to be continually competing for the title of curmudgeon of the week. A week ago, Jim had fallen off the back of his lorry and sprained his ankle.

Ellie gave him a wry smile. "If it's all the same to you, getting along with Gladys Finch three days a week is about all the goodness I can muster." From the window, she could see that the rain had slowed to a drizzle and patches of blue sky were beginning to appear among the billowing grey clouds. "I'd rather take Hector for a walk while it's not raining."

Hector's legs quivered slightly at the word "walk," but he didn't open his eyes. Ellie got up and gave him a gentle poke with her toe. "Up and at 'em," she said.

Chapter 4

When Graham left to visit the Finches, Ellie set off too, following a route that he had shown her on the ordnance survey map. She was just beginning to learn her way around the network of footpaths and bridleways that threaded across the countryside around the village, but Graham assured her that she couldn't get lost with Hector. He always knew the way home.

The dog raced ahead of her as Ellie walked briskly down the high street of the village. In Little Beecham, the Vicarage, church, and cemetery were at one end and the village school and library at the other, as if the community were book-ended by religion and education. In between, the high street was lined with buildings constructed from the local honey-colored limestone and boasted a village store, a few shops and a pub called The Three Lambs. On each side, narrow lanes of stone cottages jutted off the high street then gave way to countryside.

Compared to city life, the quiet of a Sunday afternoon surprised her. They didn't meet a soul in the village, and not even a car went by as they followed the single-track road past brown fields and bright green pastures where sheep grazed. Brilliantly colored berries and rosehips dotted the hedgerows and shrubbery, while, along the horizon, the leaves wove a tweedy pattern of brown and orange.

Released from his thralldom to the fire, Hector darted from side to side following the scents of rabbits and pheasants and a host of other delicious things. After about a quarter of a mile, Ellie left the road and climbed over a stile to pick up a footpath that wound through a dense wood and then along the edge of fields. When they arrived at a high point, she perched on a stone wall to admire the view across a checkerboard of fields, hedges, walls, and distant villages, while Hector continued his explorations.

This was the idyllic England she had imagined herself fitting into with ease, but, as she drank in the sweet air and peaceful atmosphere, she wondered if that would ever be true.

Not that anything had happened to make her doubt the connection she felt with Graham. That had been instant and unreserved since the day they met at her parents' home in Berkeley when he was on sabbatical. They had first become friends, then lovers, so when he proposed that she come back to England with him as his wife, she had been happy to accept. And why wouldn't she be?

But since she'd arrived, she'd begun to realize that she had underestimated the task she'd set herself. She and Graham on their own were one thing. Now she was married, and not only to the man, but also to his daughter and his dog, his house, his church, his parish, and his country. And, as if that weren't enough to take on, she was also becoming aware that she had an unreachable, irreproachable rival, the very thought of whom still affected so many people so strongly: the beautiful, understanding, and oh-so-English Louise.

Ellie did not like or approve of the part of herself that could feel jealous of Louise, whose death had brought her a new love and a new life. The problem was she couldn't figure out what she should feel: Gratitude? Pity? Kinship? None of them seemed quite right either.

Restlessly she got up and called to Hector, who immediately came running as if he really were her dog and stood at her feet, panting. When she squatted down to pet him, he licked her cheek vigorously with his soft, warm tongue, and suddenly what had seemed impossible a moment ago seemed possibly possible, and she gave the dog a hug. As they set off again together, she decided that whatever was ahead, she had a man and a dog on her side, and that was good enough for now.

Graham had told her that if they followed the ridge she'd be able to see the ruins of Beech Hall, the Rutherford family's Tudor manor house. She knew the house had burned in the 1930s, but when she saw the crumbled walls and chimneys surrounded by overgrown trees and barely discernible gardens, she was struck by how fresh the feeling of catastrophe remained.

She was also surprised that one wing appeared more or less intact. For a moment, the setting sun flashed on fragments of window turning them gold, as if life were still going on there: Tea about to be laid before the fire, and lamps lit in the many beautifully appointed rooms. She wondered if the haughty Emily Rutherford Hughes ever stood here longing to catch this illusory glimpse of her family's glorious past. But then the sun shifted, and the ruins blackened—dust to dust—and the dimming light reminded Ellie that she and Hector had better start for home.

When they re-entered the woods, the darkness thickened, and she wished she'd had the foresight to bring a flashlight. The bridleway was wide enough for a horse, so it was easy enough to follow Hector, who trotted ahead like a small white beacon. But when bridleway became a footpath, it was just that—in some places little more than a gap in dense shrubbery that clawed at her clothes—and the dog kept disappearing from view. Graham had said he wouldn't run off, but he was a dog after all.

She hurried after him on what she thought was the path until she found herself at a dead end. That is, a point at which she had to face the fact that she was completely surrounded by trees and bushes, and there was no path in front of her. No dog either.

She looked uncertainly back the way she thought she'd come. Shadows were filling the gaps quickly, and she was about to call for Hector to come and rescue her, when she heard someone—or something coming. Not, she hoped, a wild boar or some other denizen of the English woods.

She was relieved when a tall man with a backpack came into view, not only because he was human, but also because she could see that the path she'd been looking for was only a few feet away from where she stood.

She waited unmoving in the shrubbery—hoping not to be seen herself—but the man stopped directly opposite her. His thick white hair and beard glimmered in the fading light as he turned and gazed at her.

His expression was like that of a hunter who has sighted his prey, not like a neighbor meeting another on a walk. Ellie froze and didn't even think of smiling or saying hello, though he seemed to be taking in every detail about her. And no doubt understood exactly why she was standing there in the bushes. Before she could think what to do, he turned and disappeared into the darkness.

He was no sooner out of sight, when Hector trotted back into view with an expression on his face that suggested he could not imagine why she was taking so long to follow him when there was supper at home ahead.

Ellie clambered through the bushes to the path and put on the dog's leash to avoid any more separations. She felt relieved when they reached the fields where the sky offered more light—and gladder still when she spotted the lamp-lit cottages of Little Beecham ahead.

"Did you and Hector have a good walk?" asked Graham, as they sat down to the meal he called supper in the kitchen warmed by the red enameled cast-iron Aga stove. They were eating sandwiches made from leftover Sunday lamb at the long pine table that doubled as a worktop. Hector, sat by their feet, watching their every move in hopes of a falling tidbit.

"We did. He smelled everything and I looked at everything." Ellie had no intention of mentioning that she'd also gotten lost in the woods. "How was Jim Finch?"

"He was having a fit about not being able to patrol the churchyard enough tomorrow night."

"Why would he want to do that?"

"Last year some kids made a dreadful mess tagging the gravestones, and he's certain that, without him there, all hell will break loose."

"Really?" She slipped Hector a piece of lamb, which he gobbled up in a flash. "That sounds positively Biblical. I can hardly wait."

Monday, October 31 (Halloween)

Chapter 5

The next day Graham had a diocesan meeting in Oxford and needed to leave right after breakfast. When they had kissed goodbye and Ellie and Hector had returned from escorting him to the door, the click of the dog's claws on the stone kitchen floor made the house feel even emptier.

Ellie had a momentary pang for her life in San Francisco, when she had her own reasons to rush out the door, but back then, she'd longed for freedom—a change from the endless round of classes and papers to grade and the nitpicking politics of academia.

"Be careful what you want, because you'll get it," her mother used to warn when she was young, and Ellie had always been quick to retort, "Try me!"

Now as she made herself a mug of chamomile tea with honey and watched the wind whip the trees from side to side, she decided it was actually great not to have to go out. In fact, it was a perfect day for writing—something she always claimed she'd spend more time on if she had the chance—and here it was, so she should get on with it.

But, up in the small study she had created in a room under the eaves, she spent the entire morning alternately watching leaves spiral off the trees and aimlessly deleting words from an unfinished paper on the role of gossip in Jane Austen's novels—and then adding them back in again. Her brain wouldn't produce a single complete sentence, so she finally shut down her computer.

She didn't know what was the matter with her until she came downstairs and heard Mrs. Finch running the vacuum in Graham's study. The machine's contented humming grated against her nerves and brought to the surface images of cakes and puddings and jellies and the smiling faces of the kind of woman she couldn't and wouldn't ever be. Nothing in her marriage vows had mentioned baking!

With no car, her options were limited, but she decided she had to get out of the house immediately, regardless of the weather. She had some books to return to the library, so she ran back upstairs to get them, and slipped out.

The rain-drenched high street was deserted, although the shops were open, their windows lit against the gloom. Cold rain bit her cheeks and burrowed through any gaps in her raincoat, but she didn't mind. It was distracting. Cathartic.

The Little Beecham Library was on the ground floor of an old stone house and boasted four rooms crammed with well-thumbed books. Ellie inhaled the familiar dusty smell of books with pleasure and shook off her wet raincoat.

Charlotte Worthy, the great-niece of Priscilla Worthy, sat at the main desk so engrossed in reading that she didn't hear Ellie come in.

"Hi, Charlotte," said Ellie, setting down her bag on the desk.

The girl looked up and closed her book, which showed a buxom, scantily dressed young woman on the steps of a manor house, gazing up at a sky full of German bombers. Charlotte herself might have been pretty, but at 16 she'd already had a baby and now buried her English rose looks in a mish-mash of Oxfam clothes.

Blinking as she returned to the present, she said: "Hullo, Mrs. Kent. I didn't think anyone would come in today. It's so beastly out."

"It is, but maybe that's a good thing. Maybe it will keep the troublemakers home tonight."

"No chance," said Charlotte sourly, as she began checking in Ellie's books.

"Really? At home, Halloween is such a nice tradition."

"I thought it was just about sweets."

Ellie laughed. "It is that, but there's also jack-o-lanterns and costumes, ghosts and witches...people have a great time."

Charlotte shrugged. "My nan used to say a tradition's worth naught, if it's just for a laugh."

"Did she believe in Halloween?"

"She did. She believed the dead come back, and she would never let me go out of the house."

"Well, I don't believe in ghosts, but I do believe in celebrating Halloween. Does that count?"

"I guess. I mean, it's like what Ramona Blaisdell-Scott always says, isn't it? 'Do what you believe in. Believe in what you do.'"

"Right. So who's this Ramona Blaisdell-Scott anyway?" Ellie asked, tapping the gold-embossed name on the book Charlotte had been reading. *Love and Desertion.*

"No one knows," said the girl, as she reached behind her for some books on literary criticism that Ellie had requested from the Oxfordshire library service. "Her true identity is a secret, for all she's so famous."

"Lots of women writers have done that. Did you know? It wasn't safe for them otherwise."

Charlotte looked astonished, so apparently this information about some of England's most renowned authors had never reached her.

Hit and run, thought Ellie, as she began putting the new books into her plastic bag. It was sometimes a very good teaching technique.

"I don't see that new biography of George Eliot," she said. "Didn't it come?"

"No," said Charlotte, as the front door opened and a group of boys in school uniforms tumbled in. "But here come some troublemakers, so I'm in for it now."

Ellie laughed. To her, English schoolboys looked angelic in their blazers and shorts, but then what did she know? She was a foreigner.

At home, Hector greeted Ellie enthusiastically, racing up and down the front hall of the empty house, which Mrs. Finch had left clean and tidy. There was a beef stew simmering in the Aga, and Ellie was ashamed that she couldn't adore someone who took such good care of the house, Graham, and, by extension, her.

But there it was, perverse human nature. Instead of appreciating it, she peeked at the rich stew and felt a pang for her former diet of tofu, vegetables, and rice. Just thinking about eating stew made her feel heavy. It had finally stopped raining, so she changed into running clothes and took Hector for a run that left them both panting, windblown, and tired.

At teatime, Graham came home and told her about his day consumed by the administrative minutiae and political maneuverings of the diocese, and Ellie was about to propose some pleasant ways that they could put the day behind them when he reminded her with a rueful look that it was his Morris side's practice night.

"You could come along," he said, but she'd already attended a couple of the Beecham Morris sessions, and, while she was sure an evening spent leaping around to jaunty music and smacking sticks together was good therapy for someone whose profession required politeness, her part—sitting on a folding chair for two hours—was not much fun.

"I think I should stay home with Hector," she said, as a volley of firecrackers went off nearby.

The dog yelped and Graham scowled. "That would be brilliant actually, if you don't mind. It sounds like the illegal firecrackers are back this year, so I guess Jim Finch was right to be worried."

"Of course, I don't mind," said Ellie, who was always pleased when doing what she wanted was interpreted as selfless, "but you watch out for the headless horseman."

Once Graham had left, Ellie took her new library books into the sitting room and lit the fire that Mrs. Finch had so thoughtfully laid. Before long Hector scuttled in from the kitchen and curled up under the sofa in a knot.

The blaze was cheerful and bright, and she pulled her chair up close to its warmth, but she found it was not easy to read. Outside the wind howled around the house and bursts of rain hit the windows like gravel thrown against the glass. On top of that, the pop and bang of firecrackers coupled with

Hector's howls made her feel like she was in a war zone. A comparison of the Brontë sisters' writing styles was no match for Halloween in Little Beecham.

She closed her book and restlessly paced around the room until her gaze happened to fall on the row of small ceramic pots that stood on the mantel over the fireplace. Over the weekend, she had re-arranged them, but someone had put them back the way they had been before.

Suddenly her boredom was replaced by an invigorating irritation. She was sure the culprit must be Mrs. Finch, who must be determined that Ellie not change anything in this house, especially since she had no opinion regarding whether they ate toad in the hole or bubble and squeak for dinner.

Determined to assert herself, she went to the mantel to put the pots back the way she thought they would look better. She picked up one—a delicate globe, built by hand, not thrown, and with a glaze that shone on its surface like dew. The style was almost Japanese, and she wondered where Graham had bought it.

She turned it over to look at the bottom and was surprised to see, not a maker's stamp, but a pair of tiny initials incised into the clay: L.G.

L.G. Before she'd even turned over the next pot, she was sure this was not a coincidence. L.G. must be Louise Greenhall, and the little pot that now rested in the palm of her hand had been made by Louise's living hands.

The feeling this gave her was almost like touching her, but not in a hands reaching from the grave way. Instead it was more of a gift. In that moment, Louise became a person. A woman like herself with a history before she married Graham, who kept her potter self right before her eyes at all times, perhaps as a reminder that she too was more than just the vicar's wife. That paragon who produced perfect cakes and was loved by all.

If indeed, as she now suspected, it was Louise who had arranged the pots just so on the mantel, then Ellie agreed. They should stay exactly as they were.

A fresh burst of firecrackers saluted this decision, as Ellie set the pot she was holding back in place. "OK," she said to

Louise, since it was, after all, Halloween, "the pots will stay the way you want them. And, by the way, I think they are very, very nice."

When she turned away from the mantel, she wondered what more she could learn about Louise from this room, but that was almost a joke. She was the one who was invisible here. Everything from the rugs on the floor to the tiny plaster Christmas angel that hung year-round from the hook that must have once held a light fixture would have been chosen by Louise and Graham.

The only overt evidence was a photo of Isabelle and Louise on the bookshelf. The girl had been about twelve at the time and looked remarkably like her blonde, fresh-faced mother but with Graham's sparkling blue eyes. Ellie studied this for a moment, then moved on to a small desk at the far end of the sitting room that she had never seen Graham use. His desk was in his study, so this might have been Louise's.

She was just about to open the first drawer, when the doorbell rang, and the sound made her jump, as if she'd been caught in the act of doing something illicit. Hector began to bark as the bell rang again.

Ellie looked at her watch. 8:30. It seemed a bit late for calling, but wasn't the vicar always supposed to be at home? Always ready to help a parishioner in distress?

She supposed so, but when she opened the door, it was not a parishioner but a hooded faceless figure that greeted her. Hector went berserk until the figure turned slowly and showed it was only Charlotte Worthy, wearing a billowing hooded brown cloak.

"Charlotte, you practically scared us to death!" said Ellie, grabbing hold of the dog.

"I'm sorry, Mrs. Kent, but that book you wanted came after you left, and I thought you might need it." The girl pulled the Eliot biography from under the voluminous folds of her cloak and held it out.

"Why, thank you. That was awfully nice of you to bring it."

"It's no trouble. I always go for a walk after the baby's in bed."

"Even on Halloween?"

Charlotte grimaced. "The dead would be an improvement over the stupid prats I've seen about."

"Well, for a second there, Hector and I both thought doom had arrived on our doorstep. Do you have time to come in?"

Ellie caught a flash of longing in the girl's blue eyes, but she said no. "I can't be away long in case the baby starts crying. Mum doesn't mind, but Dad gets stroppy."

"Another time then."

"All right. Thank you." She hesitated, as if she might want to say something else, but decided against it, and fluttered off into the night.

Ellie had just returned to the sitting room to resume her exploration of Louise's desk when a long and noisy round of firecrackers culminated in an explosion and the lights went out. She stood in the dark wondering if God were trying to tell her something.

A glance out the window showed that the other houses at this end of the village also had no power, so somewhere a line must have gone down. The fire in the fireplace cast enough light for her to find some matches, and she was lighting the candles on the mantelpiece, when a prick of light piercing the darkness outside caught her attention.

Much to her surprise, she saw that it was inside the church. A small beam illuminated first one then another of St. Michael's tall windows as if someone were looking at them. Or doing something worse. Breaking hell loose.

Ellie knew instantly that, if that's what was happening, there was no time to call Graham or the police for help. If anyone was going to do something, it would have to be her. It took only a few moments to find the key to the church and a flashlight. Then she put on her raincoat and hurried back to the sitting room. The light was still visible. She was not too late.

Ellie stepped outside into nearly total darkness. Clouds blocked the moon, and she could only see the soft glow of a candle here and there in the other houses. The tiny light inside the church was still moving as if the person were looking for something. She didn't turn on her own light for fear of warning him and hurried across the slippery grass, avoiding the noisier pebbled path.

Her heart was beating fast by the time she reached the church entryway. She paused to listen, but she couldn't hear anything except her own excited breathing. She grasped the iron ring on the door and turned it, only to discover that the door was still locked. The intruder must have broken in through the vestry.

She took out the key and unlocked the ancient door, which shook and scraped across the stone floor as she shoved it open. The noise sounded thunderous, so it was no surprise that when she entered the nave, the light had gone out.

"Hello?" she called. "Who's in here?" But there was no reply. No sound at all. Not even a distant firecracker.

The church smelled of dust and candles, not paint, but she shone her flashlight beam over the walls and windows carefully, then began to advance slowly down the center aisle. Her rubber-soled shoes lisped against the stone floor as she checked the pews, lighting up the scattered needlepoint kneeling cushions, prayer books, and hymnals, but no cowering vandal.

She swept the light across the silent organ and the font. She lit up the altar and the silver cross hanging above it. She had almost concluded that nothing had been disturbed when she noticed that Emily Rutherford Hughes' posy had fallen off the window ledge. The vase was broken, and the flowers lay scattered on the floor in a pool of water. That was odd, but, as a prank, it wasn't much of one.

She clutched her flashlight, ready to use it as a weapon, as she approached the vestry room door, but she pushed it ajar only to find the room empty and a cold draft coming from the open window. Outside she saw a dark figure moving silently away through the gravestones. Ellie quickly re-fastened the window, wedged an old notebook into the frame of the broken pane and ran back through the church.

Outside the tombstones were ghostly, pale and sorrowful, in the rain and darkness. The firecrackers, she noticed, had stopped. In fact, all she could hear was the dripping rain, as she walked carefully from one end of the churchyard to the other, shining her flashlight across stones. Although she felt certain she was being watched, she saw no damage and no sign of anyone living or dead.

By the time Graham returned home, she and Hector were snuggled together on the sofa in the sitting room under a blanket, sound asleep.

"This is a pretty picture," he said when he came into the room.

Ellie opened her eyes. "You have no idea what a night we've had. It's a concession for both of us that we are on the couch and not under it."

Tuesday, November 1 (All Saints Day)

Chapter 6

Ellie awoke to a world mysteriously muted. Silvered and still. Overnight the temperature had dropped, and leaves brought down by the wind lay crystallized on the ground. Frost glittered on the gravestones where the morning sun touched them.

She went downstairs to put the kettle on the Aga, while Graham dressed. The Aga emitted a slow constant heat that kept the kitchen warm, but the stone floor was cold. When she let Hector out, she could see her breath plume out in front of her.

She made the tea, then stood sleepily at the window, marveling at the beauty of the morning. Outside, the dog nosed around the graves and marked out his territory in a way that probably would not be approved of by the deceased.

She had just poured tea for herself and Graham, when she heard the dog begin to bark. Loudly. She could no longer see him from the window, so she went to the back door and looked out, calling: "Hector! Come!" But, of course, he didn't come, and he didn't stop barking either,

Finally, she grabbed her coat and slipped her feet into one of the pairs of old rubber garden shoes heaped in the entryway. The air felt wintry as she crunched across the frozen grass to see what was going on.

The barking was coming from the far side of the graveyard, beyond the church. Hector must have heard her coming, because he suddenly appeared, gave an anxious little yip, and then disappeared again. It wasn't until Ellie rounded one of the larger monuments that she caught sight of him again, guarding what looked like a dark lump in the grass.

"Hector!" she said, admonishing him and bracing herself to see what it was he had found. It looked too big to be something he had killed. At least she hoped it was, and, as she drew closer, she saw that she was right. It wasn't a rabbit or a pheasant, or, thank God, a cat.

It was a man.

And not only that, it was a man she recognized.

Only two days ago, she had seen him striding through the woods. Now he lay on his back next to one of the gravestones, partially covered by leaves that must have blown over him during the night. One arm was flung out, and she could see the palm of his hand. Frost lay in the web of tiny lines there and caught in his eyelashes. The eyes that had stared at her no longer saw anything. Only the thick white hair stirred in the light breeze created by the rising sun.

She knelt down and touched his hand. The flesh was cold, but she saw no sign of injury—no indication of how he died. His clothes gave off the scents of wood smoke, wet grass and whisky. That was all.

She regarded his lifeless face. Their first encounter had been one of life's many forgettable moments. Now his features would be imprinted on her memory forever.

She rose to her feet and picked up Hector. "Good dog," she said. "Good dog." His damp paws clung to her shoulder, and she could feel both their hearts beating fast as she carried him home to the Vicarage.

When she reached the study, she sat down, still clinging to the dog. Graham was on the phone, but he soon hung up and said, "The window will be fixed this morning," before he registered her expression.

"Ellie, what's the matter? You're completely white."

"It's not good news. Something more than a break-in happened last night. There's a dead man in the churchyard over by the yew hedge."

"Are you joking?"

Ellie shook her head. "I'm definitely not joking. Hector found him."

"Do you know who it is?" Graham asked, already on his feet.

"No, but I've seen him before, so you probably do."

A moment later, they were hurrying back across the churchyard, their footsteps marking a trail across the frosted grass.

"Good Lord," said Graham, when they reached the body, and he knelt down beside him. Already the rising temperature was turning the frost to beads of water on his face.

"Who is he?" Ellie asked, then mentally corrected herself: *was he.*

"I've no idea." Graham gently closed the man's eyes, made the sign of the cross, and bowed his head in prayer.

She bowed her head too, but, now that the first shock of finding him dead had passed, curiosity took over, and she studied the man more closely. She was struck first by how handsome he must have once been. His high cheek bones, fine straight nose and square jaw were evident beneath the lined, weatherbeaten skin, and the white hair must have once been thick and dark.

His worn body contrasted sharply with his heavy tweeds, which were obviously new—the little plastic string that had held a price tag still dangled from the sleeve of his jacket. His heavy walking shoes were new too, the soles only slightly stained with mud. Whatever he was doing in Little Beecham, he had put on new clothes for the occasion.

When Graham stood up, he sighed. "We'd better inform the police. I was going to call them anyway. About the break-in." He put his arm around Ellie. "Are you all right? You still look very pale."

"I am pale. Do you realize this man could have been the intruder I chased out of the church?"

"I really doubt that," he said, considering the size of the man. "I suppose he could have squeezed through that window, but why would he want to?"

Back in the kitchen, Graham called the police, while Ellie drank a cup of sugary tea, huddled close to the Aga for warmth. Hector was subdued too, watching them with big eyes from his basket.

"They're bringing the pathologist and undertaker," he said.

"A pathologist?" That had an ominous sound.

"It's perfectly routine," Graham assured her. "He has to come for any unattended death."

The words made her wince. "You know, I can't stop thinking of him dying out there while we slept."

"But we had no idea he was there, so how could we have helped him? He smelled like he'd been drinking, so I think he probably crashed his car on the B road and lost his way in the dark trying to find help. The power was out, after all."

"Maybe," but she wasn't convinced.

"Look, you stay here and drink your tea. I'm going back to keep an eye on things. Other dogs and people could come along, and we don't want the body to be disturbed."

No sooner had he left than the doorbell rang. Two men were on the doorstep, and although they had come in an unmarked car and wore no uniforms, they were still unmistakably policemen. They gave off the energy of men moving through the world as observers and enforcers, not participants.

They introduced themselves as Detective Inspector Derek Mullane and Detective Sergeant Alan Jones. Mullane was a solidly built man in his late-30s, whose English schoolboy good looks had thickened and hardened with maturity. He had a brisk manner that suggested the discovery of dead bodies was routine for him. Jones was a thin, long-faced man with pale eyes and pale brown hair, who continually glanced at Mullane for direction.

"Sounds like quite a Halloween down here, Mrs. Kent," said Inspector Mullane. "The church wasn't the only place vandalized. Someone smashed the antiques shop window too."

"No kidding," said Ellie and saw them immediately take note of her American accent, mentally adding "foreigner" to the list of details about the situation.

"Yes, someone's had a little spree. Whether that's connected to this other business remains to be seen. Now if you can just show us where the old gent is, we'll take care of everything from here on."

As she again crossed the churchyard, Ellie saw Mrs. Bigelow riveted to her front window watching. From her vantage point, she would not be able to see the body, but the parade of people across the churchyard—including two official-looking strangers—signaled that something out of the ordinary was happening. She would not want to miss it.

The three men greeted each other tersely, then Mullane put on thin plastic gloves and knelt by the body. He searched the pockets with deft fingers.

"Nothing," he said to Jones, who'd taken out a small notebook. "No I.D. Nothing." He bent lower and sniffed the man's clothes. "Probably legless."

"Legless?" asked Ellie.

"Drunk," said Mullane. "He's a well-dressed bloke though, so it's a bit odd that he doesn't have a wallet or keys in his pockets." He stood up. "We may be dealing with a crime here, as well as an accidental death, so if you don't mind..." He nodded toward the Vicarage, showing white even teeth. You couldn't really call it a smile. "We'd like to get on with our business. We'll be in to take your statements when we're finished."

"Of course," said Graham, putting his arm around Ellie's shoulder. "We have our arrangements to make as well."

"What arrangements?" she asked, as he led her away. She would have preferred to stay and watch what the police were doing, even if from a distance.

"I have to call the insurance company, for one thing, and the Parish Council."

This had nothing to do with her, but she gave in and fixed breakfast, while he began making calls.

Death made her unexpectedly hungry, and she ate three pieces of toast standing at Graham's study window. From there, she saw the undertaker's van arrive, then a short, stout man with a black bag who came in another car—no doubt, the pathologist.

The ambulance attracted a small crowd of villagers. They stood on the sidewalk, craning their necks to catch glimpses of what was going on. Two more constables arrived to help Jones search the churchyard and the church. Bright yellow crime scene tape soon marked off the place where Ellie had found the body and the back entrance to the church. Finally, the ambulance crew carried the shrouded figure on a stretcher to the waiting vehicle, and then, she thought, the incident was over.

The two detectives appeared to think it was over too, when they joined them in Graham's study to take their statements. Mullane sat on the edge of his chair, as if he had to be ready to rush off to his next call at any moment. His strong thighs strained the fabric of his trousers, and he cupped one fisted hand inside the other in his lap. Jones sat next to him, quietly taking notes.

"The pathologist says your man might have had a heart attack, but the cause of death appears to have been exposure," Mullane said. "It was a cold night after all, and he had been drinking. Of course, these points are just based on observation. We'll have to wait for the post-mortem report to learn what really happened," he added.

"And the break-in?" asked Graham.

Mullane glanced from Graham to Ellie. "We're exploring the possibility that he was your intruder as well, but if you would explain what happened, Mrs. Kent, that would be very helpful." His tone was polite, but his eyes were sharp and inquisitive.

"Last year some kids spray-painted the churchyard, so when the power went off and I saw a light in the church, I went over to be sure nothing like that was happening again," said Ellie.

"That was rather reckless. Why didn't you call us—or your husband?"

Ellie shrugged. "That would have taken too long, and anyway I assumed it was just some of the kids from the village."

"And then what happened?"

"Nothing. Whoever it was had already gotten out. All I found was the broken window."

"And the broken vase," added Graham.

"A broken vase?" asked Jones, pencil poised over his notebook.

"That's right. A small vase had been knocked off one of the window ledges, and it broke."

Mullane looked impatient. "OK, and then what happened this morning."

"This morning, when I let Hector out, he found the body and started barking to let us know."

Jones was writing furiously, and Mullane paused to drink his tea.

"And when you saw the man, did you recognize him?"

"Yes, I think so. I mean, I don't know him, but I saw him in the woods on Sunday. It was just about dusk and he was walking away from the village with a full backpack."

Mullane told Jones to remind the men outside searching the grounds that they should be looking for a flashlight, a backpack, and anything else that might have belonged to the dead man.

"And you didn't know him either, Father Kent?" he asked Graham, who shook his head. "Well, he may have been a visitor who stopped in at the pub, had a few too many, and passed out on his way to wherever he was staying."

"Then someone robbed him and left him there?"

"We're not talking about the good Samaritan, Mrs. Kent."

Ellie blushed. "Of course not. But the thief might also have been the one who broke into the church."

"What I can't imagine is how this man wound up in the churchyard in the first place," said Graham. "I would have been less surprised if he were by the road."

Mullane shrugged. "We'll check with your local. As to the break-in, I suppose you have some usual suspects when it comes to mischief in this village?"

"No, we don't," said Graham stiffly.

"That's not a very helpful attitude, Father Kent. I would think you'd be as eager as the next person to see this kind of vandalism stopped, but I suppose you have your scruples. I expect your neighbors will be more forthcoming. We'll have your statements typed up by this afternoon. Please come to the station in Chipping Martin to sign them.

"That will be all for now, unless you remember something or hear of anything that could shed light on the dead man's identity. We'd like to know that right away."

"What do you mean about all for now?" asked Ellie.

"You'll have to give evidence at the inquest. Whatever else is required will depend on the results of the post-mortem." And, with that ominous remark, he departed.

Graham spent the morning fielding calls from the worried and the curious while Ellie re-arranged his library alphabetically by author. She wanted to stay close to him, but she couldn't just sit there and do nothing. Surrounding herself with piles of books seemed like a good antidote to an overdose of reality.

A surprising number of people turned up to put posies and bouquets on the graves of their loved ones. Graham said this was traditional for All Souls Day, but Ellie observed that almost without exception they also stopped to look at the spot where the body had been found.

The people who called all asked the same questions, so Graham was forced to repeat over and over:

"Yes, a man was found dead in the churchyard."

"No, I don't know who he was."

"No, I don't know how he died."

"Yes, there was also a break-in."

"No, we don't know if the two events are connected."

Ellie could tell when it was a reporter on the phone by the sudden coldness in his voice: "Yes, my wife and dog found the body. No, none of us has any comment." After one of these calls, he put the receiver down and massaged his forehead with his fingers. "That one wanted a photo of you and Hector in the churchyard."

Ellie laughed for the first time all day. "It must be a slow news day."

She had reached the S's—Schweitzer, Schleiermacher, and Swedenborg—and Graham had gone to refresh the teapot, when the phone rang and she answered.

She heard an anxious wheezy breathing, then "Is this the Vicarage?"

"Yes," said Ellie. "May I help you?"

"I've only just heard about the man you found today. Could you tell me please...what he looked like?" The voice sounded muffled, as if the woman were in bed under the covers.

"Are you worried about someone? Is someone you know missing?"

"Please. Just tell me. What he looked like."

"He was quite tall, with thick white hair and a full beard."

Ellie heard a sharp intake of breath. "Do you know him? We're very anxious to find out who he is," she said, but there was no answer, only the sound of the receiver dropping before the connection broke.

"I think that caller knew our man," she told Graham when he came back. "She asked me to describe him, and when I did, she dropped the phone."

He set down the teapot. "The sad bit in these situations is that someone's worst fears will be confirmed. But maybe she'll call the police now, and the whole thing will be sorted quickly."

In the afternoon they drove to Chipping Martin, a market town about six miles from Little Beecham. As the green and rolling countryside whizzed by, Ellie tried to absorb some of its tranquility, but she hated sitting in the passenger seat of Graham's Mini Cooper. She clutched the dashboard and pressed her feet against a non-existent brake every time a car passed them going the other way as if a head-on collision were imminent, and she got out of the car with relief when they arrived.

The Chipping Martin police station was a stone building set slightly apart at one end of town. Although West Oxfordshire was never a hub of crime, this was the day after Halloween, and the officers were busy following up on missing bicycles, overturned trashcans, spray-painted walls and other mischief.

DS Jones came to meet them after they'd waited on a wooden bench in the small entryway for about 15 minutes. He acted more confident away from Inspector Mullane and escorted them into an interview room. There he handed them their typed statements, which they read and signed.

When they were finished, he thanked them, and, with an embarrassed expression, said, "DI Mullane needs your fingerprints. Strictly for purposes of elimination, you understand. We're trying to learn what we can about the dead man's movements through his fingerprints."

"Of course," said Graham. "We'll do anything we can to assist you."

Ellie couldn't help thinking of the paranoid stories she'd read about the British—how they used any excuse to collect information for their vast security files—but there was nothing she could do; she could hardly refuse.

Jones was about to dismiss them when she remembered the phone call.

"By the way, a woman called the Vicarage who was very upset. I think she knew the man."

"Did she give her name?"

"No. Actually she hung up as soon as I described him."

Jones gave her a patronizing smile that did not suit his thin weak face. "I wouldn't worry about it then. Once news like this hits, we get lots of callers. Most of them are lonely people with nothing better to do. If she really knows him, she'll call us."

"Did you find the man's car?"

"No, but it's early days, Mrs. Kent. When we hear from the pathologist we'll know what we're dealing with." And then he ushered them firmly out the door.

"What do you think he meant by that?" asked Ellie, as they walked to the Mini.

Graham shrugged. "I assume he's referring to the cause of death. Whatever it was, I hope they find out enough to remove that crime scene tape before tomorrow."

"Tomorrow?"

"The All Souls service."

"Oh, right. Of course, I knew about that."

It was late afternoon before they heard anything further. DI Mullane called to tell them that the investigators had not found the man's fingerprints in the church.

"So he either wasn't the person who broke in or he wore gloves," Ellie said to Graham. They were in the kitchen, where she was making lentil soup while he gave Hector a thorough brushing.

"But his hands were bare," said Graham.

"True, but the second thief could have stolen his gloves, as well as his wallet, his backpack and his flashlight."

"I suppose. After all, a dead man doesn't need to keep his hands warm."

"I wish we'd hear who he was. You'd think that woman would have called in by now."

"She was most likely some nutter."

"I don't think so. She sounded genuinely scared," said Ellie, putting the lid on the soup. "That has to simmer for an hour. Do you have time for a walk?"

Graham released Hector, who barked and shook himself vigorously. "Walk" was a word he knew well.

"I think I'd better revise my sermon for tomorrow before it gets too late," he said, so Ellie put on her jacket and set off with Hector alone.

They were again on the path through the woods and had just reached a point where two paths intersected, when a golden retriever came around the bend and rushed toward them. Hector began to bark wildly, and Ellie held tight to him as he twisted and lunged under her grip.

The dogs continued to make a terrible racket, but the retriever's owner looked totally unfazed when he appeared: a handsome man in his mid-30s, who was dressed like an ad for expensive country wear, from his designer wellingtons to his tweed cap. Ellie noticed that a dog's leash dangled from his pocket, and also that he was carrying a plastic trash bag, which seemed very incongruous with his otherwise impeccable image.

"I say, I'm sorry if Whistler is causing a dust up with your dog," he said, but he made no attempt to control the retriever, who was now tearing up and down the path inciting Hector to join him in a game of chase.

"If he's in the habit of attacking people, maybe you should keep him on that leash."

"Leash? Oh, you mean, the lead." He set down the trash bag and took the leash out of his pocket, but he made no move to try to catch his dog. "Let me guess. You must be our new resident American. I've heard about you," he said, appraising her. "Do allow me to introduce myself. I'm one of your flock. Michael-John Parker."

"I don't have a flock," she said, but before he could reply, Whistler came bounding back to see why they hadn't followed him. Michael-John grabbed at his collar and, with Ellie's help, put him on the leash.

"I suppose this is better as long as you don't mind plunging into the bushes every few feet," Michael-John said over his shoulder as Whistler pulled him down the path. "I hope you'll forgive us. He only came to live with me a couple of weeks ago, and he hasn't accepted me as the alpha dog, or whatever it is, yet. So you don't see yourself as our village shepherdess?"

"No," said Ellie, who followed along behind them. "And my name is not Bo Peep."

"Despite rounding up the odd dead sheep."

Ellie blushed. "So you've already heard about that."

"*Bien sûr*. Everyone has heard about that."

"Well, I assure you it was a one-time event."

"How can you tell? You've only been here, what, a month? Two? I've been here a year and nothing exciting happened until you arrived. Now I've had my window broken, and a mysterious dead body has been found in our otherwise bucolic village."

"Your window was broken? Does that mean you run the antiques shop?"

He nodded. "Something of a retirement project, you know."

"You seem awfully young to be retired."

"My dear, I was a femme fatale on the stock exchange." He smiled a brilliant smile that showed off his very expensive teeth. "You should come and see my shop. It's in the old blacksmith shop and very nice when there isn't broken glass everywhere. I've preserved the forge, but, I promise you, I do not dress up in soot and a leather apron."

"I'd like that. So what are you doing now? Collecting refuse to sell?" she asked, pointing to the trash bag.

He laughed. "Now there's an idea. But no, I've been out to Beech Hall. I try to keep the old heap clean. It's my bit of public service, you know. You'd be aghast at what people dump there."

"I thought it was fenced off."

He shrugged. "That's never stopped anyone. People treat it like a public lounge and snogging ground."

"Not very hospitable, I should think."

"There's no accounting for the taste of the English. If I had my way, I'd buy it and restore it, but Mrs. Rutherford Hughes would rather die in genteel poverty. You know that family lived there for more than four hundred years and never accomplished a thing except to burn down their own house."

Ellie laughed. "Surely that can't be true."

"Well, nearly. I'm considering writing a monograph about them. What do you think? Doesn't that sound like something a country gentleman would do?"

"I suppose, but Mrs. Rutherford Hughes strikes me as a pompous bore. Her family's trust supports St. Michael's though. That's something good they did."

"Guilt money. At least I hope it was. Otherwise my future may lie in garbage collection after all."

By this time, they'd reached the Vicarage, and he held out his hand. "Thank you for your help with my bad dog. Don't forget to come for a visit. We incomers have to stick together too."

Ellie thanked him and watched as he headed down the high street toward his shop with Whistler straining at his leash. He mimed a person being dragged off his feet, and she laughed again.

She was still smiling when she noticed Mrs. Bigelow watching from her window. Ellie waved to the older woman, who scowled like a gargoyle.

"All the world's a stage," she thought, *was clearly written by someone who had lived in an English village.*

Wednesday, November 2 (All Souls Day)

Chapter 7

The next day started badly. It wasn't that Ellie and Graham had a fight. Not on the outside anyway. But there was a definite and bruising collision.

The trouble began while they were eating breakfast and a florist's van from Chipping Martin arrived with a large arrangement of yellow roses. Mrs. Finch signed for the delivery as if this were a routine event, but Ellie missed that cue and made the mistake of thinking the flowers were for her. To cheer her up after yesterday's ordeal. Or to celebrate their two-month anniversary. Or just because. Wasn't that what romantic new husbands did? Of course it was. Her assumptions had not been unjustified.

But that was because she'd forgotten about All Souls Day, an occasion she'd never even heard about until recently. It wasn't until Graham got up from the table with an embarrassed glance and hustled the flowers back out the kitchen door that she realized they weren't for her at all— they were for Louise.

She concentrated on eating her oatmeal and tried to keep her expression neutral when he returned, but she must not have been entirely successful, because he looked uncomfortable and whispered behind Mrs. Finch's back, "Honoring Louise's memory does not mean I love you any less, Ellie."

"You don't have to say that," she whispered back, but she knew she sounded surprised and sulky.

He'd said "Good," and swallowed the last of his tea.

Before they could talk further, they heard the honking horn that signaled the arrival of Graham's ride, and he went off to some meeting or other, leaving Ellie all in pieces. She retreated to her study the moment he was gone, but every time she looked out the window, she saw the roses, bright against the green grass, a vivid reminder that death did not part.

At least today she had the car, so she scooped up Hector and drove off to Chipping Martin for market day. Shifting with your left hand and driving on the wrong side of the road with cars, trucks, motorcycles, and vans barreling down at you on a narrow country road is a good way to clear your head. Nothing less than total concentration will bring you through alive, and, despite the chilly day, Ellie was sweating when she arrived at her destination.

Chipping Martin didn't have as big a market as some of the other Cotswold towns, but about 30 stalls were set up in the middle of the high street every Wednesday morning, and people came from the surrounding villages to buy everything from cheese and vegetables to baskets and baked goods.

Ellie felt better once she saw the crowd of people thronging the street. It didn't bother her at all that she had to drive around in circles to find a parking space. Parking was a city problem she understood.

She was surprised to discover that the market's biggest attraction that day was a fireworks stall. A line of people waited to stock up on rockets, sparklers, and other garden fireworks and walked off carrying armloads of explosives for the upcoming Bonfire Night. It amazed her that such lethal pleasures were distributed so liberally, even though you had to be 18 to buy them. Theoretically.

At a baked goods stand, she paused to study the display of unfamiliar pastries: biscuit-like scones, raisin-studded rock cakes, round flat soul cakes, and something called Parkin.

"Parkin's traditional for Bonfire Night, but the soul cakes are for today," said a voice from behind her. Ellie turned to face a dark-haired cheerful-looking woman with schoolboy tortoiseshell glasses, wearing a wool poncho and jeans. "People used them to pay the poor for saying prayers for their dead. I think you must be Ellie Kent."

"Yes, I am," said Ellie, "but how did you know?"

The woman laughed. "It wasn't just a good guess. I've known Hector since he was a pup." She bent down and rubbed the dog's head, then stood and held out her hand. "I'm Morag MacDonald. I live in Little Beecham too."

"I don't think I've ever seen you before."

"I'm not a churchgoer so our paths haven't crossed. You should try some of these," she said, filling a bag with soul cakes for herself. "They're quite good even if you don't subscribe to their magical powers. Parkin's not bad either. Sort of like oatmeal gingerbread."

"All right. Thanks for the tip," said Ellie and bought some of each.

After that, she wandered on from stall to stall, adding to her purchases a round of real Cheddar cheese made in Cheddar, a bag of homemade dog treats for Hector, and a bunch of fresh-dug parsnips, but, at almost every turn, she bumped into Morag, until finally she asked, "Do you have time for a cup of tea or something?"

Morag smiled and said she did.

They made their way to a crowded teashop with a low-beamed ceiling and ordered tea. As Ellie settled herself into a chair overlooking the 300-year-old market square, she felt her bad mood had left her completely.

When the fat stoneware pot of Indian tea and two slices of Victoria sponge arrived, Morag filled their cups. Under the table, Hector sat quietly, as ever alert for crumbs.

"Have you always lived in Little Beecham?" Ellie asked, stirring milk into her tea.

"No," said Morag. "I grew up in Oxford. My ex-husband was from here, but in the end, he moved to London, and our son Seamus and I stayed. I taught at the village school until last year."

"What are you doing now?"

"I received an inheritance from an aunt, so I decided to try something different."

"And..."

"So far I've ruled out future careers as a novelist, gardener and weaver. How do you like your new career?"

Ellie looked away at the framed watercolors of sheep lining the wall by their table. "I love the vicar," she said, "but I'm still figuring out the other parts."

Morag nodded sympathetically as she ate a bite of her cake.

"I've had some real surprises," Ellie went on to say. "Did you know I found a body in the churchyard yesterday?"

"You mean that old bloke whose photo was on the news last night?"

Ellie nodded.

"That's brilliant. Not, I mean, that the man is dead and it must have an awful shock for you, but Seamus will be so chuffed to know I met you. He was shattered that a body had been found in his very own village, and he missed it. He fancies being a detective and goes around the house examining fingerprints."

"I don't think Sherlock Holmes is called for in this case. It was more unnerving than dramatic. To find him lying there. Just, you know, dead."

"Poor you. Poor him too." Morag poured them both some more tea. "You know I would hardly have described vicar's wife as an exciting profession, but Louise had some pretty odd experiences too. Anonymous letters, things like that."

"Really? So you knew Louise?"

"In such a small village it would have been hard not to, but, in fact, we were good friends. I think she liked that I was not involved with St. Michael's. There, everyone wanted to talk to her. She needed someone she could talk to, if you know what I mean."

"Yes, I can see that," said Ellie, and she found herself studying the honest, confident face of her new acquaintance more closely. She saw that Morag was studying her too, leaving an opening. "Sometimes I find Louise is a pretty tough act to follow," she added.

"I can imagine," said Morag, pulling money out of her purse to pay the bill. "But I know she'd be rooting for you. She would never have wanted Graham or Isabelle to mourn endlessly over what happened."

"Really?" She pictured those yellow roses. "Sometimes I think he still is."

"But that's only natural, isn't it? I still miss my mother terribly sometimes, and she's been dead for years."

"Yes, of course, you're right."

"Absolute fact. Listen, I have to shove off, but it's been a pleasure meeting you. Let this be my treat. A welcome party. And you'll have to come round to the house for tea soon. I know Seamus will be dying to meet you too."

Ellie's spirits remained high until she reached Little Beecham and saw two police officers working their way down the high street, apparently doing a house-to-house search for information.

They sagged even further at the sight of Graham's face. He met her at the kitchen door, and even her cheery, "You're home early!" had no effect on his expression.

"Inspector Mullane called," he said. "The preliminary blood tests showed the man was not only drunk, he'd also consumed a large quantity of sleeping powder."

Ellie set down her packages. "You mean he committed suicide?" She had a sudden vision of an unhappy man wanting to die in the church...and being forced out into the cold and damp instead.

"It's not the most likely scenario for a suicide, so I actually think Mullane suspects something worse."

"As in someone doped him, robbed him, and dumped him off in our churchyard to die?"

"Something like that. He couldn't have walked terribly far in the condition he was in, and they still haven't found his car."

"Oh my God, and when did all this supposedly happen?"

"Between nine and eleven o'clock, but apparently the body could have been dumped in the graveyard a bit later. They're interviewing people now to see if anyone saw or heard anything."

Ellie slumped down into a chair at the kitchen table. The last of the morning's good cheer had totally evaporated.

"Could it have been random? Opportunistic? Like, the power's off here, so this would be a perfect place to shove my victim out of car?"

"I don't think so. He was apparently seen around the village during the day."

"So I might have been searching the churchyard under the watchful eye of a murderer."

"That does not even bear thinking about," said Graham, who stood at the kitchen window, looking out at his roses for Louise.

There were only a few people in the church when Ellie arrived for the All Souls Day evensong service, but as the bells tolled, more and more poured in.

She sat down in a back pew and watched her neighbors arrive, while the organist played suitably doleful music. The regular churchgoers were there, such as the Bells, Mrs. Rutherford Hughes, and a whole pew full of Worthys, including Charlotte and her baby. Mrs. Bigelow turned up with a purple shawl wrapped dramatically around her ample body, and Ellie also recognized the butcher John Tiddington, Mrs. Wiggins from the village store, and Mrs. Teaser from The Three Lambs. She wondered if this many people always came or if some were attracted by the novelty of a service for the dead with a crime scene outside.

Most people were casually dressed, but Emily Rutherford Hughes sat in her front pew wearing a severe black dress as if she were at an actual funeral. Her posture was as unbending as ever, but she did turn around once, and Ellie observed that black was not a color that suited her. She looked pale to the point of being ill.

Michael-John Parker created a wave of whispers when he arrived with Whistler on a leash. He looked solemn, but stunningly handsome in a black suit, and both he and Whistler wore red AIDS ribbons. They paused as he cast around for a seat, and Ellie gave a little wave to invite him to join her.

When he caught her eye, Michael-John smiled that radiant smile and slipped into her pew. "Now don't worry about the dog. I've had a very strong conversation with him about how to behave in church," he said, as Whistler jumped up onto the pew between them. Whistler sat down and leaned comfortably against Michael-John, shedding generous amounts of golden fur onto the black suit.

"He had to come, you see. His owner only passed a few weeks ago, and we were once, you know, partners, so that's how Whistler ended up with me."

"I'm sorry for your loss. Both of you."

"Thanks," he said. Then the organist began to play the opening hymn, and they all rose, including the dog.

If Graham were surprised or pleased by the additions to his congregation, he didn't show it. The flickering candles created a solemn atmosphere that matched the dignity of the evensong service, and when it was time for the sermon, he spoke to the congregation without referring to his written text:

"Death is one of the central mysteries of life that Christianity—and all other religions—seek to explain. We talk about it, think about it, fear it, but faced with the reality, our explanations fall away."

"What we do know is this, that if we stop, as we do on this day, to remember our dead, in our hearts and minds they are very much alive. Their love, their humor, their little quirks and failings, their pain, their achievements, their well-remembered faces are all vividly with us—and we need never lose them.

"When the priest-poet John Donne said, 'Every man's death diminishes me, because I am involved in mankind,' he wanted us to consider our connection and responsibility to each other. To understand that 'no man is an island.'

"I believe in this connection and responsibility between the living, but I do not see death as a dividing line." He seemed to be speaking directly to Ellie, and she blushed when he said, "I am enriched by all the people I have known and loved, and those who have died continue to live as part of me."

Then he read out the names of the dead submitted by the villagers—including Louise Greenhall Kent—and concluded with, "I would also like us to say a prayer for the stranger who died in our village this week. It's a painful fate to die alone and unknown, no matter what the circumstances."

The congregation shuffled in their pews, and some got on their knees for the final prayer and blessing. Ellie bowed her head, while Michael-John stared at the ceiling, one arm wrapped tightly around Whistler. Then they sang another hymn, and the service was over.

Afterward people were reluctant to leave and stood chatting in the pews and aisles. Whatever private reflections they had on their own losses, the big topic of discussion was the death in the graveyard. Many of them had been visited during the house-to-house questioning that had taken place that day, and they wanted to compare notes.

"Far be it from me to say the Vicar's wrong," said John Tiddington, "but I don't think that fellow died alone or unknown. I'll wager someone gave him a helping hand."

Mrs. Wiggins shuddered. "I thought I would faint when the policeman came around with that photo of him dead."

"I recognized him straight away, and I wasn't at all surprised to hear he'd come to a bad end," said Mrs. Teaser, who looked pleased when all eyes swiveled toward her. "He was in the Lambs on Monday and Ralph pegged him for a thief, he acted that strange."

Miss Worthy stopped daubing at her nose and eyes with her handkerchief and asked, "Why? What did he do to make you say that?" Today she was wearing sweaters in three different shades of blue that highlighted the blue of her red-rimmed eyes and a grey wool skirt that looked about 50 years old. Ellie thought the effect was somewhere between carelessly frumpy and highly artful.

"It were the way he smelled. Damp and smoky like he'd been living rough. And the way he looked at everything. Like he wanted to eat his food and us along with it," said Mrs. Teaser.

Ellie almost laughed when she heard that; she'd seen the same look herself.

"On top of that," went on Mrs. Teaser. "There was all them euros. Where did a bloke like that get so much money?"

Miss Worthy snorted. "I've never known you to be critical of a customer with plenty of cash, Ginny Teaser."

Mrs. Teaser bridled. "There's hard-earned money and there's the other kind," she said. "Anyway, this bloke was foreign, I'm sure of it."

"Did he speak English at all?" asked Mrs. Bell, cutting in. "So many of these people don't speak a word of English. I don't know why they bother to come here."

"His accent were very queer," said Mrs. Teaser, "but I'm sure I couldn't tell you where it was from."

They had all fallen silent, reflecting on the mystery of the stranger, when at last Emily Rutherford Hughes rose from her pew. They watched as she went to the war memorial window, where there was a fresh posy in a new vase on the windowsill, paused reverently and crossed herself before walking out without a word to anyone.

It took another moment, after the door closed behind her, for speculation to resume. No one else had spoken to the man as much as the Teasers had, but numerous people claimed to have seen him over the course of Monday afternoon. If all the reports were true, he'd been very busy: crossing fields and lurking in back lanes, as well as eating at the Lambs and walking right down the high street.

Mrs. Bigelow thought he must have been casing out the church for the break-in when she saw him.

"But I thought that was someone else," said Miss Worthy.

"Who else?" said Mrs. Bigelow with a scowl. "A local could rob this church any weekend with the doors left wide open the way they are. So it stands to reason, it was someone who didn't live here."

"Now really," said Graham, stepping in. "I think we should all try not to get ahead of the police investigation. They have better means than we do of tracing the man's movements and actions and will no doubt sort out the whole story soon."

Far from settling everyone down, this led to a fresh burst of speculation about what the whole story might be. And, while Graham was able to shepherd them out of the church, many of them agreed to adjourn to The Three Lambs.

The possibility that the man may have been murdered became general knowledge in no time, so the phone rang all evening: The press again, eager to cash in on a Halloween murder story, but also old people living alone who wanted Graham's reassurance that no killer was on the loose in the village.

When the phone rang at ten pm, Graham dutifully picked up the receiver. This time, however, his voice and face instantly brightened, and Ellie knew it must be Isabelle.

From Graham's side of the conversation, it became clear that she had read the news. "In the *Telegraph*? No, I didn't know that," he said. "I haven't had a minute all day to look at the paper."

Ellie listened as he told her what had happened, and then they moved on to other topics. How her studies were going. How her digs were working out. And so on.

As the conversation continued, she began to get restless. She was sure she'd never talked to her own father for more than ten minutes, and she was annoyed to find herself feeling new twinges of jealousy—and this time not of a dead rival, but of a young and vibrant living one.

At last, Graham said: "I think Ellie wants to say hello," and handed the phone over.

Ellie could not think of a single topic that hadn't already been covered in detail, but she said, "Hi, Isabelle, I guess you've heard the news."

"You could have knocked me down with a feather when I saw that story in the paper," said her very-English stepdaughter. "It must have been dreadful."

"It was pretty awful. A dead body is so, I don't know, dead."

"I know," said Isabelle, and suddenly Ellie realized she'd blundered again.

How could she have forgotten the story? How Graham and Isabelle had gone to visit Louise at the hospital and a parishioner had stopped Graham in the corridor so it had been Isabelle who discovered her mother, utterly unexpectedly, dead.

"Of course you do. I'm sorry. I know," and then she wrapped up the conversation as quickly as possible.

She had expected Graham to say goodbye when she handed back the phone, but instead they moved onto to yet another topic, and his expression grew somber. She couldn't hear what Isabelle was saying, but the gist of it was clear.

"I've been thinking about that today too, sweetheart," he said. "Yes, I got the yellow roses. Just the kind Mummy liked. No, I didn't forget. That's good. She would be very happy about that. She was always so proud of you. Yes, I know. All right. Yes. Goodbye. I love you too."

Ellie had picked up a book and was pretending to read. She looked up when Graham was off the phone, but he didn't notice. He was busy at his desk tidying things up, and the minutes ticked by. She turned pages without grasping what they said.

Finally, he came over to the sofa and sat down next to her, so Ellie put her book down. "Should we go for a walk before bed?" he asked.

Ah. How could she have never before noticed the beauty of the word "we"? How evocative and seductive it was. Suggestive of the French word: oui.

"Yes, we should," said Ellie. "Yes."

Outside the air was chilly, but it was a clear night, and, far from the ambient light of any city, the stars were dazzling. There were no cars on the road, and they walked down the middle of the high street with Hector trotting before them.

Most houses were already dark, but here and there lights sparkled and thin plumes of smoke trailed across the sky. Through the diamond-paned windows of The Three Lambs, they could see a convivial crowd surrounding Mrs. Teaser who obviously enjoyed being the center of attention. Ellie guessed she was telling again the story of her encounter with the bearded man.

Michael-John Parker's shop was dark, the broken front window covered with plywood. The curtains on the windows of the upstairs flat were drawn, but they could hear faint strains of music. They stopped for a few moments to listen. Was it opera? No—the Mozart *Requiem*.

Ellie shivered.

"Are you cold?" Graham asked, slipping an arm around her.

"No. It's this music. 'When the judge takes his place, what is hidden will be revealed; nothing will remain unavenged.'"

"I didn't know you could quote the requiem mass."

"There are lots of things about me you don't know yet," said Ellie. "But there's no mystery about this bit of arcane knowledge. I sang the *Requiem* when I was at school, and they made us memorize the text in English so we'd know what we were singing."

"I see. Well, I prefer the closing lines: 'Let perpetual light shine on them, as with your saints in eternity, because you are merciful.'"

"So you don't believe in vengeance?"

"No. I believe only people are vengeful; God is not."

"Really? Is that a fact? Tell me more," she said, as she leaned into his sheltering warmth

Thursday, November 3

Chapter 8

DI Mullane called the next morning to set a time to interview Ellie and Graham again. The house-to-house interviews had produced some information about where the stranger had spent the day of his death but they still had not identified him.

"All we know for certain is that he was wearing new clothes and shoes made here, but his underwear was old and Italian."

"So what does that mean?" asked Ellie.

"We don't know yet."

"What about his teeth? I thought you could learn all sorts of things from people's dental work."

"We're investigating every angle, I assure you, Mrs. Kent, and we'll know more when we get the full toxicology report. Meanwhile we want to do follow-up interviews with anyone who actually had contact with the man. That's why we need to talk to you and your husband again."

"Well, he's in a budget meeting right now, and I know he has a busy afternoon too. Can it wait until tomorrow?"

Mullane said it could, and they set the time for 9 a.m.

Mrs. Finch did not come on Thursdays, so Ellie had the kitchen to herself. She planned to fix a nice dinner and hoped that the demands of cooking would distract her from speculations about suicide or murder.

It was a clear autumn day with no wind, and on the high street people were out shopping and chatting in the sun. At the butcher's shop, Ellie found John Tiddington eager to engage her in conversation about the death. He was a vigorous-looking man in his early 40s who wore a traditional white butcher's coat and kept a sign in the window that said:

"You Are What You Eat, So Buy Good Meat." He was also the foreman for the Beecham Morris, and, according to Graham, the best dancer among them.

"The whole village is convinced it was murder," he said, as he whacked the head and feet off a chicken. "They're chuffed because we haven't had a murder here since 1955. Can you believe it? Of course, there're some who'd say it's only that we haven't had one where the murderer was caught." He laughed heartily. "I guess we've had our share of unexpected deaths and disappearances."

"I suppose so," said Ellie, who tried to listen without being too obvious about the fact that she didn't like watching him work. The English custom of hanging dead rabbits, pheasants, ducks, and other animals in the window of a butcher's shop was unnerving to her. She knew it was avoiding reality, but she was used to buying packaged meat that was only identifiable by its color and label.

John wrapped white paper around the beheaded chicken and tied the bundle with a whirl of string. "They're saying someone got him blotto, poisoned him and then dragged the body into the graveyard. Or brought him by car. Did you hear a car in the night, Mrs. Kent?"

"No, I didn't. I didn't hear a thing, but he was on the far side of the church. Not in sight from the house."

"Nowadays they can identify a car by the tire marks on the ground. "

"I know. Anyone who watches TV knows that, including the murderer, if there was one."

"Still, once you've got a body on your hands, you've got to get rid of it. It would be like lifting a pig or a side of beef to shift a full-grown man. That takes a lot of strength."

"I've never tried it myself," said Ellie.

"No, you wouldn't have, would you? But I have. Maybe the police will fix on me as a suspect." He laughed again. "Still it must ha' been someone local. After all, plenty of folk saw the fellow here during the day. Ginny Teaser took a real dislike to him. Maybe it was her."

"Personally, I think the man was drunk and took an accidental overdose," said Ellie firmly.

"Now don't go disappointing everyone with that theory, Mrs. Kent. Just when they've got a good story to tell." He pushed the package of chicken across the counter, and said, "Thank you for your custom."

In the village store, Ellie ran into Mrs. Bell. She looked neat and perky as a new doll in her navy wool skirt and matching sweater and carried her groceries in a rush basket over her arm.

"Good morning, Mrs. Kent. How are you and the Vicar faring with all this unpleasantness?"

"Oh, we're fine. We just hope the police will clear up everything quickly."

"I quite agree, although I don't see why some people are set on finding a local connection between that man and Little Beecham. With the way people from all over Europe are pouring into this country, I'm sure it's only a coincidence that he met his end here."

The storekeeper Mrs. Wiggins was far more interested in joining the conversation than in ringing up their purchases.

"I don't believe he was foreign like Ginny said. When I saw that awful photo, I thought there was something familiar about him."

"Oh, well, when it comes to that, to me all men with beards look alike," pronounced Mrs. Bell. "Who could say what he really looked like?" She began taking items out of her basket and laying them on the counter. "Mr. Bell wanted to grow a beard once, but I wouldn't have it. I told him if I'd wanted to marry Father Christmas I would have."

"Maybe that's who he reminded me of," said Mrs. Wiggins with a laugh.

Ellie was not able to finish her shopping and escape from the store without first hearing a detailed description of Mr. Bell's latest gout attack and an account of Mrs. Wiggins' mother's problem with varicose veins.

Outside, she noticed Michael-John Parker sweeping the sidewalk in front of his shop and waved. He waved back and gestured for her to come and join him.

"Aren't you the tidy shopkeeper," she said when she reached his door.

"Actually, the chaps who installed my new window didn't clean up very well. They left behind little bits that can chew up Whistler's paws. And my carpets." He squatted down to study the sidewalk. "I may actually have to vacuum."

"Did a lot of things get stolen?" asked Ellie.

He shook his head. "No, the berk who did my shop wouldn't know what to steal—or what to do with it. This was more of a statement, if you know what I mean."

Ellie nodded. "So you know who it was then?"

"The type, yes. The perpetrator, no," said Michael-John, standing up again. "And don't get me started on whether the police will do anything about it. I hope the investigation into your crime is going better."

"So far, lots of fuss. No results."

"Isn't that the way of things. Millions die from poverty, and no one lifts a finger, but an old sot snuffs it in the wrong place, and the taxpayers shell out for a full-scale investigation. The miscreant, if there is one, will be tried and sentenced to prison for shaving a few months off a wasted life, costing thousands more pounds, and this is what our society takes pride in calling justice."

"When you put it like that, it does seem skewed, but...I don't know. You can't ignore murder, can you? If that's what it was. Personally, I don't believe it."

Michael-John lifted one eyebrow. "Don't you? Well, good on you. A streak of optimism is probably needed in your job. Will you stop for tea? I think I'm finished here."

"Next time," she promised, shifting her packages from one arm to the other. "I have a cooking project to get on with."

But before she made it back to the Vicarage, Ellie ran into another acquaintance: Charlotte Worthy walking her baby in a stroller. Today she had abandoned the long cloak in favor of a bright green windbreaker and red Capri pants. The baby was covered up to his nose with a blanket, but he looked up at Ellie with a blue-eyed stare remarkably similar to his mother's.

"Hello Charlotte, not working today?" she asked.

"I'm off sick, Mrs. Kent. I only came out to pick up a prescription that the surgery in Chipping Martin sent over to the shop for me. I haven't been able to sleep a wink ever since that murder."

"No one knows for sure if it was murder yet."

"If it wasn't murder, why are the police asking so many questions and following people about?"

"Following people? Who are they following?"

"Me, Mrs. Kent," she said. "I think I'm a suspect."

"Why would they think that?"

"Everything would have been all right if Mum hadn't told that detective that I went out that night. He grilled me for ages. Who'd you talk to? Where'd you go? What did you see? I thought he was going to take *me* to jail, the way he carried on. But I said nothing."

"Did you have anything to say?"

"No. Nothing." She announced this loudly enough for anyone passing by to hear, then began rummaging in her pockets with an important air, pulled out a tissue, and wiped the baby's perfectly dry nose.

"That's all right then, isn't it? So, why don't you introduce me to your baby. He's very cute. What's his name?"

Charlotte squirmed and fussed with the tote bag over her shoulder. "Dolphin," she said quickly. "Dolphin Worthy." She glanced up to gauge Ellie's reaction and then returned to digging in the bag.

"That's unusual."

"I know," said Charlotte, flaring up again. "Mum and Dad say it's not a name at all, and they won't call him anything but Boyo. But it's a name. It's his name."

"I like it. What made you think of it?" Ellie expected to hear that it came from some romance novel, but Charlotte surprised her.

"Dolphins are smart and loyal, and that's what I want him to be. I'd say that's better than being named after a pudding." At last she pulled out a teething ring and slipped it into the baby's mouth. He obediently began sucking on it, but he continued to stare at Ellie. "Did you know if you're drowning, a dolphin will rescue you?"

"I have heard that."

"Well, it's not just some story; it's a scientific fact. There've been hundreds of cases. Thousands. And those are just the ones they know about."

"That's a good omen then," said Ellie. "We all need rescuing once in a while."

Charlotte looked mollified, but as Ellie watched her trundle down the street, she wondered whether the girl really had seen anything on Halloween night. Obviously she had some talent for keeping secrets, since, from what she'd heard, no one had a clue as to how, where, or with whom Dolphin had been conceived.

When Ellie got back to the Vicarage, Hector greeted her with a happy bark that seemed to echo in the empty house. She put her groceries away and tried to think what she should do next. It was too early to start dinner, and she didn't feel like working in her study.

She'd never had free time to worry about in what she thought of as her previous life. Then she was always rushing to keep up with class preparation, reading students' papers, going to committee meetings, writing articles. Now she had to plan each day to stave off feeling at loose ends.

She made herself a cup of tea—that "when all else fails" activity—and sat at the kitchen table, looking out into the yard. In the ten days since Finch had sprained his ankle, no one had raked any leaves. They lay in coppery drifts across the grass, clumped along the church foundation and around the flowers on the graves.

Ellie had lived all of her adult life in cities, and she was no gardener, but she thought she could hardly go wrong with raking leaves. Even Finch, possessive as he was about his territory, couldn't object to a little help with that.

In the entryway off the kitchen, she found an old sweater of Graham's that he used for outdoor work and a pair of small leather gardening gloves—probably Louise's—that were in a basket on the floor. Thus prepared, she went out to the garden shed and found a rake.

Once she began, she discovered she enjoyed raking. It reminded her of her childhood and the neighborhood of old houses and big trees where she'd grown up in Berkeley. Here, however, the leaves accumulated not only from the trees in the yard, but also from the woods adjacent to the churchyard that enclosed the spacious property of Emily Rutherford Hughes.

She worked hard, building up a sweat, and the piles of leaves grew. Before long the yard was dotted with mounds of leaves and began to resemble some kind of earth art installation or prehistoric site.

She had gone into the house for a drink of water before beginning the next task—picking up the piles—when the phone rang.

"St. Michael's Vicarage," she said and waited for a reply. Instead there was silence, then fumbling sounds that she recognized immediately.

"Am I speaking to the vicar's wife?" said that same under-the-blanket voice.

"Yes. This is Ellie Kent. May I help you?"

"I'm just calling to give you a message. You need to tell the police that that man was not murdered. The whole idea is completely wrongheaded."

"How do you know?"

"I can't explain, but it's very important that you tell them. There's nothing to investigate. It was all a mistake. He made a mistake."

"But how do you know? Who are you? Why don't you tell them yourself?" she asked, but the caller had hung up. Ellie stood looking at the old-fashioned wall phone and wished there were some way to retrieve her number.

She picked up the receiver again to call Inspector Mullane and then thought better of it. Jones was probably right. This woman was just a crackpot who wanted attention. Otherwise, why wouldn't she call them instead of her?

She decided to put the whole issue out of her mind, but when she returned to the shed to get the garden cart, she discovered something that brought it right back.

Tucked behind the cart, she found an upturned pail, a candle stuck in a coffee can, several empty beer bottles, a pile of well-thumbed girlie magazines, and another can full of cigarette butts.

Her first reaction was amusement that the dour and elderly Mr. Finch was using this place to while away his time instead of working. But when she jerked on the cart to free it from a tangle of hose that had fallen to the floor, she found two fresh packages of firecrackers. These, she was sure, had never belonged to Mr. Finch.

She sat back on her ankles and considered the possibility that someone else might have been using the shed while Finch was laid up. Surveying the contents—tools, flower pots, drop cloths and paint, canning jars full of nails and screws on a narrow shelf lining the wall, the lawnmower, the ladders—she couldn't see why anyone would bother. It was not an inviting place. But it was private.

She picked up one of the beer bottles and tipped it upside down. A small amount of liquid trickled out. Wasn't that evidence that someone had been using the shed more recently than ten days ago? Carefully, she put the bottle back and, with another glance around, returned to the house.

In the kitchen she washed her hands and face, then picked up the card that DI Mullane had given them and dialed his number. He wasn't there, but she left a message saying she'd found something she thought he should see.

Within less time than it takes to boil water, a police car pulled up in front of the Vicarage.

"We've set up an incident room in the Village Hall," explained DI Mullane, who strode across the lawn so quickly that Ellie had to hurry to keep up.

"I'm not sure if it's connected to anything else," she said, "but it looks like our gardener has a little hangout that other people have been using since he's been off sick."

"Let's have a look," said Mullane.

When he opened the shed door, he became very still and alert, his eyes moving slowly over the jumble of objects. He crouched down to look at the things Ellie had found, but he didn't touch them.

"Did you touch anything?"

"I picked up one the bottles to smell it," she said, pointing to the one.

Mullane gave her a peculiar look: politeness bordering on suspicion. "I'd like your permission to search this shed thoroughly right away."

"Of course. I'm sure that would be all right."

He took out his phone and was calling for assistance, when Graham pulled into the drive. "What's happened?" he asked, trying to put together Mullane, Ellie and the piles of leaves that were beginning to be blown about by a fresh wind.

"Mrs. Kent found something that could prove important," Mullane told him, stuffing his phone back into his front pocket. He was the kind of man who wore his pants too tight and kept too many things in his pockets.

"Someone's been using the shed as a hang out," said Ellie.

Graham looked surprised. "But Finch always keeps it locked, and I checked it myself the other day."

"Is there another way in? A window?"

Graham nodded and they all walked around to the back of the shed where they discovered a window that was closed but unlocked. "Oh Lord, I never even thought about checking that."

"A boy—and possibly a man—could get in through that," said Mullane, as he slid the window shut.

"The same as the church."

"Exactly," said Mullane. "And what was he up to?" They went round again and into the shed to look at the cache Ellie had found. "Would these things—the magazines and so forth—belong to your Mr. Finch?"

"I don't know about the magazines, but I've known Finch for nearly twenty years, and I've never known him to go in for on-the-job tippling."

"You wouldn't be the first to be deceived about something like that, Father, but as your wife so quickly determined, the beer in those bottles was consumed quite recently, so it was probably our prankster. I'd like to search the shed to see if there's any evidence that might be connected to the events of the other night."

"Do you think the dead man might have been using the shed too?" asked Ellie.

"I don't know."

Graham ran his fingers nervously through his hair. "I had rather hoped this business would be settled quickly," he said.

"The sooner we investigate, the sooner we'll be able to piece together what happened."

At that moment, a police car pulled up, and two more men jumped out.

"If you don't mind," said Mullane, "we'll get on with it. And perhaps before our meeting tomorrow, you'll think back over the past few days to see if there's anything else relevant you might have forgotten to mention."

"Of course, Inspector," said Graham. "We'll cooperate in every way possible."

Under Mullane's direction, the two men spread tarps on the grass and proceeded to remove every single tool, pot, canning jar, bag of manure, can of paint, and rag from the shed.

"I had no idea there was so much junk in there," said Graham, as he and Ellie watched from the kitchen window.

Every now and then, the men stopped to confer with Mullane over some object, but all of the things Ellie had found had already been bagged and taken away.

The police car in front of the Vicarage attracted an audience, including a gang of boys on bicycles. The oldest— a lanky boy whose red hair was moussed into aggressive little spikes—led them across the churchyard—no doubt to see where the body had been. Then they returned and parked themselves as close to the police operation as they could get without being shooed away. As they watched the search, they provided their own commentary on the items carried out from the shed, which they apparently found hilarious.

Finally one of the policemen started over to speak to them, and they took off.

Ellie gave up watching then and turned her attention to dinner. If they were ever going to eat, she'd better get started. She unwrapped the chicken and found, to her dismay, that it was still dotted with bits of feather. These she attacked with an unnecessary and unproductive vengeance until the chicken's skin was pockmarked with holes and sagging as opposed to merely feathery.

"What are you making?" Graham asked, coming into the kitchen at an inopportune moment.

"A mess," she said, with a sigh.

He looked from the battle-weary bird to the backyard where the police were now searching the empty shed with high-intensity lights. "You know that business is really getting on my nerves. Would you mind if we went out for dinner instead? There's a new place I've been wanting to try for ages."

Ellie thought she'd never heard a more brilliant idea. "Not at all," she said, rewrapping the chicken in paper. "I can be ready in ten minutes."

The Horse's Head outside of Stow-on-the-Wold was an old pub that had been done over into a posh restaurant-pub. It had the atmosphere created by the heavy beams, old stone walls and vast fireplaces, but the tables were covered with white linen cloths and the food came artfully arranged on glistening white porcelain plates.

Over dinner, aided by candlelight, good food, wine, and the convivial sounds of other diners, Ellie and Graham were able to forget about the day, and tune back into their own private channel. The one that had charged between them when they first met.

"Do you ever think about how much we owe my mother's gall bladder?" Ellie asked. They'd reached the coffee stage and were sharing an upscale version of sticky toffee pudding. "If she hadn't had an attack, I would never have stopped by the day you came to visit my father."

"True, but I think the debt really goes back to the applications committee at Cambridge," said Graham, scooping up a spoonful of toffee sauce and custard. "If they'd accepted me, as I wanted, I would never have been at Oxford when your father came to lecture."

"Right. And I remember thinking I would never forgive him for going on that trip because he missed my tenth birthday."

They smiled at each other across the table, and Graham signaled for the check.

Much later, Ellie woke up thirsty and went to the bathroom to get some water. It was only then, as she filled her glass, that she remembered she'd been doing the same thing that afternoon when the phone rang.

"It was a mistake," the woman had said. Or no: "He made a mistake." That was it.

Was it possible that she was not a nut after all? That she really knew something? If so, what was it? And what could she have meant?

Ellie couldn't help pausing to glance out at the dark and silent graveyard as she tiptoed back to her bed. There, safe and warm, she thought how unfair it was that some accidents could lead to love and some could end in death.

Friday, November 4

Chapter 9

Promptly at 9 o'clock the next morning, DI Mullane and DS Jones arrived for the interview. They all sat at the big table in the kitchen, where Ellie had set a pot of tea and a plate of McVittie's digestive biscuits. Jones had his notebook in front of him and a serious expression. Watching Mullane drink tea with milk and three sugars, Ellie was surprised he had any teeth at all, much less the pearly whites that appeared when he presented his even, emotionless smile.

He told them that the search of the shed had produced no physical evidence of the dead man having been inside it and nothing to suggest that the hideout was connected to his death. There were many different fingerprints in addition to those of Mrs. Kent. An officer was on his way as they spoke, to take Jim Finch's fingerprints for elimination purposes, but it was clear that a number of other people had been in the shed.

"Not our dead man though, unless he wore gloves. We didn't find his prints in the church either."

"So it's a double dead end," said Ellie.

"I prefer to think of it as inconclusive," said Mullane. "Merely something we do not yet understand. Meanwhile, we're following up a number of leads. The photo of our dead man has been published here and in Italy. His Italian underwear, you know. We're also looking at connections between local people and that country." He paused for effect then added, "So, what about you, Father Kent? Do you have any connections in Italy?"

"I've been there on holiday a few times, but I wouldn't say I'd made any connections to speak of."

Mullane nodded then turned smoothly to Ellie. "Mrs. Kent? I believe you once held a U.S. passport in the name of Helen Ruggieri," he said, and the face of her ex-husband, Vito Ruggieri, floated up before her like the answer in a Magic 8 Ball. Dark-eyed, handsome, and indisputably Italian.

"Yes, but that was years ago, and, anyway, my ex-husband was American. We once spent a few months in Italy, which you obviously know since you've researched my passport records, but he was born in America."

Mullane's eyes did not leave her face: "Were you visiting his family?"

"No, Vito is a poet. We went there so he could write."

"Do you speak Italian?"

"I studied it in college."

"So you can converse and read in Italian."

"With a phrase book and a dictionary. Like everyone else!" She got up from the table and went to the sink to refill the kettle. "What exactly are you hinting at, Inspector? That some relative of a man I haven't seen in six years turned up, so I killed him?"

Just then, there was a muffled clunk from the other side of the kitchen door. Graham opened it and found Mrs. Finch hurriedly picking up the broom off the floor.

"I was coming to get a fresh bottle of Dettol, Father Kent," she said quickly. "I didn't realize you were in the kitchen."

"Please focus on the upstairs for now, Mrs. Finch," said Graham.

"Of course, Father," replied the housekeeper, but not before taking in as much as she could of the scene.

"Great," said Ellie, under the whoosh of running water. "My past will no doubt be a hot topic of conversation at The Three Lambs tonight." She set the kettle down on the Aga with a bang.

Graham closed the door and came back to the table, while DI Mullane leaned back in his chair and regarded her with his arms crossed.

"You see, the problem is, we only have your word for it that you didn't know the man, Mrs. Kent. You've admitted meeting him on Sunday, and there's no one to corroborate your account of what happened then or on Monday night."

"I never said I *met* him; I said I *saw* him. There's a difference."

Graham gaped at both of them. "Now wait a minute, Inspector. Surely you're not accusing my wife—"

"No one's accusing anyone of anything, but if Mrs. Kent could just describe her movements on Monday night again, it would be helpful.

"My movements," Ellie repeated. "I didn't have any movements. I was here all evening except when I went to search the church."

"And you had no visitors. No phone calls."

"One visitor. Charlotte Worthy, as you already know." Ellie imagined Charlotte being cross-questioned to see if their stories matched. No wonder the girl was upset.

"And what time was that visit?"

"Around eight thirty and the lights went off a few minutes later."

"How long did she stay?"

"Not even five minutes."

"And where did the visit take place?"

"At the front door."

"So you stood in the doorway talking to her."

"Yes. I invited her in, but she said she didn't have time."

"And what were you doing the rest of the evening?"

An image of herself searching Louise's desk flashed into her mind, and she knew she blushed. Really, she'd to have to learn how to control that if she were going to continue to be interviewed by police.

"Reading in the living room," she said.

"All evening?" He sounded slightly incredulous.

"Yes, Inspector. I was a professor of English literature before I came here, so I read a lot."

"And how long were you away from the house when you went to search the church?"

"I'd guess about fifteen minutes, max."

"Did you see or hear anything—anyone?"

"When I got to the vestry window, I thought I saw someone and I did sort of have the feeling I was being watched as I searched the churchyard."

Graham looked surprised at this revelation. She'd neglected to mention this before because she didn't want him to worry. Now she saw how tricky the question about telling the truth, the whole truth, and nothing but the truth could be. Usually people didn't.

"It was just an impression, and I was very wound up. I'd forgotten about it, actually."

"You were frightened and thought someone might still be lurking in the graveyard, but you didn't call your husband when you got home. Didn't you think you *should* call him— or us—right away?"

"I couldn't call Graham. He'd left his cell phone on the charger, and there's no phone in the hall where he was. And no, I didn't think of calling you. I assumed it was some kid making mischief, that's all. Nothing seemed to have been damaged or taken."

"Except the window and the vase," said Jones, flipping through his notebook.

"So your husband also told us." Mullane looked at them skeptically as if he thought she—or they—might have had another motive for not wanting the police around that night.

"All right. So you returned to the house after this break in. What did you do then? Weren't you worried that the same intruder might break into the next available building— the Vicarage?"

"No. Why would kids break into the Vicarage? Anyway, I assumed that, having nearly been caught, the person would have hightailed it away from the area as fast as possible."

"When, in fact, the person most likely returned to your shed."

"Oh," said Ellie. "I suppose that could be."

"So you went back to the sitting room and resumed reading."

"No. The power was still out. I had a stiff drink and then I fell asleep. Which is how Graham found me when he got home."

"What time was that?"

"About ten thirty," Graham said. "Ellie and Hector were asleep on the sofa."

"Hector is the dog, I take it?" asked Jones, his pencil poised in the air, and Graham scowled at him.

Reluctantly Mullane turned his attention from Ellie to Graham. "All right. What about you, Father Kent? Could you please describe what you did that evening?"

He explained that he'd been at his Morris practice and had gone for a pint with the side afterward. "I can give you their names, if that's necessary," he said stiffly.

"That would be excellent. And did you travel to and from Chipping Martin alone?"

He nodded.

"You understand, I hope," said Mullane, "that in a murder investigation we have to ask questions without regard to people's positions and reputations."

"So you're sure it was murder?" Graham asked.

"We're proceeding on that basis, given the unlikeliness that the old man could have made it to the churchyard off his own bat. And there's also the robbery to consider. So you can appreciate the situation. You were both close to the scene and neither one of you has an alibi for the entire period of nine to eleven o'clock."

"But we have no motive," said Ellie.

"So you say. There's one more question. Do either of you use sleeping pills?"

Graham said no, and Ellie did her best not to blush this time.

"I have some. And I suppose that shows I had the means as well as the opportunity to commit the crime."

"If I might just see them," Mullane said coolly.

Ellie shrugged and led him upstairs to the bathroom, with Graham and Jones following along behind.

As she rummaged through the bathroom cupboard on her hands and knees, she was very conscious of the men standing over her, watching. Finally her travel bag tumbled out onto the floor along with a hot water bottle, American cold medicines, and extra bottles of her favorite shampoo. She took the pills out of the bag, hastily shoved everything else back into the cupboard, and stood up.

Mullane took the bottle and studied the American pharmacy label carefully, before he twisted open the lid and looked inside. "There aren't very many left."

"Really? I didn't know. I hardly ever use them. They're probably out of date."

"No, they're not."

Ellie shrugged. "Well, I haven't taken any since I got here, which I would have thought was fairly obvious."

"You could also say they were hidden."

"Yes, I suppose you could," she snapped, "but they weren't. Look, if I'd used them to poison someone, wouldn't I have thrown the bottle away?"

The inspector said nothing.

"Oh hell, why don't you just take them and test them? If they aren't the same, I hope you'll get over this idea that I had something to do with that man's death."

"But they are the same, Mrs. Kent. I can see that already from the label."

Then, as Ellie watched open-mouthed, he dropped the bottle into a plastic evidence bag and sealed it shut.

"Well," said Graham, who'd turned very pale. "Is there anything else we can help you with, Inspector?"

"No, that's all for the moment."

"You seem to be attempting to build a case against me and my wife based on extremely flimsy and circumstantial connections. We both have very sensitive roles in this village, and I'm sure you realize how damaging rumors and false accusations can be."

"I'm aware of that, Father Kent. Unfortunately in this kind of case there's often collateral damage. We do our best to avoid it, of course."

Graham's face was now stiff with anger. "I should certainly hope so. In the meantime, I'll be contacting my solicitor to discuss the matter with him."

"That's your prerogative," said DI Mullane. "Sergeant Jones will type up your new statements, and I'd like you both to come down to the station to sign them. This afternoon would be fine.

"There's just one other thing. Could you tell me again how long you've been married?"

Graham looked livid. "Two months. Though I can hardly see how that's relevant."

Mullane said nothing, but Jones made a note.

"It's our job to decide what's relevant, sir, and I hope it's not too inconvenient, but until this is cleared up, I must ask you both not to leave the area without notifying us."

After the detectives had left, Ellie sat at the kitchen table, unable to summon the energy to move. Graham collected the tea things, and finally she rose to help him with the washing up. Neither of them wanted to wait for Mrs. Finch to remove the evidence of their visitors.

The dishes clinked noisily in the sink, and Hector's toenails clicked on the stone floor as he paced back and forth between them. From upstairs, they could hear the whir of the vacuum cleaner as the housekeeper worked. It was a normal everyday sound, but the possibility of this ever feeling like a normal day had vanished.

"It's amazing how they can manage to make you feel like you did something wrong, even when you didn't," said Ellie at last.

"I know. I think they take a special course in that."

She made the effort to laugh, but it came out half-heartedly. "So what are you going to do for the rest of the day after this fine start?"

"As usual, I have a sermon to write."

"Maybe you should take the text, 'Thou Shalt Not Kill'."

"Let's not even joke about that."

"You're right. It's not funny."

But what else could they do? Ellie looked at Hector who was waiting anxiously to be noticed. "I guess my philosophy is, when in doubt, run. Does that sound good to you, Hector?"

The weather was totally out of sync with her mood. The air was crisply cool and still, and it was so clear that every leaf and blade of grass shone brightly in the sun. Ellie turned right and followed the road away from the village to get out into the countryside as quickly as possible. Beyond the last house, she turned down a single-track road that wound up a hill, and soon Little Beecham was out of sight.

As she puffed along, with Hector running before her, all she could think of was how you could go along imagining that you knew what your life was about—what your challenges were—and then all of a sudden something would happen that showed you didn't have a clue.

She didn't believe for a minute that Mullane suspected Graham—unless he thought of him as a love-besotted accomplice—but the way he'd lined up the elements of the story, she was a perfect suspect. And the fact that the trail of coincidences led straight back to her ex, Vito Ruggieri, was too ironic for words. He would be tickled to discover that his long shadow could still reach her—especially in such a public and discomfiting way. The most she could hope for was that he'd never find out, but her eagerness to keep Vito and everything that reminded her of him out of her life would no doubt only strengthen the argument that she had a motive for killing the unknown presumed-to-be Italian man.

Ellie had fallen in love with Vito Ruggieri when they were both graduate students at Columbia. He was already a prize-winning poet, and she imagined they had a brilliant future ahead of them, joined perhaps by two or three beautiful children with Vito's dark eyes and sparkling laugh.

She believed he shared this vision when he married her at the City Clerk's Office right before they graduated. She hadn't known then that he'd also been having an affair with his advisor's teenage daughter and was on the verge of being booted out with no degree and no references. Ellie had been his clean slate.

They spent their first summer together in Tuscany in a beautiful but dilapidated stone house, where on a good day you had running water or electricity, but you never had both at the same time. Ellie had struggled to keep house and finish her dissertation on "Jane Austen's Rebels," while Vito drank wine and flirted with girls in the village cafe rather than writing the book he was supposed to produce. The café owner's daughter wept when they left, so maybe there was someone from those days who had grounds for blackmailing Vito, but it had nothing to do with her anymore.

In the fall, they'd started teaching jobs at Baldwin College, a small progressive school in Massachusetts. Ellie had plunged into the demands of her new life, while Vito finally sat down and wrote another book that won an even bigger prize. He used that as an excuse to shirk every other responsibility except to teach a couple of poetry workshops, which were filled with Vito worshippers.

It took four years to make up her mind to quit. The marriage. The job. The town. She thought she'd be the one to make the clean break until she returned to their home one spring afternoon to discover that her husband had left for New York with a 19-year-old linguistics major in tow. Ellie had had to face the unpaid rent, the bills, the packing up, the goodbyes. Once she'd moved back to California and the divorce went through, she cut off all contact with Vito, including his family.

She'd not forgotten the years she'd spent as Ellie Ruggieri, but it was outrageous that anyone might think she was "the Italian connection." It was even more outrageous that Graham and her new life should be touched by her past in this way.

She finally picked up the pace of her running so that the sound of her own beating heart would drive all thoughts from her head. When she reached the top of a second long slope, she stopped, panting, to catch her breath. Her route had taken her about three-quarters of the way around a five-mile circle that would lead back to the village, and she'd once again reached an overlook with Beech Hall below her.

She sat down, leaning back on her elbows, to rest, and Hector lay down beside her, his tongue lolling and his eyes bright. Together they surveyed the pastoral scene with something close to lazy satisfaction.

She'd been near to dozing off when she caught a glimpse of a figure flitting back and forth between two of the windows in the intact part of Beech Hall. She sat up, and, when the figure went by a second time, she had no difficulty identifying Michael-John Parker. He must be doing his research. Or gathering trash. Or whatever it was he did down there.

She decided to find out and hurried down the sloping bank to the lane below with Hector scrambling after her. The gates to the drive were locked, but there was nothing much left of the stone wall that had once enclosed the estate. It was easy enough to climb over and cross through the wood to reach the drive. Closer in, a chain link fence around the house itself was in equally permeable condition.

When she and Hector arrived at the weedy gravel circle in front of the ruins, she found Michael-John standing in the doorway, smoking a cigarette. As ever, he was immaculately dressed—a sharp contrast to Ellie with her old running clothes and sweaty hair. Nevertheless, he smiled and stepped forward to greet her as if he were the lord of the manor and she a special guest.

"You look like you were expecting me," she said.

"I was," he said. "I saw you start down the hill from upstairs. The view from there is breathtaking." He ground out the cigarette with his shoe and then carefully put the butt into his pocket.

"Cleaning up again today?"

He nodded. "I was just about to start back, but I can give you a tour first if you like."

"I'd love it," she said and followed him through the doorless doorway.

They entered a hall that must once have been gracious and now opened to the sky with the remains of a marble staircase curving upward to nothing. Whoever had once lived there, the spiders had now taken over. Their elaborate webs hung in every corner and waved gently in the breeze.

Ellie found herself gaping.

Michael-John smiled. "'Last night I dreamed I went to Manderley again,'" he said, quoting the opening line of the gothic classic *Rebecca*. "Don't you think?"

"It reminds me more of an architectural version of Miss Havisham's wedding cake. You know, stopped time. Nothing changes. How could the family leave it like this for 75 years?"

He shrugged. "Believe me, the Rutherfords seem to have been a remarkably ineffective group of people. I've discovered the only reason they acquired all this was because some murderously violent ancestor did well by King Henry at Agincourt."

Ellie laughed. "I take it you don't approve of the feudal reward system?"

"My own people were more the type whose bodies were left trampled in the mud at the end of the battle."

"I suppose mine were too—if I had a clue who they were. But now at least you have one heroic deed to report in your monograph."

"Exactly. And apparently the latter day heroes did plan to restore the house, but, you know, there was the Great Slump, and then the brothers were killed in the war. Emily was the only one left, and she had to sell most of the land to pay death duties and debts. She's hung on to the house though. I'll give her that. And if I'd grown up in a place like this, I'd fight for it too. Even in the state it's in, it's lovely," he said, running his fingers down a smoke-streaked wall.

Ellie climbed over a fallen beam to enter the wing that was still standing. "You really have fallen hard, haven't you? It would cost a fortune to repair this."

Michael-John shrugged. They were standing in a doorway that opened into a drawing room with a huge stone fireplace. Everything of any possible value that could be removed—floor tiles, moldings, doors—had been scavenged, adding to the ravaged look of the place. French doors must have once led onto a flagstone patio, but they were gone and leaves had drifted through the opening to clot along the walls. "I have a fortune," was all he said. Then, "Let me show you the best part."

They climbed a stone staircase that led to the wing that was still standing and followed a dark hall with rooms off either side. He led her into a spacious corner room with six windows, where golden light streamed in, warming the stone floor, and you could look out at a panoramic view of fields and woods that stretched to the horizon.

"Imagine waking up here every day."

"You're right. Breathtaking is the word," she said. "And I see what you mean about people making themselves at home." She pointed to the blackened hearth of the fireplace. "It smells like someone burned a fire in here recently."

Michael-John frowned. "I know, and I've just spent half an hour cleaning it up."

"Here's something you missed though." She bent down to pick up a small pearl button that lay caught in a crack between tiles and handed it to him.

He inspected the button. "Hmm, a lady. Must have been ripped off in a moment of passion."

"Not a very comfortable place for it."

"But very private. And with a great view."

"Do you think they were looking at the view?" said Ellie.

"P'rhaps not," said Michael-John with a smile.

When they'd descended the stairs and come back out to the drive, he called for Whistler, and the retriever came bounding out of the woods with Hector racing after him. Hector looked like he'd been rolling in dirt and leaves.

"Shall we go?" He picked up his bag of trash. "I should get back to the shop. You never know when a customer might wander in."

Ellie fell in beside him. "Wouldn't it be easier to drive out here? Rather than carrying all that stuff back to the village?"

Michael-John shrugged. "I have to walk the dog anyway. This way we both have a purpose." He looked her up and down as if noticing how she was dressed for the first time. "I used to be a runner," he said. "But it was a time in my life when I had a lot to run away from."

Ellie stiffened. "Really. Well, I do it because it feels good. It clears my head."

"So it has nothing to do with our friendly detectives hovering around your house?"

Ellie gave him a long look. His expression was interested. Non-judgmental. "Most of the time, no, but today, yes," she admitted. "Inspector Mullane seems well on the way to deciding that I'm as good a suspect as he will find."

"Oh, dear. I knew there must be a reason for the high rate of unsolved crimes in this country. All our best detectives are fictional."

Ellie laughed. It felt good to have said the words out loud.

"Just out of curiosity, what was your motive?"

"Stopping the old geezer from blackmailing me about my past life."

"Do you have a past worth blackmailing you over?"

"Only a ne'er-do-well ex-husband who's quite a well-known poet, but I got rid of him long ago."

"Really? And exactly how did you get rid of him, Mrs. Kent? We may be getting to the root of the problem here. I myself have, as you say, gotten rid of a number of exes, but you do have to be careful how you go about it."

Ellie laughed again more heartily and thankfully he changed the subject to his own amorous misadventures.

They took a shortcut across the former gardens and through the encircling woods following a narrow path that Ellie would never even have even noticed if Michael-John had not been leading the way. Consequently, she was surprised to see a woman coming the other way using a walking stick to poke at the grass on either side of the path. She wore a head scarf and carried a long flat basket over her arm.

As they got closer, Ellie recognized Miss Priscilla Worthy, bundled up in her usual layers of sweaters—pink today—and an old tweed coat and wellingtons.

"Mrs. Kent, Mr. Parker, what a surprise! Not many people use this old path any more," she said.

"I came across it returning from Beech Hall one day," said Michael-John.

"Returning from Beech Hall!" Miss Worthy glanced from one of them to the other. If Michael-John had been some other kind of man, Ellie could tell that their being caught together would have been very suspect.

"I was out running, and we met by chance," Ellie said. "Mr. Parker has just been kind enough to give me a tour of the ruins."

"*You* gave a tour of Beech Hall?"

"Yes," said Michael-John, attempting to win the old lady over with one of his smiles. "I've become something of an expert on the place. I also clean up."

Miss Worthy's expression changed from surprise to utter dismay.

"I assure you, I only meant that I pick up the rubbish," he said, holding up the garbage bag. "I hope you won't turn me in for trespassing."

She hitched her basket up into the crook of her elbow. "No, of course not. If it comes to that, I'm trespassing too, but I've picked mushrooms here since I was a girl."

"Is it a good place?" asked Ellie. There were only a few mushrooms in her basket.

"Usually, yes," she said a little defensively. "And do you find a great deal of rubbish, Mr. Parker?" she asked, eyeing the heavy bag.

"Absolutely oodles. People have no respect for private property any more."

"Quite. I guess we're all proof of that, but I must get on. I'll see you this afternoon at the committee meeting, Mrs. Kent?"

Ellie assured her that she'd be there, and they made way for Miss Worthy to continue down the path.

"Committee meeting?" said Michael-John, when they were out of earshot. "Are you sure they'll let you in? I mean, after they find out about...you know."

"Maybe not. Which would be fine with me. I don't expect a coffee morning to be a revelatory moment in my life. Look, do you still have that button? The one I found?"

Michael-John reached into his vest pocket and pulled it out. Ellie took it and rubbed its pink pearly surface with her finger. "I thought so," she said.

"What?"

"Miss Worthy was wearing a sweater that was missing a button exactly like this!"

"Get on with you! That old pussycat? You think she's been having trysts at Beech Hall?"

Ellie closed her hand around the button. "I don't know, but she didn't really seem to be looking for mushrooms. There are tons of them around that she hadn't picked."

"Maybe they're all poisonous."

"Or maybe not," said Ellie. "Maybe the poisonous ones were the ones in her basket."

"You are desperate to pin this murder on someone. I'd better watch out. I suppose next you'll be wanting to solve the mystery yourself."

"Do I look like Miss Marple?"

"No, I guess not."

"It's not a bad idea though," said Ellie suddenly feeling more cheerful. "I could start right now by questioning you. I'll bet you've been to Italy."

"I have," he said. "Many, many times."

"And what was the nature of your business there, sir?"

"Love. Only ever love."

"Really? You quite surprise me. I thought it would be for art or antiques or something."

"I don't care for Italian antiques. Or food. It makes you bloated. But Italian men. Now that's a different story. You know what I mean?"

Ellie stiffened a bit and said: "All too well, I'm afraid."

Chapter 10

Being a detective sounded much better than being a suspect, Ellie thought as she made her way home. Research was one of the things she was good at, and she figured she was in a position to gather information, even if she weren't yet privy to everyone's secrets the way Louise had been. Mentally she began toting up what she already knew and the questions she'd need to answer.

At the Vicarage, she opened the front door to find Emily Rutherford Hughes ranting at Graham in the entry hall.

"There have to be limits," the old lady was saying. "You simply can't let people get away with such an outrage!"

"Oh, hullo," said Graham, who gave her a quick smile then bent to pat Hector.

Mrs. Rutherford Hughes turned from Graham to Ellie, took in her running clothes, and said: "Mrs. Kent," in a tone heavy with disapproval. "I hope you haven't forgotten our meeting this afternoon."

Ellie adopted her most bulletproof smile and said "Of course not. I've just been getting in shape for it."

Mrs. Rutherford Hughes stared at her, then looked down at her watch as if she were setting a timer. "Good," she said. "Then I'll be off. And since we're in agreement, Vicar," she added to Graham. "I'll assume that I will hear no more about this appalling idea."

"What appalling idea was she referring to?" Ellie asked after she'd left. They had gone up to the bedroom, where Ellie stripped off her clothes and turned on the shower in the adjoining bathroom. She put her hand under the thin stream of water, waited for it to heat up then stepped in.

"A proposal has been put forward that our stranger be buried in Little Beecham if he's not identified. She wanted to be sure I knew that she's vehemently opposed."

"Whose idea was it?"

"Mary Bell called, but that usually means Priscilla Worthy wants to do something that Emily won't like, and she has persuaded Mary to make the case. Mary being somewhat more influential as the wife of the church warden, but also someone who shares Priscilla's resistance to Emily always having her own way."

"Lucky you. And I suppose Emily sees the churchyard as her property."

"Correct. She views it as her family burial ground," said Graham, who stood leaning against the bathroom doorframe. "The other people are her guests."

Ellie laughed. "So do you really agree? About the old man?"

He shrugged. "With Emily, I pick my battles very carefully. Speaking of which, I'd recommend that you do the same. She has some rather fixed notions about how the coffee morning should go."

"That won't be a problem," she said, pushing aside the shower curtain to grab a towel off the towel heater. "I have no notions about the coffee morning at all."

Still she found herself wondering what a murdering vicar's wife/detective ought to wear on such an occasion, and Graham watched with amusement while she rifled through her small collection of trousers, skirts, and dresses. When she'd finally decided on a grey wool pencil skirt, navy cashmere turtleneck, and navy pumps, with a necklace of silver beads, she asked, "What do you think? Do I look harmless and helpful?"

"I'm not sure. I need a closer look," he said and stepped forward to embrace her.

"Wait a minute. I really need to know," said Ellie, pulling back to look at his face. "Do you think they'll have heard? That Mullane has decided I'm a suspect?"

"No. And I don't believe he really has. He's just probing in every direction. No one in their right mind could think we'd commit murder," he said and kissed her.

Ellie kissed him back, and she fully appreciated the loyalty behind that "we," but she was still sure that Mullane saw in her a tidy solution to his problem.

As she walked to the home of Mr. and Mrs. Bell on the outskirts of the village, she imagined an elderly man buying new clothes before visiting someone. Her own parents hadn't bought any new clothes for years. They said there was no need; they could get along with what they had.

So was that significant? Were the clothes a disguise? Or was he trying to impress someone? If so, who? And why didn't it work? If he'd been welcome, would he have ended up sleeping rough as Ralph Teaser claimed? Would he have ended up dead? She thought about the woman who called and wondered what mistake he'd made and whether it was in coming to Little Beecham at all.

She was walking up the drive through the Bells' large well-tended garden when suddenly Miss Worthy appeared as if from nowhere. This was the second time in a single day that she'd surprised her, but this time the surprise was only on Ellie's side. Miss Worthy had been waiting for her.

"Hullo, Mrs. Kent," she said, falling in beside her. "I was hoping to see you."

"That's nice," said Ellie, hoping it was true.

"I know it's none of my business, and I'd hate you to think I'm one of those interfering types, but I have to say I was quite shocked to see you out with Mr. Parker today. It occurred to me that you must not know him terribly well, and so you might welcome a word of caution."

"I wasn't 'out' with him, Miss Worthy. We just happened to run into each other, and as we were both returning to the village we walked together. I think he's very nice."

"Do you?"

"Yes," said Ellie more firmly. "Why?"

"It's just that ever since he came here people have had questions. About his money. His lifestyle. And some of his pre-occupations are quite peculiar, wouldn't you say?"

"Not particularly. Why? What are you really asking, Miss Worthy?"

"Well, all that business about cleaning up Beech Hall. It's quite absurd. If I weren't certain the place had been stripped bare years ago, I'd suspect him of stealing something."

Ellie suppressed a small pang of agreement and said: "He told me he's fallen in love with the place, that's all. He'd like to buy it and restore it, but apparently Mrs. Rutherford Hughes won't sell."

Miss Worthy stepped back so fast she nearly tripped over a tree root. "Buy it! But that's unthinkable."

"I don't see why not. It will be a pile of rubble if no one does something soon. Michael-John is rich and he'd make it into a home again. Wouldn't that be better than letting what's left collapse?"

Miss Worthy clutched at her coat as if a cold wind had just blown through her.

"No," she said in a more assertive tone than Ellie had ever heard her use before. "It would not. And this fantasy," she continued, "only shows how little he understands the situation, if you'll pardon my saying so. You don't think he's mentioned this to Emily, do you?"

Ellie shrugged. "He might have. Does it matter so much? I mean, of course, neither one of us can fully appreciate what it means to her, but, after all, something has to happen to it when she's, well, gone. Wouldn't it be better to know it was entrusted to someone who would care for it?"

Miss Worthy shook her head emphatically "I'm sure this sounds rude and arbitrary, Mrs. Kent, but the answer is no, absolutely and finally no. If Mr. Parker is a friend of yours, you'd be doing him a service to tell him to forget any notion of buying that house—and never to say a word about harboring such ambitions to anyone, much less Emily."

Ellie thought calling the ruins a house was a wild overstatement, but they'd reached the door of Castor House, the Bells' imposing Georgian home, and Mrs. Bell opened it before they even had time to knock.

"Hello, Mrs. Kent. Priscilla, what on earth have you been doing out here? Emily has been waiting these ten minutes, and you know how she gets."

"We were just chatting, Mary, and we're not late," said Miss Worthy staunchly.

"How very nice, I'm sure, but the time is getting on. I've just been hearing all about her visit to the Vicar," she said, as she led them through a hall lined with oriental carpets.

"And—"

"What do you think?!" hissed Mrs. Bell, and Miss Worthy's brow wrinkled in an angry frown.

In the drawing room, Mrs. Rutherford Hughes sat in front of the fireplace at a low table, set with a silver tea service and plates of delicate tea sandwiches and Victoria sponge cake. Although she was only in her early 70s, she looked older, and Ellie thought she appeared even more gaunt than she had a few days before. Her high-collared silk blouse hung loosely around her long neck and bony wrists. Nevertheless, she maintained a ramrod straight posture as she held her cup of tea, and her expression made it plain that she was annoyed with them for keeping her waiting, despite the fact that the clock chimed two at that very moment.

"Here we are," said Mrs. Bell in a bright, artificial tone. "They were here all the time, right outside, having a chat. Now who would like tea before we begin? Priscilla, you look a little peaky. Let me get you a cup. Mrs. Kent, please take any chair."

Mrs. Rutherford Hughes looked from one to the other of them suspiciously, set down her tea, and picked up a pen and a leather folder of papers while Mrs. Bell bustled about pouring tea and passing the refreshments.

When they were settled, their chairperson said, "I'm sure I'm glad that you've found so much to talk about, but I trust we can focus on the topic at hand now. I have apologies from Mildred." She looked at Ellie over her half glasses and explained, "Priscilla's niece Mildred Worthy will be in charge of decorations, but today she is babysitting for that so-called grandchild of hers."

"There's no call to put it like that, Emily," said Miss Worthy irritably. "The baby most certainly is her grandson, and Charlotte is ill. Of course Mildred has to step in."

Mrs. Bell looked surprised by this outburst, but Mrs. Rutherford Hughes only glanced sourly at Miss Worthy and continued on. "Since this is our first meeting, we should set some goals for this year. Receipts from the coffee morning have gone down over the past three years, and it has become too much like a party for the village, rather than a fundraising event. I think we need to set our sights higher, and that one thousand pounds in receipts is a reasonable target."

"A thousand pounds?" said Mrs. Bell. "But the most we've ever made was six hundred fifty."

"Exactly. So we'll have to exert ourselves rather more this year."

"I'm sure we have always worked very hard to make it a lovely event, and the people who come enjoy it," said Mrs. Bell in an offended tone.

"If it's such a popular event, as you say, then maybe we need to consider putting up the prices. We can double the door fee, and charge more for everything. After all, why should we be selling homemade cakes for five pounds? They cost twice that at any shop."

"We can't do that," said Miss Worthy. "If we do, our pensioners won't be able to afford anything, and they love the coffee morning."

"Then we'll have to come up with some other strategy," said Mrs. Rutherford Hughes. "The parish is falling short on its contributions again this year, and that money has to be made up somewhere."

Ellie didn't really understand the financial—or any other—aspect of how the church was run as a business, but the others looked chastened.

"Now, I took Mildred's report over the telephone. She's planning her usual bits and bobs, as you might expect. I suppose there isn't much we can do there, since the goal is to raise more money, not spend more. She says Jack will donate a tree for us and deliver it the day before."

"As usual, we'll all gather items for the tombola. No junk, please. We need clean, quality items. Mary, perhaps you will be so good as to tell us what you have in mind for the home produce stall."

Mrs. Bell picked up a small sheet of notepaper and began reading from it, but her face was pink with irritation. Ellie listened to her recount who'd already volunteered to make marmalade, who would bring a lemon drizzle cake and so on, trying to imagine how this would add up to more than about £300.

"You'll need to involve more people to reach our goal, and they should diversify. We can't have a table with forty jars of orange marmalade. There has to be variety," Mrs. Rutherford Hughes pronounced.

Miss Worthy opened her mouth to say something, but instead turned abruptly to look out the window. She had changed from her mushrooming clothes, but Ellie noticed that she was twisting her buttons as she stared out into the garden. It was the very habit that must have caused her to lose the pink button at Beech Hall.

And what had she been agitated about then? Had she had a rendezvous with someone there? The person who built the fire? And could that have been the man with the white beard who was thought to have been sleeping rough? He might well have been walking to Beech Hall when Ellie saw him in the woods.

Ellie was almost convinced she could see these scenes, when Mrs. Rutherford Hughes's barking voice brought her back to the meeting. What, she demanded to know, was Miss Worthy planning to do about the teas?

Miss Worthy blinked as if she too had to remind herself where she was. "I haven't thought about it yet," she admitted. "When the time comes, I'll make biscuits and probably a few cakes. We'll borrow the urns from the church as usual."

"Your biscuits are always lovely," said Mrs. Bell hurriedly. "I hope you make those smashing sugar stars again. And your shortbread of course."

"Just don't put too much sugar in everything, Priscilla," said Mrs. Rutherford Hughes, writing on her pad. "And don't give away extra biscuits with the tea. One is enough. If there are any left over, we can sell them."

Miss Worthy scowled and turned back to the window. The wind had picked up, and the beech trees were beginning to sway.

Ellie knew her turn was next, so she was ready when the cold grey eyes focused on her. "Now, Mrs. Kent, you've heard our little plans. Have you anything to contribute?" Mrs. Rutherford Hughes managed to sound accusing and dismissive at the same time. A fine art.

Ellie set down her teacup and said, "It sounds like you have everything taken care of, but I'd be happy to pitch in wherever I can help. Make a poster, perhaps?"

This offer was greeted with silence, so she plunged in and added, "Also, you didn't mention a raffle. I could ask local merchants to make donations."

She saw Mrs. Rutherford Hughes write down 'Poster and Raffle' next to 'Mrs. Kent' on her pad.

"The raffle could include more than just donations," she added. "I could ask people to donate services like hanging Christmas lights and wrapping presents."

Miss Worthy shifted her gaze from the garden to Ellie. "I knew you'd have some new ideas," she said.

"A raffle is hardly a new idea," said Mrs. Rutherford Hughes. "We used to have one every year."

"Oh, Emily. I don't know why you have to be so discouraging and negative," said Miss Worthy. Mrs. Bell shot her a warning look, but she'd discovered defiance and went on recklessly. "*We* are trying to cooperate and help the church, and *you* are making it very unpleasant."

Mrs. Rutherford Hughes's expression became icier than ever: "I merely stated a fact, Priscilla. A fact is neither positive nor negative."

"That's nonsense, and what's worse is you believe your opinions *are* facts," said Miss Worthy.

Mrs. Rutherford Hughes ignored her and told Ellie, "In the past, Louise handled the raffle. We haven't had one since she died. I suppose it's fitting that we take it up again, now that we have a new vicar's wife."

Mrs. Bell jumped in again, saying "I think the idea of raffling off services is brilliant. I'd buy a chance on help with wrapping presents. Charles has so many nieces and nephews. After a while it's not fun anymore."

Miss Worthy said nothing. She'd worried her button to the point that it was hanging by a single thread.

"That's settled then," Mrs. Rutherford Hughes said. "You can tell us next week how you're getting on, Mrs. Kent. And all of us should be thinking of how our activities can earn more than before. Since Friday is Remembrance Day, we will meet Saturday week at Priscilla's cottage. And please let's be ready to start at two pm sharp."

With that, she announced that she had another appointment and stood up. The others rose too, and the meeting ended with cursory, chilly, goodbyes.

Outside, the sky had grown ever-more threatening, and Mrs. Rutherford Hughes sped away in her ancient black Mercedes as the first rain began to fall. Miss Worthy looked at them as if she'd like to say something, but instead pulled a scarf out of her pocket, tied it around her head, and, with a hurried goodbye, set off, unfazed by the storm.

When only Ellie remained, Mrs. Bell said, "I'm sure you know, Mrs. Kent, that even the very oldest of friends squabble now and then, but it means nothing. In no time, it's forgotten and they move on."

Ellie concurred politely, but she was relieved to see Graham's Mini pull into the drive, ending the conversation. She and Mrs. Bell shook hands formally, as the old friends they were not should do, and thanked each other. Then Ellie ran out into the cloudburst and jumped into the car.

"Am I ever glad to see you," she said to Graham, as they pulled away from Castor House and took the B road toward Chipping Martin.

"Was it really that bad?" asked Graham with twinkling eyes.

"Aside from the fact that they all seem to hate each other, and Mrs. Rutherford Hughes has set an impossible goal for the event, it was fine. The tea sandwiches looked delicious, but I was afraid to eat one, in case the dragon spoke to me while I had a mouth full of fish paste. Anyway we all survived. And I may not have to bake after all. I'm going to arrange the raffle."

"Really? That was something Louise always did, did you know?"

"No, no thanks to you, but, believe me, I was told. Mrs. Rutherford Hughes certainly has a way with words. She can make any remark sound like a threat or an insult. I thought she and Miss Worthy might come to blows."

"Over what?"

"Ostensibly over the number of cookies given with a cup of tea, but I think it might really have been about her opposing the burial. Mrs. Bell let her know that she opposed it. What I don't get is why Miss Worthy should care what happens to him?"

"I believe Mary said something like it's where his soul left this earth. That's definitely not an idea she would have come up with, so it was probably Priscilla's."

"Lordy. By that logic, if you dropped dead in the street, you should be buried under the sidewalk."

"Exactly. But I suppose she thinks of it as poetic."

"Yes, I can see that. She was rhapsodizing about the ruins of Beech Hall today as well."

"I'm surprised that was mentioned at the meeting."

"Oh no. It wasn't. This was outside, when Miss Worthy accosted me on the way in to warn me that Michael-John Parker was an unsavory character and I should avoid him," said Ellie.

"My goodness, you have had an eventful afternoon."

"Yes, well, I ran into him on my run and we ran into her, and he made the mistake of going on about how he loves that old heap of stones." For the time being, she thought it was better not to mention the button, the fireplace or the fact that she planned to try to solve the murder herself.

Graham shifted gears and sped along the rain-drenched road. It was slippery with wet leaves, but most vehicles didn't bother to slow down. They hurtled past, throwing up blinding sprays of water, and Ellie flinched every time, clutching the dashboard. Trees flashed by in a tweedy blur.

"I can understand Mrs. Rutherford Hughes having strong ties to the place," she went on when there was no immediate threat to their lives, "but what's that got to do with Miss Worthy? She was practically apoplectic over Michael-John's dreams of buying the place."

"The story I've always heard was that, after the fire, Emily and her brothers and their friends used to play in the ruins—knights and ladies and that sort of thing. And they believed that when the house came to their generation, they'd right the wrongs of their elders," said Graham.

"Like a pact, you mean?"

"Yes, some childish form of that."

"And instead, Emily's brothers died, and she was the only one left."

"Exactly. Whatever money was left went to death duties and unpaid debts. The house she lives in belonged to her husband's family."

"So what will happen when she dies?"

"Only her solicitor knows that secret."

"Who's that?"

"Mr. Bell, of course. He's everyone's solicitor," said Graham, as he pulled into the police station car park. He shut off the engine and Ellie felt herself precipitously dropped back into the present and her own uncertain future.

In the station, Sgt. Jones escorted them to the now familiar interview room and treated them with a dour courtesy. He gave them tea in Styrofoam cups that tasted of plastic and handed them their statements from the morning's interview.

Ellie felt a surge of anger as she read the summary of what she'd said typed on an official police department form. Nothing was untrue, but the way the facts were put together made it possible to think she could be guilty.

Graham looked tense and withdrawn when he handed back his form. They both waited for Sgt. Jones to say something, anything, about what was going to happen next, but he only glanced at the signatures and said thank you.

On the way home, Ellie started a dozen conversations in her head, but couldn't think of a thing to say aloud. Graham drove with preoccupied concentration through the darkening countryside. At last she said, "So speaking of Mr. Bell, did you ever talk to him about all this?"

"No, I decided to wait. I suppose I'm naïve, but I can't believe they won't find some clue to what really happened soon and leave us in peace."

How naïve became more evident soon after they returned home. They'd just settled down by the sitting room fire, when the doorbell rang. Ellie went to answer it and there was their neighbor Mrs. Bigelow waiting on the doorstep, wrapped in a large caped mackintosh.

Reluctantly, she invited the woman in, and Graham offered her a glass of sherry. Mrs. Bigelow accepted and settled her large body into an armchair close to the fire with obvious satisfaction.

"This is very cozy," she said, looking around her. Then after a good slug of her sherry, she leaned forward confidentially and said, "I don't want to intrude on your personal time, Vicar, but I thought you ought to know what happened this afternoon while you were out."

Ellie and Graham waited while she took another drink and paused to heighten the dramatic effect of whatever it was she was about to say.

"Those police officers came back, you know. They knocked on your door, but even after they saw that you weren't home they went right ahead with their work. I don't know what they were doing, but it involved a great deal of pacing and measuring, and they went into your shed again too."

Ellie wondered how Mrs. Bigelow could know that, since the shed was not visible from her windows.

"I thought it my duty to come over despite the rain." Here she took out a crumpled handkerchief and blew her nose noisily. "Just to make sure, you know, that they didn't do anything illegal. Nowadays, you can't trust the police at all. They're as bad as criminals when it comes to search and seizure.

"They assured me that they had your permission to go into the shed, but I kept watch to make sure they didn't take anything." She sniffled a bit and finished her glass of sherry, which Graham promptly topped up.

"And did they?" he asked in his perfectly noncommittal vicar's voice.

"No. But they asked me if they could come back to interview me again since I live so close to the scene. They said they could tell that I'm a good observer, which I thought was very perceptive of them.

"I agreed, of course, but I never expected to get the third degree. You wouldn't believe all the questions they asked me about you and Mrs. Kent. Was I surprised that you'd gotten married after such a short acquaintance? Was that—I think the word they used was—characteristic? How did Mrs. Kent seem to be settling in? Did you have many visitors? What kind of schedule do you keep? Have you seemed any different in the past week than formerly? And any details about the period around the murder. After they finally left, I had to take one of my calming pills."

Ellie sipped her own sherry, resisting the temptation to slug it down and pour herself a large whisky—her own idea of a calming dose. It was bad to be discussed in the third person as if she weren't there, worse that the person involved was a busybody like Mrs. Bigelow.

Graham rose to the occasion better than she did. He calmly crossed his legs and regarded Mrs. Bigelow with his clear, honest blue eyes.

"That sounds most unpleasant," he said, "but I'm sure you gave them what information you could and that will be the end of it. I can't see any reason why they should bother you again. Inspector Mullane has assured us that this kind of detailed questioning is typical and necessary for the police to develop a full picture of what happened. I'm sorry that they upset you."

"Oh, they were polite enough. It was what they seemed to be implying that upset me." She glanced at Ellie to make sure her point was not lost on either of them.

"I don't think it pays to read too much into any one aspect of the investigation," Graham said smoothly and, as soon as he could, he thanked her for coming by and ushered her out the door.

"Ugh! That was horrible. Hideous! Disgusting!" said Ellie when they were alone again. "I feel like I need a shower. That woman was reveling in every moment, and I'm sure she's been on the phone telling everyone in the village."

"I'm afraid you're probably right. But, if it's any comfort, no one in the village likes her or listens to her."

They managed to eat the steak and kidney pie Mrs. Finch had made in peace—if a preoccupied silence could be described as peace—and afterward Graham retired to his study to work on a text he was translating from medieval Latin. Ellie believed this was a sure sign that he was more upset than he let on.

Her own solution lay in studying the present, not the past. She brought her laptop to the sitting room and curled up in an armchair to summarize her views on the case.

She created a file named *Investigation.doc* and typed: Who was the dead man?

Then:

Tall, handsome, in his 70s. Walked vigorously. Healthy?

Italian? (underwear, accent. . .)

Stranger (according to Graham, Wiggins, Three Lambs, police)

NOT a stranger (knew way through woods)

Why did he come? (Lover friend, ex-wife, business partner, relative?)

Where did he stay? (Beech Hall??? Elsewhere?)

Miss Worthy's button...is it connected? (If she knew him, then others must too?)

She'd just pulled out the local newspaper to check ads for campsites and B&Bs in the area, when the phone rang.

"Mrs. Kent?" said a breathless voice. "Is that you?"

"Yes, Charlotte. How are you?" From the sounds of traffic, Ellie deduced that she was not at home.

"I've had a spell, but I told Mum I needed some air. I just had to call you."

"Why?"

"Those policemen came back today."

"The ones following you?"

"No, that detective and his partner, and they went on at me about every detail of that night. Like how fast did you answer the door, and why did I think you didn't invite me in? Did it seem like there was anyone else in the house? Were you like nervous or anything?"

"So what did you tell them?"

"I said you were fine. I didn't want to come in. But I thought you ought to know that, like no matter what I said, they seem to suspect you!"

"I know."

"You do? But how can that be? I mean I never thought it could turn out like this."

"What do you mean by 'it,' Charlotte?"

There was a pause before she said, "Nothing. All I ever did was take a walk and bring you that book."

"If that's true, you have nothing to worry about."

"Of course it's true," she said defensively, but then in a rush, she added, "Look, Mrs. Kent, I'd help you if I could, but I have my baby to think of. I'm all he's got in the whole world." Then she began to cry and the line went dead.

"I've just had the most interesting conversation with Charlotte Worthy," said Ellie, going into Graham's study.

He looked up dreamily, as if returning to the 21st century took a long time. "Charlotte? What did she want?"

"She called to say the police questioned her again and wanted to know every detail about her visit here on Halloween night."

"Oh, Lord," said Graham. He put the cap on his fountain pen and ran his hands through his hair wearily.

"But that's not the point. The point is I'm sure she knows something. Or saw something."

"What?"

"She wouldn't say. She started to cry and hung up."

"I thought she was here before anything happened."

"She was. But she might have noticed something odd. Or someone."

"She hasn't told the police?"

"She seems to be afraid to tell anyone."

"I wish she would. I suppose by now there's no chance the police will conclude it was an accident after all."

"No. Although that's what the mystery caller wants us to think."

"Mystery caller?" said Graham, surprised.

"Didn't I tell you? That woman who called the first day called again. She told me to tell the police it was all a mistake. Or the man had made a mistake. I guess that was it."

"But Ellie, this is very important! Did you tell Mullane?"

"No. I figured they'd think either I'd made it up or she was crazy. I mean, why tell me? Not them?"

"But they have to check it out. This could be the solution to the whole thing," he said, closing his translation folder. "If you won't tell them, I'm going to." He reached for the phone, but before he could begin to dial the Chipping Martin station, they heard a voice call, "Hello?!" and Hector leapt to his feet, barking.

"Who's that?" asked Ellie.

"Oh Lord," Graham said again, putting down the phone. "I've been forgetting to tell you something too. It's Isabelle. She always comes for Bonfire Night. I tried to talk her out of coming this time, but she insisted."

They both went into the hall with Hector dancing around their feet, and there was Isabelle, the stepdaughter Ellie barely knew.

"Hello, darling," said Graham, embracing the girl, who threw her arms around him and called him "Daddy." Then she bent down to pick up the wriggling little dog, and they lavished kisses on each other's faces. Finally, she turned to Ellie with a friendly smile and reached out to hug her too. "Hello, Ellie. How are you? It's good to see you again."

Isabelle was not as tall as Ellie, but nearly, and, as they hugged, her bones felt fragile and light beneath the skimpy clothes she wore: a cropped sweater and skintight jeans. She had Louise's beautiful fine features and clear fresh complexion, but Graham's lankiness and shining intelligent eyes.

"Let's not just stand in the door. It's freezing out there. I hope you brought a coat," said Graham, picking up Isabelle's laptop and backpack from the floor.

Isabelle laughed. "Oh, *Dad*. I was in the car. I didn't need a coat. Anyway I have plenty of clothes here."

"Are you hungry?" asked Ellie. "Mrs. Finch made a huge steak and kidney pie for dinner."

"Did she now?" said Isabelle. "Well, isn't she a good egg! I'm famished, and that's my favorite thing in the whole world."

What a coincidence, Ellie thought, but she only smiled, and, as they trooped off to the kitchen, she was struck by how much more noisy and crowded the house suddenly seemed.

Isabelle slid into the spot at the table where Ellie usually sat—at Graham's right hand, so she sat down opposite, on his left. She and Graham shared a beer, but his eyes never left his daughter's face, as she chatted about what she called "uni" and ate her way through a giant serving of pie.

Ellie kept smiling and thought about all her friends who'd struggled to connect with stepchildren. How she had always imagined that if she were in that position she'd do better, and now here she was faced with the chance to prove it. If she could.

When Isabelle had finished eating, she pushed back her plate, looked from Graham to Ellie, and said, "Right then, now I want to hear all about this murder."

"I hope you didn't come home because of that," Graham said.

"Dad, I came because of Bonfire Night. You know that. But now I'm here, I want to know about the biggest news ever to hit Little Beecham. Especially since it touches my own family. If you don't tell me, I'll only hear at the pub, so let's get on with it."

"All right," he said. "I'd rather you hear about it from us."

He glanced at Ellie, who was picking at the drips of candle wax on the candles, and Isabelle waited expectantly until she said:

"I guess you could say it all started on Halloween night, when someone broke into the church. Your father was out, but I noticed the light and went to investigate. When I got there, I didn't find anything except the open window in the vestry."

"And Emily's broken vase," added Graham.

"You mean that little vase she always sets on her window sill?"

"Right. It was on the floor, broken."

Isabelle shivered with pleasure. "That sounds like a ghost!"

"But a ghost wouldn't need to break the window to get in."

"No, you're right. It must have been Jackie Henning then. Knocking over the vase just for the hell of it sounds like something he'd do."

"Who's Jackie Henning?"

"Little Beecham's number one aspiring yob. Age fourteen. He undoubtedly was behind the mess last year, but no one could prove it because no kid would dare grass on him. He's quite the little bully," said Isabelle.

"We never proved that, Is, so there's no point in demonizing him, as some people seem very quick to do," said Graham.

"With good reason. But, of course, you-know-who gives him the benefit of the doubt," said Isabelle. "Didn't they find any fingerprints?"

Ellie shrugged. "We only know they didn't find the dead man's. But someone broke in, and someone robbed the man, and somehow he died in the churchyard."

"Quite a satisfying little mystery. So what's the village opinion? Who was he and who did it?"

"You know, that's another odd thing. I haven't heard a single theory about who he was," said Ellie. "Have you, Graham? Everyone says he's a stranger. A foreigner. And they all seem pretty happy with that explanation."

"No, I haven't heard anything either," said Graham.

"When people in the village don't express their opinions, it means they either all know something so there's no point in saying it or they really don't know," said Isabelle. "That foreigner business sounds like a blind. I mean, what would a foreigner be doing here in Little Beecham? Present company excluded, of course."

"That's what the police are trying to figure out."

"Where's he supposed to be from?"

"Italy," Ellie and Graham said simultaneously.

"The police have been frantically trying to find some link between this Italian stranger and the village. One of the things you'll undoubtedly hear is that a front-runner for the honor is me."

"You! You're a suspect! Dad, you never breathed a word about that. No wonder you were trying to keep me away. And I thought—well, never mind what I thought."

She sat back, wide-eyed, and, in a gesture that Graham also used, ran her fingers through her long blonde hair. "That's totally daft! What could you possibly have to do with some stranger?"

"That's the big question. But I'm a stranger too, after all. No one knows that much about me. Where I come from. What my past is."

"Wow," said Isabelle, but Ellie caught a fleeting exchange of looks between daughter and father.

"Of course we know you," Graham said staunchly. "And your father before you. You're just making a good story, Ellie. I didn't tell you, Is, because I'm sure the whole thing will be sorted any day now. Nonetheless, it's been very difficult."

"I'll say. It sounds absolutely beastly."

"It has been pretty awful, and it has been a long day, so if you don't mind, I'm beat." Ellie began collecting the dishes from the table.

Isabelle jumped up. "I can do that," she said. "Please let me, and don't let me keep you up."

"OK," said Ellie. "I'm sure you two have a lot of catching up to do anyway."

Graham got to his feet too, and they both kissed her goodnight, but Ellie thought she saw something like relief in their faces. They were glad she was going, so they could be alone. Hector looked from her to them and then settled back into his basket. Of course, when it came to loyalties she knew where he stood.

She went to the sitting room to collect her laptop. The *Investigation.doc* file was still open. She glanced at it again then pressed delete, as if this could erase the past few days from her memory as well.

As she climbed the stairs to the bedroom alone, she suddenly felt incredibly tired and lonely. She was reminded of her first days living in the Vicarage when she'd felt rather like a houseguest whose length of stay had not yet been determined.

Saturday, November 5 (Bonfire Night)

Chapter 11

In the morning, Ellie came down to the kitchen fully dressed and braced for a family breakfast, but Graham was there alone, in his old navy plaid woolen bathrobe stirring a pot of porridge that had been cooking slowly in the Aga overnight.

"We sat up until two," he said, excusing Isabelle's absence. "She's writing a paper on the Civil War."

"Really? She's interested in that?" asked Ellie, pouring herself some tea.

"The English Civil War."

"Oh, right. I forgot you had one too."

He plopped some porridge into a bowl and handed it to her. "More than two centuries before yours, as a matter of fact," he said. "There's hot milk in the microwave."

"So you didn't confine yourselves to local gossip?" she asked, as they sat down at the table.

"No. She wanted to know why they would suspect you, and I made it clear that they don't know anything for certain—not even that the man was really murdered."

"You're probably the last person clinging to that hope."

"Anyway, the coroner will decide. Not the village or the police."

Ellie began to eat, but he stirred his porridge around and around until the oats, treacle, milk, and butter were all mixed into a thick syrupy concoction.

"I feel like a total prat for forgetting to tell you that Is was coming," he said. "I put you both at a disadvantage— especially you—and I'm grateful you handled it so well." He was so contrite that Ellie decided to pass over the fact that

Mrs. Finch had obviously known, making her the only one who didn't.

Instead, she turned her head. "See this," she said, tapping her left cheek with her forefinger, "I'm turning the other cheek. And I forgive you. But personally, I think letting your spouse know when company is coming should be one of the marriage vows."

Graham laughed and looked relieved. "Agreed. So where are you off to this morning? You're looking very...British today," he said, taking in her grey tweed jacket and conservative wool trousers. She had pinned her red poppy to the lapel of her jacket.

"I'm glad you noticed. Not that it will fool anyone. I'm off to solicit donations for the raffle. I thought I should try to look the part of a coffee morning committee member." She didn't mention that, refreshed by a night's sleep, she was determined to continue her private investigation.

Graham wished her luck, and shortly after breakfast she set off for the village shop. There she found Mrs. Wiggins poring over her copy of the weekly *Oxford Times*—which carried a front-page photo of the dead man.

"Good morning, Mrs. Kent," she said. "I was just wondering how you and the Vicar were bearing up, what with all this nonsense about murder."

"We're fine," said Ellie, "we just wish the police were making more progress."

She shook her head. "I know. Seems like nowadays you can't pee without the government knowing when, where, and how much. So how can a man walk into the village, be seen by everyone, and get killed without anyone knowing a thing about it? If we had them CCTV cameras like they have in Chipping Martin, this would all be done and dusted by now."

"I doubt the cameras cover the graveyards though."

"That weren't where he was killed. Someone had taken him and fixed him good and proper with a few stiff drinks, and it weren't the Teasers at The Lambs. Nor you! I hope you know that not everyone in this village is daft enough to believe that."

Ellie smiled ruefully. "Thank you."

"What I say is that, if the vicar married you, I know all I need to know about your character, foreign or not. The very idea that they would suspect you shows they haven't got a clue what happened."

"The other day you said the man looked familiar. Did you ever remember who he reminded you of?"

She studied the man's face for a moment then closed the paper. "No. He looks a bit like Charlie Withers, but he's been dead ten years or more. He don't look Italian to me, but what do I know." She laughed and leaned forward, tapping her finger on the counter. "I've never left home myself. Too busy!"

"But if he were a local like your Mr. Withers, a lot of people would know him, wouldn't they?"

"Not necessarily. We've had a lot of incomers in these last years, and the old timers have long memories, but not necessarily about anything useful. That Doris Finch can't seem to forget that I once sold her a tomato with a worm in it. Thirty years later she looks suspiciously at every veg she buys here, and I have to be glad she still comes. But that's neither here nor there. What can I do for you today?"

"I'm on church business actually," and Ellie went into her pitch about the coffee morning.

Mrs. Wiggins was eager to put weight behind her view that Ellie was innocent and immediately offered to make up a food basket for the raffle. "It's only what we did for the first Mrs. Kent, so why wouldn't we do the same for you?"

Why not indeed? thought Ellie as she dropped a two-pound coin into the Poppy Appeal box.

However, she found village opinion was more mixed than her encounter with Mrs. Wiggins would suggest.

At Tiddington's, she had to listen to John's summary of the case as determined by the Friday night tipplers at The Three Lambs.

"There's two camps, really," he said, settling himself on a stool as if he had all day to talk. "Some think the old git was blackmailing someone—that's how he got the cash Ginny Teaser saw—but he wanted more, and his victim did him in on account of his demands. And took the money back to boot."

"So who do they think that was?"

His eyes glittered mischievously. "Some says this one and some says that. But they're certain the person lives in this village or hereabouts and is most likely a woman. Sleeping pills being a lady's way of going about it."

"I see. And what does the other camp think?" Ellie asked, careful to keep her tone unconcerned.

"The other camp holds to his being a sot who wandered into our village and topped himself by mistake—or on purpose—while he was pissed. That camp was outnumbered four to one though. And judging from the way the police have been questioning everyone, I'd say they fall into the first camp."

"I think you're right, except that the police theory seems to be that *I* did it, so I can't say I'm impressed with their detecting skills."

John crossed his beefy arms and laughed, his belly shaking. You would never guess that such a large meaty man could be so light on his feet, but Ellie had seen him dance.

"I told them the same thing. I said that Mullane has his head up his arse. If Mrs. Kent wanted to get rid of someone, she wouldn't have left the bloke lying in her own backyard."

"Is that a compliment?" she asked, and he laughed again.

"They thought it was, so I hope you won't take offense."

"I won't, if you promise the Beecham Morris will perform as one of my raffle prizes."

"More folk would pay not to see us," said John, but he told her they'd be glad to help and offered a goose. "Something that will bring in some real money."

She had intended to ask the Teasers for a donation, but, as she walked past the windows of The Three Lambs, she saw Ginny stop talking in mid-sentence and the two people at the bar turn to stare at her in a way that made her think better of it. She would try to catch Ginny somewhere else. At church or on the street. There was no reason to risk public humiliation.

At the charity shop, a prim little woman named Sylvia Martin looked at Ellie with distaste and said it wasn't up to her to make such decisions, she'd have to ask "management." And, at Fab Nails and Hair, the purple-haired proprietor Cherie Jones-Hill was more interested in where Ellie had her hair done ("I s'pose you go to Londin") and what was it like to be fingerprinted ("Is it really like they do on the telly?"). Ellie escaped from her as fast as she could with the promise of a set of false fingernails.

The secondhand bookshop was only "Open sometimes" and this Saturday morning was not one of those times. She peered through the dusty windows at the heaps of battered books piled on the floor and concluded that this was not a big loss.

She had saved The Chestnut Tree for last. There she found Michael-John Parker peacefully listening to Bach and reviewing auction websites on a laptop in the office at the back of the shop. Whistler lay curled on a monogrammed dog bed by his feet and barely bothered himself to open his eyes when she came in.

"Hello. Have you come to interrogate me?" Michael-John asked, setting his computer on sleep.

"No, I'm on church duty today, looking for donations for the Christmas coffee morning raffle."

"Delighted, I'm sure," he said, "Do you want to pick something yourself or would like a suggestion?"

"A suggestion would be great," said Ellie, looking around at the array of furniture, paintings, crockery, silver, and memorabilia in the shop.

He led her across the shop to a corner cupboard that held about 20 music boxes, ranging from feathered birds in cages and carousels to inlaid wooden boxes. Among them was an enameled Christmas tree about 12 inches high.

"If it were up to me, I would pick this," he said, giving the tree a gentle twist.

He handed it to Ellie who watched it turn in slow circles as it tinkled out the melody "Joy to the World."

"That's totally perfect," she said. "Are you sure you want to give it away? Surely this will sell."

"It would, but I'm happy to donate it. Always glad to curry favor with the higher ups, you know, especially in these perilous times. Now that we've done our business, will you have a cup of tea?"

Ellie said she would, and while he brewed the special blend he said he ordered from Mariage Frères in Paris, he asked her when she was going to solve the mystery so the police would leave Little Beecham in peace.

"I think we've seen enough of them to last a lifetime," he said, handing her a mug of delicately fragrant tea.

"Have they been bothering you?"

"They have, but I refused to confess. Sorry."

"You only have to apologize if you did it," said Ellie, sizing up the possibility. Michael-John and an elderly blackmailer. Why not?

"Oh, no," he said. "I recognize that look."

"Do you? You're an experienced suspect then?"

"I refuse to answer on the grounds that it might incriminate me."

"You can't plead the fifth. This is England."

"And a bloody rotten place it is too. So, seriously, how is the detective work going?"

"So far, I've accumulated an impressive list of questions and not a single answer."

"The mystery of the missing button remains unsolved?"

"That I'm pretty sure about, at least in terms of who, where, and how, but not the why and when. That button could have been there for months."

"Not, I should think, without my seeing it."

"Then is there any way you could narrow down when she might have dropped it?"

He shook his head. "Unfortunately, I'm not that systematic."

"What about the fire in the fireplace then? Yesterday you said you'd been cleaning it up. Does that mean it wasn't there on Tuesday? That was the day we first met. "

Michael-John set his chin in his hand and thought. "Tuesday. I don't think I went upstairs that day. There was a particularly nasty mess of beer cans and bottles in what I call the drawing room leftover from some Halloween party. Or so I assumed."

"All right, but what about the time before that?"

"Lord, you're worse than the police." He clicked open his computer calendar and studied it. "I went to London on the Saturday and came back on Tuesday morning. It was a bloody miserable drive. Whoever designed the roads around London deserves to be drawn and quartered."

"So you don't think you were up in that room for a week? But before that, surely you'd have noticed the remains of the fire?"

"Yes, I guess so. Does that help?"

Ellie shrugged. "It creates a window of possibility that the man spent the night there. And that Miss Worthy visited him. That's all."

"If you had one of those Little Detective fingerprint kits, you could go out there and check."

"If I had his fingerprints! And if you hadn't cleaned."

"There you go again. I'm not sure you're a safe person to befriend," he said. "If you promise not to turn it into evidence against me, I'll show you something I found that might be another clue."

"Really!? What is it?"

He began to rummage through a box of old books on the floor by his desk and pulled out a small thin book. "This," he said, handing it to her.

It was a chapbook, bound with a heavy blue paper cover embossed with gold: *Memorie del mio paese* by Angelo DiGuerro.

"It's very pretty," said Ellie, admiring the design and typography of the little book. "And it's in Italian. So what?"

"Look inside. I'm dying to know what it says," said Michael-John, leaning against the desk. The smile in his eyes was mischievous.

"The title means memories of home," she said. Then she opened the flyleaf and saw there was an inscription written in an old-fashioned calligraphic hand: "*Cara Mia, Ricordarsi del passato, sognando del futuro, Con amore, Angelo.* That means, more or less, 'My darling,

Remembering the past, dreaming of the future. With love, Angelo.' Very romantic." Under the signature was a date. One week ago.

"This was only signed last week. Where did you get it?"

"The way I get everything. I just came across it. But, in this case, the circumstances were rather unusual since it was actually Whistler who found it. I mean, he was trying to pull me off the path so he could kill something and there it was."

"Are you kidding? That's really weird. Where?" She studied the book more closely. On the back there was a stain from dampness, but otherwise it looked brand new, unread.

Michael-John described a spot that was just outside the village on his regular route to Beech Hall.

"When was this?" she said, flipping through the book again.

"Recently, but before all this mania for anything Italian started, so I guess it might have been last Tuesday."

"Tuesday? I'm surprised it wasn't soaking wet."

"It was in one of those plastic bubble envelopes. No address. I almost put it into my bin bag, but when I saw what it was, I kept it. And before you even ask, I can tell you Angelo DiGuerro is not famous. At least I Googled him, and I didn't find anything. No smiling photo of our man. No handy bio linking him to our village."

"That would have been nice. Still, it's an odd coincidence that something like this should turn up right now. And, if it were connected to the death, it points to a motive, don't you think? Our man comes bearing a sentimental gift and is rejected. Ends up sleeping rough. Tries again and gets topped for his efforts."

"So Cara Mia tossed the book after their rendezvous in the woods?"

"Maybe. Or maybe he never had a chance to deliver it. Are you sure you found it on Tuesday?"

He made a show of thinking then said, "Yes, but in my life, one day tends to be the same as any other."

"Even in that envelope, it couldn't have been on the ground very long. It has rained off and on a lot this week."

"True."

"Don't you keep a record of when you acquire things?"

"Now you sound like my accountant. And yes, I do, but not every little thing, and I didn't actually expect anyone would buy that. I just couldn't throw it away."

"The poetry isn't as good as the binding," she said, skimming the first poems.

"It's not by the notorious husband then," he said.

Ellie closed the book with a smack. "What's that supposed to mean?"

He shrugged. "I thought maybe you and the ex might have, you know, had a little reconciliation. The old gent witnessed something he shouldn't have seen...and with the necessity to preserve your reputation as the virtuous vicar's wife...well, you know."

"Very funny." She handed the book back to him, and he laughed. "But I'll tell you, murder is not funny, Mr. Parker, especially if you're involved with it, as you might have a chance to find out. You should give this to the police. They can check it for fingerprints. I'm sure they'll be delighted to find mine on it."

"Unfortunately it's one of my most closely held principles never to have anything to do with the police. They don't help me and I don't help them."

"Withholding evidence is against the law."

"It's just a book I found in the woods. If you like, I'll give it to you as a gift."

"And what am I supposed to do with it?"

"Turn it in to the police, if you like. Or not."

Ellie looked at the inscription again and flipped through the pages. She would really like to read it, and once the police had it, her chance would be lost.

"All right. Here's what we'll do, since my fingerprints are already on it. I'll take it and read it, and then bring it back to you. And you'll give it to the police. OK?"

"That sounds more like my favorite detective. I'll give you a brown paper bag to carry it home in. Brown paper is so good at covering secrets."

"I don't have any secrets."

"Don't you? That's a shame. Then I'm pleased to be

giving you one," he said, as he slipped the book into a bag
and handed it to her.

Lunch was nearly ready when she returned to the
Vicarage where Isabelle was bustling around the kitchen as
if it were hers—which, of course, it was. She had heated up
Mrs. Finch's chicken soup and made them each a cheese and
Marmite sandwich, so there was nothing for Ellie to do but
hang up her coat, wash her hands, and wait to be served.

She picked at her sandwich and listened as Graham and
Isabelle reminisced. They seemed careful not to mention
Louise, but their conversation ranged over events and people
that Ellie knew nothing about. Graham's animated manner
only served to highlight how tense and unhappy he'd been
for the past few days. When he'd finished eating, he showed
no signs of rushing off to work, but lingered over a cup of
tea until Isabelle announced that she'd better take Hector for
his walk.

Ellie watched Hector bound out of his basket to Isabelle's
feet with an eager look on his face and decided she'd had
enough of being the incomer in what was supposed to be her
own family and home. She stood up abruptly and said,
"Thanks so much for the lunch, Isabelle. It would be great if
you could take Hector out, because I need to go shopping.
You didn't forget, did you, Graham? That I need the car?"

"No, of course not," said Graham, who also rose to his
feet awkwardly and began gathering up the dishes and
silverware. "You both go on. I'll do the washing up."

Isabelle looked from one to the other of them curiously,
then turned to Hector.

"Whatever," she said. "Are you ready, Heckie?" and
Hector, who was always ready, raced to the door with a
joyful bark.

Once Ellie was in the car, headed to Chipping Martin at
her own version of breakneck speed, she felt embarrassed
about breaking up the cozy family scene and promised
herself she would be more patient next time. Of course, it
was a treat for Graham to have his daughter at home and

this, as he would no doubt be quick to say, had nothing to do with her or the anxieties about their current situation.

In town, she tried to distract herself by browsing through the local bookshop, which was crowded with people hoping to buy what were being trumpeted as rare, signed copies of Ramona Blaisdell-Scott's first book *Remembrance Day*. These were on display in a locked glass case, but there were also stacks of her second book, *No Regrets*, in paperback, and the latest, *Love and Desertion,* in hardcover.

A poster for *Remembrance Day* hung on the wall over the whole display. It described the book as the "breakthrough debut and international bestseller by Britain's best-kept literary secret." The art showed a woman with a bowed head, holding a bunch of red poppies, in a field of white crosses marking military graves.

A timely promotion, thought Ellie, and picked up a copy of *Love and Desertion,* the book she'd found Charlotte reading the other day. This was described as a "page turner about a young woman who risks everything to track down her brother, gone missing after Dunkirk. In the process, she stumbles on stolen art masterpieces, unmasks a treacherous British officer, falls in love with a Frenchman, and never gives up hope."

On the inside back of the cover there was no author photo or biography, only a brief statement saying that the author, who had so quickly become beloved by millions of readers, chose to remain anonymous. Despite a reward offered by the *Daily Mail,* no one had been able to discover the author's real name or whereabouts.

Ellie put the book down, thinking about how the writers she studied had used pseudonyms to disguise the fact that they were women at all. Could that be case with Ramona Blaisdell-Scott? Perhaps she was a he—and therefore needed to hide his true identity? Or maybe it was just a gimmick— as well as a way to avoid tiresome public appearances.

She ordered a latte in the bookstore's small café section and sat down. The coffee was only fair, but the satisfaction she took from ordering "a double latte" almost outweighed that fact. There were limits to the efficacy of tea, in her opinion.

She settled herself at a corner table then took out the book Michael-John had given her. It was printed on a letterpress with fine paper and beautifully bound. She smelled the ink and ran her fingers over the slightly indented letters, the roughly cut edge of the paper. Whoever had written this book had spared no expense on the printing.

She studied the inscription, which, she was sure, had been written with a fountain pen. Did that say something about the age or status of the writer? Maybe. But it yielded no new insights into the identity of Cara Mia.

She had just opened the book to begin reading, when she became aware that someone was watching her and looked up. Detective Inspector Mullane came toward her, holding a book of his own. *Love and Desertion.*

"Reading again, Mrs. Kent?" he asked as he reached her table. From his clothes—a polo shirt and jeans—she guessed he was off duty, but there was nothing off duty about his eyes or the tone of his voice.

"We're in a bookstore after all," she said, closing the book and then she blushed as she saw his glance down at the title.

"Italian, I see. I'll wager you didn't buy that in this shop."

"Inspector, you're questioning me in a public place. Is that appropriate?"

"I'm not questioning you. I'm just greeting an acquaintance."

"I'm not your acquaintance," she said, putting the book back into her bag. "And, if it's all the same to you, I prefer to be left alone. Good day." She stood up, and he stepped aside, smiling his cheerless smile, as she wriggled between the small tables and escaped.

It annoyed her that her heart was jumping with something like fear as she hurried away from the town square. She turned down a narrow street of shops, with no thought other than to put some space between herself and Mullane, but stopped short when she saw a handwritten sign in a window that said "Cyberstop" and ducked inside.

The tiny storefront shop offered four computers, three of which were occupied by teenagers deeply engrossed in surfing the Net. A slender, pale girl with a ring in her nose and what she seemed to hope were dreadlocks leaned on the counter watching them with an expression that wavered between envy and boredom. She took Ellie's two pounds as if it were a favor and pointed to the vacant stool in front of a PC. Still feeling exposed, Ellie was glad this was the one farthest from the window.

Her heart rate slowed as she watched the familiar screens open and she typed the name 'Angelo DiGuerro" into the Google search box. Sure enough, Michael-John was right. Not only was there no poet with that name, she didn't find any listings at all.

Next she Googled the letterpress printer in Rome that had produced DiGuerro's book and discovered that they had a beautiful website, although there was no mention of the chapbook. She clicked on the contact address and up popped a box in which she could write an e-mail message.

After thinking for a while, pulling up Italian phrases from her memory, she wrote:

"Dear Sir:
I received a copy of Angelo DiGuerro's book *Memorie del mio paese* as a gift and would like to purchase several more for friends. Please tell me the best way to do this. I am also very interested in the author and would like to know anything you can tell me about him.
Thank you for your assistance.
Best regards,
Ellie Kent"

She pressed send and then tried to calculate how soon she might receive a reply. Probably Monday at the earliest.

She still had ten minutes left on the computer, so she searched for B&Bs, hotels and campgrounds in the area, printed out a list, and checked her e-mail. Her parents wanted to know why she hadn't written. She began a cheery note to them and then deleted it, but before she left the shop, she carefully photocopied Angelo DiGuerro's poems so she could work on translating them into English.

After doing her grocery shopping in Chipping Martin, Ellie decided to stop at the Little Beecham Library on the way home to see if she could learn anything more from Charlotte. This might not be so easy, she realized, when, at the sight of her, Charlotte tried to hide with her book cart between two rows of shelves.

"I know you're working, Charlotte, but I need to talk to you for a minute," said Ellie, cornering her.

The girl had dyed her hair barbeque sauce red since the last time she'd seen her, and it looked as if she'd attacked it with nail scissors. "What about, Mrs. Kent?" Her voice cracked as she attempted to sound casual, and her face turned so pale that her skin looked green next to the red hair.

"When you called last night, you said something about 'it' not having anything to do with the murder in the churchyard. I'd like to know what 'it' was."

"Look, Mrs. Kent, like I said, I'm sorry the police are after you, but I can't get involved. You don't know what it's like living in a village like this. You can't be too careful about people."

"What do you mean? Are you really afraid of someone here?"

The girl's blue eyes became glassy. "I shouldn't have to be afraid. I haven't done anything wrong." Then she turned to face the bookshelf. "I just wish I never—" she started and then stopped.

"Never what?" asked Ellie, taking her by the shoulders and turning her around. "Look, I don't believe you had any more to do with this than I did. We're innocent bystanders, but I might be able to help you, if I know what you're talking about."

Charlotte did not look convinced. "I never would have thought of it if I hadn't brought you that book," she said resentfully.

Ellie's skin tingled as she remembered Charlotte with her cloak blowing around her on the front doorstep that night. "Thought of what?" she asked quietly.

"The yew."

"Me? What about me?"

"Not you. Yew. The yew hedge."

"OK, what about it?" she prompted. This was like trying to pull an answer out of a student; she couldn't allow her patience to unravel.

"It's one of those old customs Gran used to tell me about, so I thought I'd try it. I mean, what harm could it do? I only wanted to find out."

"Find out what?"

"Who's going to love Dolphin and me."

"I don't understand," said Ellie, more in the dark than ever.

"I came back, you see. Gran said the girls used to go to the churchyard at midnight on Halloween to pick yew. They would put it under their pillows, and then they'd dream about the men they were going to marry."

Ellie stared at Charlotte. "So you mean you were there? In the churchyard? At midnight? And you saw something."

She nodded, tears now spilling down her cheeks and splashing on the books she clutched to her chest.

"Not really. I swear it. I saw someone crouching on the ground. I didn't know what was there. I couldn't see what he was doing. It was dark. I never knew a thing about the body until the next day, and then. Oh, Lord. I don't think he saw me, but I can't be sure. And if I grass on him, I'm finished."

"You mean you recognized him!?"

A little sob escaped her, and one of the books she was holding fell to the floor.

"So why haven't you told the police all this?"

"Because I can't. That's what I've been trying to explain. If I tell anyone, I won't be able to live here anymore. I'd have to leave and—all for someone nobody knows."

"But what about justice? Doesn't your Ramona Blaisdell-Scott believe in that?"

"Of course she does. But even she says sometimes the wrong people get it, and I've got to put Dolphin first. Whoever killed that man wasn't in the churchyard. That doesn't make sense, and the person I saw might've just been looking. He might not have done anything at all, but once I speak it'll be all the same for me, so if you tell anyone about this, you'll have me and my baby's ruination on your conscience, Mrs. Kent."

"You don't know any of that for a fact, Charlotte. The person you saw might have been dumping the body."

"No, he couldn't have. I'm absolutely sure of it."

"Why?" asked Ellie, who suddenly thought she knew the answer, but before she could speak, the door to the library opened and a voice called: "Charlotte? Are you there? What's going on?"

Both Ellie and Charlotte jumped guiltily as Miss Worthy came around the corner of the bookshelf, carrying a basket of well-thumbed romance paperbacks.

"Aunty!" said Charlotte, flushing a mottled red. "I forgot you were coming."

"Hello, Miss Worthy," said Ellie, who was equally embarrassed.

"Hello, Mrs. Kent. Has something happened? Is there something wrong?" asked Miss Worthy, taking in Charlotte's tear-stained face.

"No, no. Charlotte and I have just been...chatting."

"I see," she said, looking skeptical. "Well, I'm sorry to interrupt, but I've brought these books for the library sale, and I hope you'll take care of them."

"Of course, Aunty. We were finished anyway," said Charlotte, who took the basket and scuttled away without looking back.

Ellie left then too, but she was not discouraged by this end to the conversation. She was sure that now Charlotte had begun talking, next time she would be able to get more out of her. Meanwhile, as she drove home, she busied herself thinking about how else she could test her new theory about the person the girl had seen in the churchyard.

Not even Hector was around to greet her when she entered the kitchen. "Graham?" she called, as she piled the bags of groceries on the kitchen table. "Isabelle?" But there was no answer.

She checked the sitting room and Graham's study. Empty. She looked in their bedroom, but it was empty too.

Then she heard a small snuffling sound, which could only be coming from Isabelle's room.

"Isabelle?" she called, crossing the hall to knock on the door. The sound stopped. "May I come in?" she asked, but paused for only a few seconds before opening the door.

Isabelle was huddled under a quilt with Hector, who had been dozing with his head on the pillow. She held a small leather-bound book in one hand and a wad of Kleenex in the other. Her eyes were teary and her nose pink. Several similar volumes lay scattered across the bed.

When she saw Ellie, she closed the book and pulled herself upright, dislodging Hector, who glared at them both indignantly.

"Sorry to bother you," said Ellie. "I couldn't figure out where everyone had gone."

Isabelle blew her nose. "Dad is at the church with some bloke. An inspector or something," she said.

"Oh," said Ellie, noticing that the word *inspector* now made her jump.

Isabelle began stacking up the books.

"What are you reading?"

"Mum's diaries," she said, sniffing and rubbing her reddened nose.

"Diaries?" By the side of the bed was a cardboard box labeled "Datebooks." The box was full, and it looked like Louise had kept one for each year.

"It's so queer. Like hearing her voice again." Isabelle's eyes filled with tears, and she reached for a tissue. At that moment, she looked more like a little girl than a young woman. "I'm sorry. I guess it's rude of me to talk about her."

"Not at all," said Ellie. "I'm very interested. Your mother was obviously a wonderful person. Everyone speaks very highly of her."

Isabelle sighed. "I'm glad if people haven't forgotten her. I mean, I was her daughter, so of course I thought she was the best, and Dad was absolutely ga-ga about her, but reading these books makes me realize how much she did for other people too."

Except for the part about Graham being ga-ga, Ellie was anxious to hear more. "Just the other day, I heard that everyone came to your mother for help. Even more than to your father. If they had a secret or something."

"I think they did," said Isabelle, in an unconcerned tone. She had gotten up and was putting the diaries back into the carton. "Not more than Dad though. I think it was different kinds of things. Women's things, you know. I doubt the men asked her for advice. This is England, after all."

She closed the box, and Ellie's eyes followed as she carried it into her closet. Isabelle's casual agreement that Louise knew people's secrets made her not just curious, but determined to see what was in those diaries.

"I have to change now," said Isabelle. "I'm meeting some old school chums at the pub before the fireworks." This was her cue to leave, so Ellie nodded and went back downstairs in search of Graham.

There she discovered he was back from the church, in his study with his translation project spread out on the desk in front of him. He turned to her, and, in the lamplight she saw that he shadows under his eyes had returned.

"So was it Inspector Mullane again?" she asked. "Isabelle said it was some inspector."

He sighed and fiddled with his fountain pen, screwing and unscrewing the top. "Right. I didn't tell her who he was. I'd like to keep her out of this, if it's possible."

"What did he want now?"

"He wanted to go over every detail of that Sunday the man first appeared. Who attended the church service. How people acted. Did I notice anything unusual. Everything."

"Did you notice anything?"

"No."

"Did he tell you anything new?"

"Only that they now know the man arrived in Kingbrook by train from London that day. He was seen walking on the footpaths toward Little Beecham." Ellie noticed that his hands were shaking when he set his pen down.

"He seemed very interested when I told him that we were not together all afternoon. I told him that I went to visit the Finches but that you hadn't wanted to come. He asked where you went, and I had to say I didn't know."

"But I went for a walk on the route you gave me. I didn't go anywhere else. And I told you both I saw the man in the woods. There's no mystery."

"No, but *he* can hardly give you an alibi, can he?" said Graham, without looking at her.

"Do I need an alibi? Don't you believe me?"

"Of course I believe you. But I'm sure he will be back to ask you about it."

"He can ask me anything he wants. It isn't going to change the facts."

Graham shook his head. "Of course, you're right," he said, turning back to his desk.

Ellie was so surprised by his tone and the sight of his back like a suddenly closed door that she didn't dare challenge him. Saying he didn't sound like he believed her would probably only drive him further away. Instead she tried to put them back on a different footing by asking when they should leave for the bonfire, but all he said was:

"I'm not going. I always stay with Hector. You know how fireworks upset him."

"Oh," said Ellie. "I didn't realize that. I thought we'd go together."

"No, but you can go with Isabelle."

"She's going with her school friends, but that's OK. I'll go on my own," she said, trying to keep her disappointment out of her voice. All week she'd been looking forward to her first Bonfire Night. Something fun and normal.

Well, she could still try to make it that way. Isabelle had put the steak and kidney pudding in the Aga to heat up for their supper, but Ellie couldn't face it. She made herself a peanut butter sandwich, then pulled on her coat and set off into the dark.

Chapter 12

It was not the kind of evening she'd imagined either. The weather had turned raw and windy. She walked along the high street with groups of people who were heading out of the village to the field where the bonfire had been laid. She had never seen so many people in Little Beecham before. Despite her efforts to pick up the excitement of the crowd, she felt very alone, and she was sure people were staring at her. The American vicar's wife. Suspected of murder.

The village had planned this year's Bonfire Night as a fundraiser for the school, so at the roped-off entrance to the field, Ellie joined a queue waiting to pay the two-pound admission fee. "That includes a cup of hot soup and a raffle ticket," said the young father whose toddler daughter handed her a ticket. He directed her to a table where a woman in a red parka was ladling steaming soup into Styrofoam cups.

Beyond the roped-off area, Ellie saw the unlit bonfire. It was bigger than anything she'd ever imagined—a mountain of boards, logs, doors, skips, and other scrap wood about 20 feet high and 30 feet long. A spotlight illuminated the pile and the cloth figure of a man tied to the top. This was "the Guy"—the effigy of Guy Fawkes who plotted to blow up the Houses of Parliament on November 5, 1605, in hopes that England would revert to Catholicism. Ever since, this failed terrorist had been burned all over the country on the fifth of November. It was the sort of behavior that made Ellie wonder about the value of religion.

Religious differences didn't seem to be on anyone's mind tonight though. She sipped her bean soup and watched the milling crowd. There were people of all ages from children in glow-in-the-dark headbands who were chasing each other up and down the grass, to old people wrapped in blankets. At first, she didn't recognize anyone, but then she heard a friendly voice say: "Ellie! Come and join us!"

She turned and saw Morag MacDonald with a lanky boy of about 14 who, with his curly black hair, fair skin, and rosy cheeks, bore a remarkable resemblance to her. "This is Seamus," said Morag. "He's dying to meet you."

When Ellie said hello, the boy looked more like he was dying from embarrassment than anything else, but she was glad to join them on their blanket. Once settled, she felt less like a lone outsider, and the crowd began to lose its anonymous aspect. She noticed familiar faces: the butcher John Tiddington with a wife and several children; Mr. and Mrs. Wiggins from the shop, sitting side by side on lawn chairs; and the Worthy clan, including Charlotte with a lump under her long hooded cloak, that was probably a well-wrapped Dolphin. She scanned the field for Isabelle and spotted her long blonde hair flashing in the light from the torches held by the men who were making last-minute preparations before igniting the fire. She was with a group of young people who were laughing and drinking beer.

"It always takes them forever to get started. Have some tea and Parkin," said Morag, passing Ellie a tin of the oat bars while Seamus poured steaming tea from a thermos into a mug. "How are you? What's been happening?" she asked.

Ellie had been hoping to take her mind off the very topic she knew they wanted to discuss, but their expressions were so friendly and eager, she leaned toward them and whispered. "Actually, if you really want the inside story, you're sitting next to a murder suspect."

"You!" Morag laughed, nearly spilling her tea. "Oh my God. They must be really desperate! Derek Mullane and Seamus's father used to hunt together, and I must say I thought he was smarter than that!"

Seamus was thrilled. "Why do they think you did it, Mrs. Kent?"

"Because the mystery man, who was found dead virtually in our backyard, wore clothes from Italy, and I speak Italian."

"And—" said both Seamus and Morag, leaning in closer.

"I was once married to an Italian-American and spent a summer living in Italy."

Morag burst out laughing again. "Oh, my! That's priceless. The poor bloke must be beside himself."

"I think the real reason is that you found the body," said Seamus. "You know the person who finds the body is always the prime suspect. It's like the murderer can't wait to get on with being caught. That would explain why you left it in your own backyard instead of hiding it like any git would have done."

"You're not really serious, are you?" asked Morag.

"I don't know," said Ellie. "I don't have an alibi for the important times, and I had Valium—the drug he was given––in my possession."

"Anyone can get that from the NHS."

"But, you see, in my case, it all comes together. Opportunity and means. No one here really knows me, so my motives could be anything. I might have mafia connections. A drug-dealing past. How would they know?"

"A drug-dealing vicar's wife. Wow. That's brilliant!" Seamus pulled a little notebook and a pencil out of one of the inside pockets of his anorak and began to write.

Morag regarded him with rueful pride. "Don't mind him," she said. "I'm afraid he read his first Agatha Christie at eight, and he's never looked back. Have they searched the Vicarage yet?"

"No, but they've gone through the garden shed with a fine tooth comb."

"That old shed where Mr. Finch keeps his dirty magazines?" asked Seamus.

"How did you know that?" Morag asked sharply.

"Everyone's been in there to have a look, at least once."

"Then I guess it's not really a clue that I found beer bottles in there."

The boy shrugged. "That could have been any number of kids, so probably not."

"So much for my investigation."

He brightened. "Are you investigating? That's brilliant! What else have you found out?"

"Seamus, this is not a detective story," said Morag. "Someone has really been murdered. It's a dangerous situation."

Seamus looked more pleased than daunted by the idea of danger, but before he could ask more questions, several men with torches ran up to the enormous pile of fuel and began lighting it on all sides. Conversations died, and everyone stood up to watch the dry wood burst into flames that leapt high into the night sky. Smoke and sparks swirled into the air.

The crowd pressed closer to the ropes, entranced as the fire gradually spread until the ring of flames reached all the way around the pile of wood and slowly moved higher and higher—closer and closer to the Guy. They sighed with pleasure when the first flames licked his legs and then whooshed up to engulf the straw-filled body.

At that exact moment the first fireworks went off. With a satisfying boom and a whistle, a rocket shot up and opened into a shower of white and red sparks. The crowd ooh-ed and aah-ed and clapped as one rocket after another went up.

Most people had their eyes focused on the sky, but as the firelight flared, Ellie caught sight of one person who was not watching the show. He stood with a group of young men, like them wearing a dark, hooded anorak, but unlike them, he was not drinking beer or laughing. His long thin face looked serious, and he was intent on something that had nothing to do with Guy Fawkes.

Ellie shivered and hunkered down deeper into her own coat as if that could hide her from the watchful gaze. Of course, it might be a coincidence that DS Jones had chosen to celebrate Bonfire Night in Little Beecham. She had no idea where he lived. But he wasn't acting like a man off-duty, and her pleasure drained away at the thought that her movements were being observed.

For a small village, Little Beecham put on a very good show that culminated in a series of explosions like thunderclaps, but now Ellie couldn't wait for it to end. Thankfully, after the last boom had faded away, the crowd began to disperse quickly. The bonfire was on the wane, awareness of the raw wind set in, and children became cranky. The show was over.

She tried to appear at ease as she helped Morag and Seamus pack up their things and joined them to walk back, but she was constantly on the lookout for the young detective.

"I didn't get to hear about your investigation," said Seamus, as they reached the lane where they would turn off.

"It's an ever-growing list of questions, mainly."

"Maybe I can help. Like one of Sherlock Holmes' Baker Street Irregulars. You need people no one would suspect of being in league with you."

Morag put her arm around him and shook him. "Listen to you! You're not going to be in league with anything but your schoolbooks until the end of term."

Seamus was not put off. "Don't mind her. She used to be a teacher, so she has to say things like that. I think I could be jolly useful, and anything you want to know about this village, I either know it or I can find out." He sounded so confident and determined that they both laughed.

"I'll certainly keep it in mind," agreed Ellie as they said goodnight.

Although the high street was crowded with cars and people, Ellie felt vulnerable when they had left her. Not that she was in any danger, since she had her own police escort, if that's what he was.

When she reached home, she turned her head quickly to the right and saw the hooded figure duck into the doorway of a cottage she knew for certain was not his own.

So. She really was suspect number one.

Sunday, November 6

Chapter 13

Ellie had finally fallen into a restless sleep haunted by hooded men when the phone rang. She opened her eyes and looked at the clock on her bedside table. Midnight. Graham yawned as he reached to answer, but then quickly sat up on the side of the bed.

"Yes. Yes. All right. Don't worry. I'll be there in a tick," he said.

"What is it?" asked Ellie, sitting up too.

"That was one of the villagers, Phyllis Henning. She says her son Jackie is missing. At any rate, he never came home after the fireworks, and it turns out no one has actually seen him since this afternoon."

"Isn't he the boy Isabelle said was always in trouble?"

"Yes, but he's only fourteen, and his father is away from home. She sounds frantic."

"What are you going to do?"

"Help look for him, I guess," he said, pulling off his pajamas.

"Then I'm coming too," she said.

Within a few minutes they'd thrown on some warm clothes and were walking side by side through the village. Graham's flashlight briefly illuminated the windows of darkened shops, the library, and the school, but they didn't see anyone, not even a cat. Only the litter from the departed crowd connected this time to the earlier hours of the evening.

"Has Mrs. Henning called the police?"

"Yes, they're keeping a look out, but you know how people are. They want familiar faces around them at a time like this."

At the school, they turned left off the high street into a short lane and then right into an even narrower cul de sac where four stone cottages huddled. There was a stile at the end of the paved road, and beyond the stile, the silvery hump of a frosted field.

Lights were on in all four cottages, as if for these neighbors trouble for one was trouble for all. Graham went directly to one bearing the name Lilac Cottage and knocked on the door.

A thin woman in sweatpants, sneakers, and a faded blue parka answered. Her hair was a colorless brown, but permed into a frizz and her naturally pale face was bloodless with stress. Ellie didn't think she'd ever seen her before, but Graham greeted her with a warm handshake.

"Phyllis," he said, stepping across the threshold. "I'm so glad you called. I don't believe you've met my wife. Ellie, this is Phyllis Henning. Her husband Jack used to farm in this area, but now he works the oil rigs. Isn't that right?"

"Farmed here for six generations," she said, resentment bringing some color into her face. "Now he's out there risking his life, and I'm left alone with these kids."

Ellie could see past her from the hall into a tiny lounge where two boys and two girls were vying for space on the sofa. The television was on, loud. They were all remarkably alike and appeared to have been born nine months apart. *Maybe, fortunately, after that, their parents' relationship had cooled off or there'd be ten or twelve of them by now*, thought Ellie. The minute she saw the mops of red hair, she recognized the boys from the gang of bicycle riders she'd seen in the churchyard the other day.

Their mother glanced at them with a sour look. "Turn that telly off. Can't you see the Vicar is here about our Jackie?"

At the sound of her voice, they turned as one and stared at Ellie and Graham. The oldest girl pulled herself out of the struggling pile and turned off the television.

"I can't get them to go to bed. Not with all this telephoning and everything going on. They want to know what's happened. Where their brother is." She introduced them as Sarah, Mike, Donny and Lucy.

Ellie didn't think they looked particularly concerned, but they squished together side by side on the sofa and faced Ellie and Graham with rather more solemn expressions, once Sarah had been sent to the kitchen to make tea.

"I called everyone I could think of before I bothered you, Vicar. I'm sorry to bring you and your missus out on a cold night like this."

"Not at all," said Graham. "Can you just fill us in? Tell us what you know?"

"I don't know nothing. That's the problem. I never know where these kids are. They scatter to the four winds the minute they're up. It's all I can do to get breakfast in them and coats on their backs. Their dad's given them all bicycles, you see. And there's no holding them back after that."

"So Jackie went off on his bike? And his bike is missing too?"

The children all nodded.

"When was the last time any of you saw him?"

"Donny saw him about two o'clock. Dint you?" said Lucy.

"He was going to buy fireworks in Chippy," said Donny, the smaller of the two boys.

"Well, he should've been home before the bonfire if that's what he was up to. I don't know. First it was the police coming. Now this," said Phyllis.

"What do you mean the police came?" asked Graham.

"Just the other day. They came to question him about where he was on Halloween. As if a fourteen-year-old who doesn't know his ass from a teakettle could've had something to do with a murder!"

The children looked uneasy. "It weren't the murder, Mum," said Mike. "It was the other stuff."

"You mean the break-in at the church?" asked Ellie. All the Hennings blushed.

"No, he never did that. I know he dint," said Mike. "He told me he broke the window of that pouf's shop, but he weren't anywhere near the church."

"The man's name is Mr. Parker," said Ellie glaring at the boy, who shrugged, unimpressed by this information.

"Well, that's not our concern right at this moment, so let's get back to where Jackie might be," said Graham. "What were his plans for the day?"

At that moment, Sarah came back in with the tea tray. She was about 13 and already had fully developed breasts. She wore tight pink pants and a cropped shirt that showed off a belly that, rather than being sexy, radiated a milky baby-like innocence.

"Jackie always had plans," she said, "but they was all talk."

"What kind of plans?" asked Ellie.

"Oh, something different every day. I'm going to visit Dad, he'd say. Or I'm going to London to get a job. He hated this village. He said it ruined Dad's life, and he didn't want to end up the same."

Graham and Ellie glanced at each other.

"I never heard him say anything like that," said his mother. "He has a good home, school, plenty to eat. His father works hard to provide for us, and he knows it."

The children's blank expressions reflected that this was a line they'd heard before.

"Do any of you think there's a chance that Jackie could have gone to spend the night with a friend in another village? In Chipping Martin, perhaps? Someone he met that maybe your Mum doesn't know yet?"

They were silent.

"Do you think he might have run away?"

The children avoided meeting Graham's eyes, and, in the silence Ellie could hear the clock ticking. If it were possible, Phyllis turned even more pale.

"He might've done. That Inspector Mullane threatened him. He said he'd get an ASBO if he didn't watch his step. Oh, my God, his father will kill me," she said more to herself than to them.

"An ASBO?" asked Ellie.

"An Antisocial Behavior Order," said Sarah. "It's the latest useless way the police try to control kids."

"Well, it's only been a few hours," said Graham. "It might turn out that Jackie is tucked up somewhere right now having a good night and just forgot to tell you where he was going, but I think we'll all feel better if we help to look."

"The police said they'd start a search, but there isn't much they can do until morning. That's why Arn, Tom, and Fred are out looking now," she said. "They're my neighbors," she explained to Ellie. "They always pitch in to help when Jack is away."

"Which way did they go?" asked Graham.

"They're checking the footpaths and bridleways, in case, you know, he had a fall with his bike or something." If the children felt sympathy for their brother, who might be lying injured somewhere in the cold, they didn't show it. The whole event was like a TV show. An exciting change from the scheduled programming.

"Then Ellie and I will head out along the road to Chipping Martin. At this hour there's no traffic, so we can go slowly and scan the sides of the road. I've got my mobile with me. If there's any news, you can call us. And we'll call you too, of course." Graham handed her a card that told how to reach him 24 hours a day. There were no "hours" with this job of vicar.

"Thank you," said Phyllis, her eyes welling with tears. "He's our first, you know. If anything happened to him, I don't think my husband could bear it."

"Don't worry about that now," said Graham. "Let's focus on what needs to be done tonight."

As they headed back home to get the car, Ellie said, "Do you know this boy? Could he have hopped a bus to London?"

"Jackie's more of a village prankster. He might talk big about London, but I doubt he's ever been there. It's as real as America or Mars, so I think it's more likely he's somewhere in the neighborhood."

While Graham warmed up the car, Ellie made a thermos of hot sweet tea and found some blankets. Just in case, as she went out the back door, she grabbed a dusty first-aid kit that looked like it hadn't been opened in years.

They set off down the empty road with the high beams illuminating the frost on the pavement and thick hedges.

Occasionally they saw the glow of a rabbit's eyes before it turned and fled back under the hedge; and once a fox ran across in front of them, its red bushy tail streaming out behind.

But there was no sign of any human being. Ellie opened the window and let the cold air rush in. She marveled at the stillness. The darkness beyond their beam of light.

It didn't take long to get to Chipping Martin. Since it was past closing time, not many people were about. They drove up and down the streets of the town, inquiring of anyone they could about a red-haired boy on a bicycle, but no one had seen him.

"It's weird, isn't it?" said Ellie, as they reluctantly turned back toward Little Beecham. "Somehow people seem so substantial. Traceable. And yet in a way, they're not at all."

"You're thinking of the dead man."

"Yes. But Jackie too."

"Maybe we should get out and search at the places where he might have had an accident. On curves. The bottom of hills. Then, if we haven't found anything, go back and wait until morning."

Graham looked exhausted, but Ellie said all right.

This time they went even slower, stopping every time they imagined there might be a hazard. A reason to fall. They searched for signs—skids marks, broken bushes—and by the time they reached the village, they were chilled and weary.

"This isn't the only way he could have come back, of course," said Graham. "He might have taken a different route."

"Well, the police will check all that, won't they? I think we need to give it up. Tomorrow is Sunday. It's not like you can sleep late."

Back at the Hennings' cottage, only the lights in the lounge still burned. Phyllis came to the door, looking ten years older than she had two hours before.

"Nothing?" she said.

"Nothing," said Graham.

She nodded, as if this were what she expected. "The others didn't find anything either," she said. Her eyes were red from crying.

Behind her the house was quiet. Sarah was curled up asleep on the sofa, but the other children must have been persuaded to go to bed.

"I don't know whether to be glad or not. All I can say is when that boy turns up, he's going to get a blistering." Then she started to cry again.

"He was always on at me about getting him one of those phones, and I said he was too young. He'd just lose it. All I can think of is him lost somewhere, and no way to let me know. If I'd only given in, he'd have called me by now."

Graham stepped forward and put his arms around her. The moment he touched her, she broke down completely and began to sob. Ellie slipped around them and went to the kitchen. It was immaculately clean and tidy, as if no trouble had hung over this house tonight.

She put on the kettle, and, while she waited for the water to boil, she looked at the photographs stuck on the refrigerator with magnets. They showed the five children at different ages, including Jackie—a cocky young teenager with spiky red hair and a new bike. He grinned at the camera as if he planned to own the world.

Phyllis and Graham were in the lounge talking quietly when Ellie brought in the tea. The exhausted Sarah slept on soundly.

"First thing in the morning, if he hasn't turned up, the police will resume the search. They have the resources to handle this kind of situation."

"Oh, my God," said Phyllis, her voice a whisper. "If he's not home in the morning, I'll have to tell Jack." Ellie could see the fear in her face and wondered if Phyllis ever got a blistering herself.

"But that's tomorrow. It's very important not to get ahead of yourself. You'll make yourself sick with worry, and that won't do Jackie or the other children any good at all. Do you understand what I mean? The best thing you can do now is to try to get some sleep. None of us ever know what tomorrow will bring, good or bad."

"Yes. I see that," said Phyllis in a flat voice.

"Good," said Graham. "Now let's say a prayer and then we'll all go to bed."

Ellie thought Phyllis looked surprised, but she stood up obediently. Graham reached out and took their hands, so they automatically grasped each other's too. Phyllis's hand was thin and shaking, but she bowed her head as Graham began to speak. Ellie could almost feel the power of hope vibrating in her fingers.

This was why she'd called in Graham, she thought. The police could search. Friends could search. But he was the expert in a form of magic that she needed, and Phyllis was praying that this magic would work.

"Dear God, we commend Jackie to your care this night and every night. Wherever he may be, we know you are watching over him. Lighten our darkness, we beseech thee, O Lord, and by thy great mercy, defend us from all the perils and dangers of this night, for the love of thine only son, our Savior, Jesus Christ. Amen."

In the silence that followed, Ellie felt a shiver go up her spine, as if there really were someone—something—attending to their prayer.

But later, back at home and in bed, it was the perils and dangers she remembered and the fact that Jackie might be in God's loving hands, but that did not mean nothing bad could happen to him, no matter how ardently they prayed.

Graham said it never worked to pray for results. You had to pray for acceptance of the results, whatever they were. Ellie could not understand that. What kind of magic was that?

Chapter 14

The police search for Jackie Henning resumed as soon as it was light. The news that he was missing had spread quickly, and a large group of volunteers showed up to help. Everyone not fit for scrambling over the countryside came to church. Or so it appeared to Ellie as she watched the pews fill up for the Sunday morning service.

Ellie and Isabelle sat together, and the spectacle of Graham's new family was enough of a novelty to attract attention until Phyllis Henning turned up with her four younger children, all looking scrubbed and pale. The casual indifference of the night before had been washed out of them by the knowledge that morning had come, and there was no word from Jackie. They sat in the back with bowed heads and slipped out the moment the service was over—with good reason.

Practically everyone else stayed for refreshments and gossip, and the cadre of women who handled the tea and coffee were quickly overwhelmed. Emily Rutherford Hughes, dressed today in a stiff grey suit that resembled sheet metal, stationed herself behind the table. She looked disapprovingly at the crowd and half-filled their cups as if there were a shortage of hot water.

Ellie and Isabelle both pitched in to help, refilling the electric kettles and handing around biscuits. In addition to being useful, this gave Ellie an excellent opportunity to eavesdrop on any conversation that interested her.

Mrs. Wiggins gave her opinion to a plump woman in an ancient rabbit fur coat, who nodded over her teacup. "I'm sure he's done a bunk. He's always been wild just like his father before him. Four walls weren't good enough to hold him in either."

"He looks older than he really is," the woman said. "He could've picked up and run off anywhere."

John Tiddington's wife told Ginny Teaser, "Phyllis looked that pale I thought she'd faint."

"Well, wouldn't you?" Mrs. Teaser said. "I can't imagine how I'd bear it if my Billy was gone all night and me not knowing where."

"It's very naughty of the lad, there's no question about that."

Miss Worthy, who was hovering on the edge of this conversation, remarked that boys were meant to be adventurous. It didn't make them necessarily bad.

Over by the baptismal font, murder was the preferred topic. Mrs. Bell declared that the police were on the wrong track if they thought the man was originally a local. "No one from our generation moved to Italy," she said to Charlotte's mother, Mildred Worthy. "It wasn't like it is now with all these holiday houses. People stayed where they belonged."

"It does seem odd that the Italians haven't identified him either," said Mildred. "I mean he must be from somewhere. Someone must know him. You can't live eighty years without knowing a soul."

"Maybe he changed his identity," said Mrs. Bigelow who'd sailed up to join them. "It's more common than you might think."

Mrs. Bell looked at her over the top of her glasses with a prim expression. "I suppose you're right. Time was you really knew who your neighbors were. Even if you didn't care for them—or they came from a different background— you at least knew what that background was."

Mrs. Bigelow scowled as if she knew Mrs. Bell was referring to her.

"If he had a village connection, my aunt would have recognized him," said Mildred. "She has an excellent memory for faces, and she's lived here all her life."

"But none of us did recognize him," Mrs. Bell insisted.

"If you had, we would know who in the village had a reason to murder him," said Mrs. Bigelow.

Mrs. Bell looked offended. "Surely you don't believe the murderer is from the village," she was saying as Ellie approached them.

They all fell silent.

"Anyone care for a biscuit?" she asked with her sweetest smile, but they all suddenly remembered their Sunday lunch engagements and began to gather up their coats and handbags. Within a few minutes, only Graham, Isabelle, and Ellie were left to finish the cleaning up.

As they walked back to the Vicarage, Ellie said: "I thought they'd never leave today with two mysteries to discuss."

"They were surprisingly charitable about Jackie," said Isabelle. "Not one said the village would be a better place to live without him. Did you know he once tried to hang Mrs. Rutherford Hughes' cat, Dad?"

"Yes, I knew."

"When did that happen?" asked Ellie.

"About a year ago. Some boys caught the cat and were trying to hang it, when Seamus MacDonald came along and created a ruckus. The cat ran off with the rope still around its neck, and Mrs. Rutherford Hughes interrogated everyone she could find until she learned who did it. Jackie was apparently the ringleader, and she wanted him prosecuted, but the police said the cat was unharmed so the case was dropped."

"Well, for once I agree with Mrs. Rutherford Hughes," said Ellie.

"I don't see what good it would have done. I think there's too much of a rush to criminalize children these days," said Graham. "There's no question he's been more wild since his father had to move away for work. But he can still turn out all right."

Isabelle did not look convinced. "Sure thing, Dad. But if he ever touched Hector, I'd hang him myself."

"No matter what he's like, I still keep hoping the phone will ring, and it will be Phyllis calling to say that it was all a misunderstanding," said Ellie.

"I know. Losing a child is one of the unthinkable things."

"Don't worry," said Isabelle, putting her arm through his. "You won't get rid of me that easily."

They went to Sunday lunch at an old-fashioned pub in Chipping Martin that offered roast beef, Yorkshire pud, and three veg for £7.99. As they ate, Ellie listened to Graham and Isabelle joke and spar, admiring the comfortable way they had with each other.

But when she left the table after the meal to go to the ladies' room, she returned to find them in an argument. Isabelle leaned across the table, her face flushed with determination, while Graham, still in his dog collar and black suit, had assumed his most stolid expression.

"Ellie," said the girl, appealing to her. "Dad doesn't want me to stay and help with the search this afternoon."

"Is there something else you need to do?" asked Ellie, wary of taking sides.

"That paper on the Civil War due Friday, for one thing," said Graham.

Isabelle scoffed. "Oh, I can do that in no time. One night."

"But there's no real need for you to stay, Is. Why add more pressure to the week by starting off tired? And I'd rather you didn't drive back to Cambridge in the dark."

"What rot. You're just trying to wrap me in cotton wool," she said, scraping back her chair. "But since you insist that I'm leaving, I might as well get on with it."

Graham looked stricken, but he rose too and went to pay the bill.

As Ellie put on her coat, she said, "If you feel that strongly about staying, Isabelle, you should stand up to him. He'll respect that."

The girl glanced up from zipping her coat and shook her head. "It's not about respect. It's this ridiculous idea he has that I'm delicate, when he's the one who can't handle things."

Back at the Vicarage, it didn't take long for her to pack, and she stumped down the stairs with her backpack and laptop still looking sulky. The goodbyes between father and daughter were subdued. She gave Ellie a brisk hug, then drove off without another word, but ten minutes later, she was back, banging through the kitchen door.

"I'm sorry, Daddy," she said, burying her face in his shoulder. "I know you mean well."

Ellie thought the relief and love in Graham's face could not have been greater if she'd been the one lost all night, and this time Isabelle departed with a teary smile and a wave to them both.

"What was that all about?" Ellie asked as they set off for the village hall, where the search headquarters had been established, side-by-side with the police's incident room. "Why not let her help if she wanted to?"

"I just didn't want her involved in this death. I didn't want to even think about the possibility that she would be the one who found him."

"Found him dead, you mean? Is that what you think is going to happen?"

"I know I shouldn't anticipate the worst, but yes. You have no idea, Ellie, what it was like for her. She had spent the afternoon with Louise. She was only gone a couple of hours. There was no reason to think she wasn't getting better. And yet she died. It was a dreadful, dreadful shock for her to discover that. How could I not want to avoid her having the same kind of experience again?"

"Do you think she knew that's what you were thinking?"

"Of course. It's always there between us."

"Yes, I can see how it would be," said Ellie and fell silent, thinking about the bonds of shared memory. Maybe, she thought, that was part of what had attracted Graham to her, a total stranger. With her, he had no such history.

At the village hall, the atmosphere was subdued and serious. The same young woman who'd been serving soup at the Bonfire Night only a few hours ago was now giving cups of tea to the chilled searchers. They spoke softly, warming their hands on their cups and stamping their feet.

DS Jones was the search coordinator, handing out maps and assignments to the volunteers. Ellie gave him a knowing look as she took her map, and a mottled red blush spread up his neck to his normally pale cheeks.

She and Graham were assigned to search along a bridle path from Little Beecham to Chipping Martin. They had to walk slowly, but keep moving to stay warm. She was surprised at the variety of lost and broken things they found hidden in the bushes and long grass—a dead fox, a crumpled McDonald's bag, a man's glove, beer cans, a blue plastic coffee mug—but none of them suggested that Jackie had come that way.

They searched on until their feet were numb, and it had begun to get dark. Back at the hall, they reported that they'd found nothing and learned that no one else had either.

At home, they found a message from Isabelle saying she'd made it back to Cambridge safely. She did not mention the search.

Graham lit the fire, while Ellie made tea. Then they settled in the sitting room, but it was hard to put the afternoon behind her, so Ellie took out the little book that Michael-John had given her. She hoped that the effort of translating the images of hot sun and tile-roofed houses would distract her from thoughts of a boy lying dead in the damp tall grass under a grey frozen sky.

She'd barely begun when the doorbell rang, and she opened the door to Detective Inspector Mullane. He looked very weary, and his pants were spattered with mud.

"Hello, Mrs. Kent," he said. "May I come in?"

"Of course," said Ellie, although she'd come to dread his visits.

He warmed himself by the fire without saying anything for a few moments, then he turned to them and spoke: "I know you were both helping with the search for the Henning boy, so I thought I should come and tell you the news myself. We've found him."

"Is he all right then?" asked Ellie, despite the evidence of Mullane's dejected manner.

"No, he's dead. He's been dead for more than 24 hours from the looks of it."

"That's dreadful news," said Graham. "What happened?"

"A bicycle accident as far as we can tell. He was on the B road to Chipping Martin, and he must have been going hell for leather. There were no skid marks. He went right off the road, hit a stone wall, and went up and over it, bike and all. That's why we had trouble finding him. Both the body and the bike were hidden by shrubbery. The pathologist says he died instantly. A broken neck. I suppose it's some comfort to the mother that it wouldn't have made any difference if we'd been called in sooner."

"No one missed him until after the fireworks."

"Precisely. I can't say I approve of parents who let their children go off all day without any idea where they are. Why didn't she miss him at teatime? A lad never comes home for his tea, and his mother doesn't even think to worry until midnight?"

"I'm sure she'll be asking herself that question for the rest of her life," said Graham.

"As well she should. But, I suppose you could say luckily in this case it wouldn't have made any difference. You know, Father Kent, you may be the shepherd, but searching for lost lambs is my patch. None of us likes it when one turns up dead."

"Oh, God," Ellie said.

"Exactly. Well, I'll be getting on then," he said abruptly. "I just wanted you to know what happened."

Ellie gaped at him, surprised that he seemed to be directing his anger at them, but when he was gone, Graham said it wasn't that. "I think, in his way, he was seeking comfort."

"You could have fooled me," said Ellie, who found that she couldn't read any more and closed her book.

Instead she gazed at the fire, listening to the crackling flames, and tried to remember back to the Sunday before. What she'd been thinking about then. How she could never have guessed what the week would bring.

That evening they went to pay their respects to the Hennings and found a neighbor fixing a meal for the children, who sat in a stunned and silent huddle in the lounge. Phyllis Henning had collapsed on hearing the news that her son was dead; her husband had been contacted and was on his way home.

While Graham talked with Phyllis privately in her room, Ellie tried to make small talk with the children, but all she could think of was the distance between expecting and knowing the worst.

Back at the Vicarage, there were a dozen messages for Graham from worried parishioners, and one for Ellie from Morag, saying, "Please call me."

It was after nine pm before Ellie reached her.

"I heard about Jackie," she said. "I feel so sorry for Phyllis. It's every mother's worst nightmare, but it's also very worrying that this happened just now."

"What do you mean?" asked Ellie.

"Seamus wants so much to help solve your mystery, and this afternoon he went round to talk to some of the boys. He thinks he found out something too. They told him Jackie had been using your shed for the past couple of weeks, and the other boys were mad because he wouldn't let anyone else in. He took it over for himself, so when he didn't show up for the fireworks, they all assumed he'd gone there instead."

"Did they know what he was doing in there?"

"No. They said they didn't."

Ellie was silent for a moment, thinking how this linked up with what Isabelle had said about Jackie and also Charlotte's fears. If she'd seen Jackie in the churchyard, she would not have wanted him to know. It also made sense that a boy like Jackie could not have moved the body.

"Did Seamus's contacts know anything else about what he's been up to lately?"

"He said they all seemed mad that Jackie had become so secretive. It was pretty common for him to brag about his exploits, as he called them, but lately he wouldn't tell them anything, and they were obviously annoyed by that. This was before they knew he was dead, of course."

"Right. Did Seamus say whether they thought Jackie knew anything about the murder?"

"He wasn't sure. He said he tried not to ask what he calls leading questions. Apparently no one volunteered anything."

"But when you said it was strange this happened now, did you mean his accident could be connected to the murder?"

"No. No. It was just a bike accident, don't you think? There wasn't anything suspicious about it was there?"

"I don't know."

Morag paused, then said thoughtfully, "Well, if it were connected, there'd be one good thing about it. You'd be off the hook, wouldn't you?"

"Yes, I suppose," said Ellie, but then she pictured herself hurtling down the B road to Chipping Martin on Saturday afternoon, and she began to wonder how well the police would be able to pinpoint Jackie's time of death.

Monday, November 7

Chapter 15

Any day that starts off with a call from your ex-husband is not likely to turn out to be a good day. Graham had left early to visit the Hennings before going with another vicar to a daylong meeting in London, and Ellie was in the kitchen finishing her breakfast, when the phone rang. Assuming the call was for Graham, she didn't get up, but when she heard the voice on the answering machine, she overturned her chair, lunging to pick up the receiver.

"Hello?" she said, hoping she was wrong and that the person she'd heard saying, "I'm trying to reach Ellie, uh, Kent," was not, in fact, Vito Ruggieri.

Unfortunately, his next words left her no doubt.

"Ellie? Is that really you?" he said, and then he began to laugh merrily.

"Hello, Vito," said Ellie flatly. "What do you want? How did you get this number?"

"I thought we should be in touch. I really like that expression, don't you? In touch?" Vito had a way of making this sound like a sexual experience. Which for him, in most cases, it very likely was.

"I don't think you're calling to discuss language with me, are you, Vito? I mean, isn't it the middle of the night where you are?"

"Nearly three a.m. But I wanted to catch you at home."

"How did you even know where I am?"

"Well, I'll give you a hint. The police didn't tell me, but your mother did. You really ought to call your parents more often, you know. They're very worried about you."

"What do you mean the police didn't tell you?"

"When they gave me the third degree. Don't worry though, I said that during our marriage you'd only become violent once or twice. Of course, it was a short marriage. And I couldn't tell them what you've been up to since. Really, Ellie, it has been too long. We should get together. I want to hear all about your life. It sounds exciting."

"Vito, you already know more than I want you to. Are you saying the police in New York interviewed you about this death in Little Beecham?"

"Little Beecham, yes," and he laughed again. "It all sounds so kinky and quaint. I never thought of you as attracted to quaintness before. But then I can't say I ever would have cast you in the role of vicar's wife either." This witty remark made him laugh as if he couldn't stop.

"So what did they ask you?"

"They wanted to know all about our romantic summer in Tuscany and what your relationship with my family was like. I told them no one in my family has vanished lately, but I don't think they believed me, because they called on my mother too."

"You're kidding."

"No. And she gave them the full-bore, immigrant Italian I-don-speaka-Eng-lish treatment."

"She didn't." Her ex-mother-in-law spoke four languages, including perfect English. "That must have been a scene worth recording. So what did she say?"

"Nothing really. They showed her a photo of the dead man, and she swore she'd never seen him before. She did think it was the most thrilling thing that has happened to her in a long time and told me to be sure to thank you."

"Oh, any time. Happy to oblige the ex-in-laws."

"Now, don't sound bitter. You have to admit your life has taken some interesting turns. Here I thought you were going to live out your days flogging Jane Austen in frontier towns, and instead you're wanted for murder. In England, no less. The *Daily Mail* will eat you up in no time."

Suddenly, Ellie recalled what a publicity hound Vito was. Any time a photo was being taken at a reception or prize giving, he always managed to be right in the heart of the action.

"I'm not wanted for murder. And the *Daily Mail* is not on my doorstep. But, if they show up, Vito, it better not be because you incited them to it."

"I can't help being involved though, dearie. I'm the Italian connection."

"That's ridiculous."

"The police seem pretty convinced."

"Well, they have no evidence, because there is no evidence. Vito, isn't it time you went to bed? Don't you have some babies that are going to wake up any minute?"

"Actually, the babies are gone. And their mother too."

"Is that so. I thought you made a point of always being the one to leave."

"Not invariably, but I'm flattered that you keep track of my activities."

"Our former colleagues still gossip about you, if that's what you want to know. Anyway, thanks for the warning, or the help, or whatever this was supposed to be."

"Sympathy. And love. I must say it puts a whole new gloss on 'til death do us part'."

"We never said that. Remember? You didn't want to."

"No. I'd forgotten. Well, send me your address at Dartmoor. Or wherever they send lady killers these days."

"You're the ladykiller, not me, Vito," said Ellie and hung up.

As soon as the connection broke, she dialed another number. "Morag?" she said, when the phone picked up. "It's Ellie Kent. Could we get together? I really need to talk."

Morag sounded surprised, but she said, of course. "Shall we meet in Chipping Martin?"

"No. How about the Arboretum? It's more private. Can you leave now?"

"I guess so. Certainly. I'll be there as soon as I can."

Ellie grabbed her purse and keys, and Hector went into full alert, barking with pleasure when he saw her pick up his leash. "Come on," she said, and he raced for the kitchen door.

Unfortunately, there they bumped into Mrs. Finch, who'd just arrived, wearing her neatly pressed work dress and carrying her lunch in a brown paper bag.

"Good morning, Mrs. Kent," said the housekeeper, as she slowly took off her coat and hung it in the entryway.

"Hello, Mrs. Finch. I'm sorry I don't have time to talk now. I have an appointment," said Ellie, who wished she weren't blocking her way.

Mrs. Finch's face registered her disapproval that the vicar's wife was off to an "appointment" dressed in jeans and one of Graham's heavy flannel shirts, but all she said was, "Very good, Mrs. Kent," in her starchiest tones.

"See you later," said Ellie, as she edged past to let herself and Hector out. Before getting into the car, she looked around carefully, but she didn't spot anyone keeping an eye on her. Nevertheless, she chose a roundabout route to Benton, watching her rear view mirror the whole way to see if she was followed.

She knew she couldn't literally run away, whether she wanted to or not, but if Mullane was interviewing people in the US, he must still think there was a case against her. And who knew where he would stop? Her only hope was that he also had some other line of inquiry that would quickly prove more promising.

Benton Arboretum was a 300-acre public park that was part of a private estate, now owned by the National Trust. She pulled into the car park and was pleased to see only a few cars—probably because the dark morning promised heavy rain. When Morag's blue Rover sped in, Ellie jumped out of her car and barely managed to keep her composure until they'd paid their entrance fees.

"So. What's going on? You look shattered," said Morag, taking hold of Hector's leash as they set off down a gravel path through the neatly labeled trees. She looked so English, so comfortable and at ease, that Ellie found herself spilling all her fears.

"I know I sort of made a joke of it the other day, but the police really do suspect me of this murder! They've had me under surveillance, and they've been interviewing people like my ex-husband, and I don't know who all. I think it's really starting to get to Graham, and I'm not sure how much more he can take. Me either for that matter."

"That's ghastly, Ellie," said Morag, "but they're just fishing, and, since there's nothing to catch, they'll have to give up sooner or later. What about Jackie?"

"If Jackie's death is really connected, it doesn't help me. In fact, it could only make things worse. I drove into Chipping Martin on that road that afternoon, so it could have been me who ran him off the road, as easily as anyone else."

"I see," said Morag. "You do have an inconvenient way of being in the wrong place at the right time. What about your own investigation?"

Ellie shrugged. "Given what Seamus found out, I'm quite sure Charlotte saw Jackie in the churchyard at midnight, so it might have him who robbed the man, but he wasn't the murderer. By then, the man was already dead."

"What was Charlotte doing there?"

"It's a long story, but she was there, and she saw someone she recognized. So far, that's all I've gotten out of her. She was too afraid of Jackie to talk before."

"Well, she doesn't have to worry about that now."

"No, but if the murderer knew that Charlotte could link the first murder to Jackie's death, Charlotte's probably right to be afraid."

"My God. You mean she could be in danger too?"

Ellie nodded. "The other thing is, I think Priscilla Worthy knows who the man was."

"Miss Worthy of the many sweaters? I want to hear more about this," said Morag sitting down on a bench that overlooked the turreted Victorian brick pile that was Benton Park. Another monument to a family's lost glory.

"When I saw the man he was heading toward Beech Hall with a backpack, and I think he might have spent the night there. Someone built a fire in one of the bedrooms and I found evidence Miss Worthy was there."

Morag's eyebrows lifted. "Evidence? Now you are starting to sound like a detective."

"Hardly. But if you really stretch you can connect the dots between them."

"Why don't you ask her? See what she says? I've always thought there was more to that maiden lady than meets the eye, but I never would've thought she was a murderer."

"It's possible," said Ellie, reaching down to pick up Hector. His feet were damp and muddy, but she hugged his warm body to her.

"My suspect would be that Michael-John Parker. He's handsome and rich—and seems blackmail-able."

"If it were Michael-John, I think the circumstances would have been less haphazard.

"Also, the way it happened, it's as if the murderer wanted the man dead, but wanted the death to happen out of sight. So somehow responsibility would be removed."

"Which sounds like a woman, although I hate to say it. It also sounds very risky. What if he'd been found before he died?" said Morag.

"True. And the same could be said for Jackie. How could you know he was going to be killed in that fall?" said Ellie.

"You couldn't."

"It's all so reckless. Almost mad."

"Oh, please. Let's not go there."

They got up and walked in silence for a while along the paths that wound through the park. The soft crunching of their footsteps, the smell of decaying leaves, and the colorful palette of Japanese maples, autumn flowering cherry trees, copper beeches, and evergreens were soothing, but the air was heavy with anticipation of the storm. The birds were quiet.

"I think I'd better talk to Miss Worthy as soon as possible," said Ellie.

"Right. You know, Miss Worthy and Charlotte might be in it together. I could see the two of them coming up with such daft plans."

"I hope it's not. I really like them both."

"But who else is there? I guess you'd better hope Derek has some information you don't. Otherwise the only alternative is to have faith that everything will work out because you're innocent, and even he can't make you guilty."

"When it comes to that," said Ellie, kicking the dead leaves on the path, "you're mixing up the vicar and his wife."

"Oh. That is tough."

They were almost back to the car park, when the slanting rays of sun that had illuminated the autumn foliage vanished, and the clouds thickened overhead.

"True. But now, I think we'd better run for it. It's about to pour."

"We didn't solve anything yet," said Morag.

"No, but I feel better, so thank you."

Raindrops as heavy as bullets began to fall, so they waved goodbye and ran for their cars.

All the way home, the rain pounded down so hard that Ellie had to concentrate fully on peering through the windshield to stay on the road and out of the ditch. She was relieved when she reached the sign that said "Entering Little Beecham," until she saw, in front of the Vicarage, not only the all-too-familiar car of DI Mullane, but also two green-and-yellow painted cars that shrieked "Police." A few villagers who enjoyed the true Englishman's obliviousness to rain were clustered on the sidewalk, trying to get a glimpse of what was going on.

Ellie began to shake so much that she could barely control the car as she pulled into the drive. She and Hector sprinted for the house, where Mrs. Finch met them at the kitchen door with a white, tear-stained face. Her voice broke as she said: "I couldn't stop them, Mrs. Kent. They have a warrant."

"Thank you for trying, Mrs. Finch. I'm terribly sorry that I wasn't here. All things considered, I think it would be best if you went home now," she said, then she rushed through the house looking for Mullane.

She found him in her study going through her papers. Her laptop was already in an evidence bag.

"What are you doing here?" she asked, although the answer was obvious.

Mullane turned and picked up an object in ⸱⸱ plastic bag that lay on her desk. "We've found a link between you and the dead man, Cara Mia. He's been recognized in Italy, and who do you suppose he was? Your beloved Angelo DiGuerro." He pronounced it Dig-er-oh.

"What!?" Ellie was so shocked, she had to sit down.

"Come now, Mrs. Kent. There's no point in pretending anymore."

"I'm not pretending and you are totally wrong. I am not Cara Mia, and, if I were, do you think I would I have left that book lying around?"

Mullane shrugged. "Maybe you figured you were safe."

"I don't see how I could have thought that with Jones following me and you hovering over us for the past week. But that's beside the point. I received that book as a gift."

"I know." He opened it and began to try to read the inscription aloud. "Even without knowing Italian I can guess what that means."

Ellie flushed. "I do not mean Angelo DiGuerro gave me the book."

"Who then? It was only signed a week ago. Right, if I might point out, the day you met your lover in the woods."

"He was not my lover!" Ellie shouted. "And he did not give me that book!"

"Then who did?" asked Mullane.

"Michael-John Parker."

Mullane looked surprised. "The chap who owns the old smithy?"

Ellie rolled her eyes. "Yes," she said.

"And when was this?"

"Saturday."

"You have a right odd marriage, Mrs. Kent, if you don't mind my saying so."

"My marriage has nothing to do with this," said Ellie, who could hear an hysterical note creeping into her voice. "Michael-John found the book, and he thought I'd like it, that's all. The inscription has nothing to do with either one of us."

Mullane sneered. "And how did Mr. Parker happen to find it?"

"He told me he found it in the woods," Ellie said, knowing this sounded totally lame.

"How very convenient for both of you. Jones! Take this book and get down to that antiques shop on the high street. I want to know exactly how, when, and where Mr. Parker claims he found it. And you, Mrs. Kent. You will kindly go back downstairs and wait in the lounge until we are finished."

Ellie glared at him, but she turned and went downstairs with what she hoped was the appearance of dignity, despite the fact that her knees were shaking in a very alarming way. In the sitting room, she found a policewoman waiting for her and silently took a seat from which she could watch the search team move through the room. Hector, she noticed, had taken up his spot under the sofa, where she could just see his dark and glowing eyes. She'd never known before that you could feel embarrassed in front of a dog, but she did.

All she could think of was how stupid she'd been to take that book and how glad she was that Graham was not there. If only this might all be over before he returned from London, she could bear it. Of course, he'd have to know what happened, but at least he didn't have to watch firsthand as the police examined every object in his home, looking for clues that his new wife had killed a man there.

Down came every one of Anthony Trollope's novels. Out came every photo and game. Ellie found it hard to imagine what they thought they were going to find—and what more damning evidence they could hope for than what she had already provided them with! Surely the next step would be an arrest.

For two hours she sat unmoving on the sofa, her brain whirling with scenarios that didn't add up. Imagining links between Jackie and Michael-John, Miss Worthy and Charlotte, and all leading back to this unknown poet.

Then she remembered the message she'd sent to the publisher on Saturday and wondered how soon she'd be able to access her e-mail. What would the police think when they found out that she'd been making inquiries? Would that add to the case against her or demonstrate that she did not, in fact, know the author?

When Mullane came downstairs carrying her laptop and handed her a receipt to sign, Ellie's panic shifted to outrage. She'd done nothing, nothing! And she was being subjected to every kind of invasion of her privacy. She forced herself to keep quiet though, until the policemen left.

Then she began to clean with a vengeance, vacuuming, dusting, and removing all evidence of the search, room by room. By the time Graham arrived home, she was exhausted, but she'd taken a long hot shower and changed her clothes, a fire was burning in the fireplace, and the table was laid for dinner.

He was unsuspecting and pleased as she poured them each a glass of sherry, but when she told him what had happened that day, he turned pale and angry.

"You should've called me! I should've been informed. I could've come back. You didn't need to go through that alone," he said.

"I didn't want you to see it. I just wanted it to be over."

"Ellie, you don't need to protect me. Whatever has happened—whatever is going to happen—I will stand by you."

Ellie tried not to show how she heard this: that Graham was worried something had happened after all. That the police must have some reason for continuing to pursue her as a suspect.

"If you didn't think anything had happened, you wouldn't need to say that."

"Nonsense; of course, I don't think you were involved in any way," he said.

But over the shepherd's pie Mrs. Finch had left them, he said: "I don't want to upset you further, but I do have to ask you one thing. Is there any reason why Michael-John Parker would deliberately try to implicate you in this murder?"

"I've been asking myself that all day too, but I don't think so. He's been very friendly. All that 'incomers should stick together' stuff. And, besides, why call attention to the book at all? He could have thrown it away, and no one would have been the wiser."

"Maybe it was a kind of insurance policy. He saw you as an easy person to shift blame to."

"But he couldn't know about the so-called evidence that Mullane has found like my marriage to Vito and the sleeping pills."

"No, of course not. You're right."

"And obviously I'd tell the police that he gave me the book."

Graham sighed. "And you're sure that you'd never met that man? Even years ago?"

"Absolutely sure. The only poets Vito ever pretended to like were ones who were more famous than he was."

"Well then, since this Mr. DiGuerro was never in this house, they won't find anything."

He made it a statement, but his face held a question that tore into Ellie's heart. Graham loved her, he was loyal, and it was his nature to give people the benefit of the doubt, but he had still felt it was necessary to say that aloud.

"As far as I know, he was never anywhere near this house. So unless you or Mrs. Finch let him in, there will be no evidence—no hairs, no fingerprints, no blood—to show that he was here."

He looked taken aback. "Ellie, don't be ridiculous."

"Then don't you be ridiculous," she said, pushing her plate away.

"Agreed; I'm sorry, but I'd better call Bell. This has gone too far."

Ellie knew he was right, but she watched him get up and leave the table with a heavy heart. He could've called from the kitchen phone, but obviously he wanted privacy. To be away from her.

She sat at her place, stirring her leftovers around with her fork until he came back.

"What did he say?" she asked.

"He said if anything else happens we should let him know right away."

"You mean like if they come to arrest me. I should make my one call to him."

"Yes." He went to the entryway and got his coat.

"Where are you going now?" She could hear the forlorn sound in her voice, but he didn't.

"It's practice night. If I don't go, people might take it as a sign that we're getting rattled. That we have something to hide."

"It seems pretty obvious that we're getting rattled," said Ellie.

"But we can't afford to be. We have to stay calm."

"Right. Calm. The police and my own husband think I'm a murderer, but I will remain calm."

"Ellie—don't be daft." He came back and gave her a kiss. "What are you going to do?"

"I don't know. Maybe I'll see if I can stop by Morag's."

"Good idea. I've always liked Morag. She's a very sensible person," he said, and she wondered if he'd still say that if he knew that Morag was helping her investigate the murder.

After she'd cleaned up the kitchen—haunted the whole time by Mrs. Finch's tearful face—Ellie rummaged through the closets until she found a dark, hooded coat that looked anonymous. "Sorry," she said to Hector, as she zipped it and pulled up the hood. "This is an adventure you have to miss."

Then she shut off the kitchen and sitting room lights, turned on the bedroom light upstairs, as if she were going to bed, and came back down to slip out of the kitchen door. Before she moved away from the shelter of the house, she waited, letting her eyes adjust, and watched for any sign of someone tailing her. The minutes ticked by slowly, but at last she was rewarded, when she saw Jones emerge from the shadows across the street and walk quickly away. Still she waited five more agonizingly slow minutes before she set off on a roundabout route to Morag's cottage.

Morag looked surprised when she saw Ellie on the back doorstep of her neat stone cottage. She was already in her flannel pajamas and robe. A cup of tea and an open copy of

Love and Desertion lay on the kitchen table and Radio 4 was playing softly in the background. Compared to the crisp night air, the room was toasty, warmed by a green Aga over which hung a row of well-worn copper pans.

"Sorry I didn't call," said Ellie, taking off her coat. "I'm being followed, so I'm afraid my phone calls are also being checked."

"That's OK; Seamus is with his father in Oxford, so I'm just lazing about. Wondering what's been happening on your end, actually." Morag pushed aside the book and teapot and brought out a bottle of whisky and two glasses.

"It was horrible," said Ellie, slumping down on a kitchen chair. "I got back to find the police searching the house, Mrs. Finch in tears, and a crowd of people ghoulishly watching from the street. If my reputation wasn't in ruins before today, it certainly is now."

"Blimey, but they didn't find anything, so then what happened?" Morag asked, pouring them each a healthy tot.

"But, that's the worst part. They did find something. What Mullane says shows the link between me and the dead man. Who, it turns out is an Italian poet named Angelo DiGuerro."

"You're kidding. And you know him?"

"No, but they found one of his books in my office."

"Among hundreds, I'm sure."

"Unfortunately, this one was inscribed to 'Cara Mia' only a week ago. But I'm not Cara Mia, and I have no idea who she is. Michael-John Parker gave me the book."

"Him again? How did he get it?"

"He says he found it in the woods, and he gave it to me, because he thought I'd like it."

"That's bizarre," said Morag, pouring herself some more whisky. She offered the bottle to Ellie, who declined.

"Actually, he said it might be a clue because of the date and the fact that it's in Italian. And I was going to turn it over to the police, but I wanted to read it first."

"Oh, dear. Bad move. So why isn't he the chief suspect instead of you?"

"I guess, if he were guilty, presumably he would have disposed of the book."

"So, how does it go then? This Italian poet came to Little Beecham with his book and gave it to someone he loved who killed him and threw the book away. It's a good argument for posting things. If he had, he'd be alive today."

Ellie leaned her elbows on the table with her chin in the cup of her hands. "The poetry is not the motive, that's for sure. The title of the book is *Memories of My Home* and it's all about nature, not Cara Mia."

"Still, you wouldn't dedicate a book to someone you hoped to blackmail."

"No. Probably not."

"So, maybe it's a triangle thing. You know, like if you were Cara Mia and Graham was jealous and killed him."

"Very funny. I can't quite see a man in his 70s producing that kind of jealousy."

"Well, Seamus says murder is about love, lust or lucre and that makes sense. So if this wasn't about lust, it could still have been about love or lucre. It's too bad we don't know more about your old man."

"He's not my old man! Which reminds me. Can I check my e-mail?"

"Of course," said Morag, who showed her into her cozy book-lined sitting room, where she had a laptop computer on her desk.

"After Michael-John gave me the book, I e-mailed the printer in Italy, pretending to be a fan who wanted to buy more copies. I asked if they could tell me anything about the author," said Ellie as she clicked open her e-mail.

She scrolled past urgent messages from her parents, several old friends, and the chair of the last English department she'd worked in, to highlight a message with the subject line: "La query".

"Aha!" she said, clicking it open.

"What does it say?" asked Morag, peering over her shoulder.

"It says," said Ellie translating, "they are pleased that I enjoyed the book, but they know nothing about the author.

All they did was the design and printing, for which he paid cash. He declined to give any contact information."

"Bugger."

"Right," said Ellie, clicking her e-mail shut. "So we're still at square one."

Morag settled on her sofa with her feet curled under her. In her robe, with her dark curly hair tumbling over her shoulders, she reminded Ellie of a college girl. They could have been strategizing about how to get a date when she said, "What's the next step then?" But, of course, they weren't.

Ellie sighed and took a sip of whisky. "I don't know. You have no idea how degrading it is to watch the police search your house. Even worse when it's not really your house. I kept thinking of Louise and how nothing like this would ever have happened to her."

"Forget that," said Morag. "Better to get on with your investigation."

"Better still, the police will discover why Angelo DiGuerro was here and that it had nothing to do with me."

"But until they do, you should press on. 'I will never give up, no matter what obstacles require surmounting!'"

"Is that a quote from something?" Ellie asked, finishing her whisky.

"*Love and Desertion.* Ramona Blaisdell-Scott," said Morag, and they both laughed.

"OK, I will surmount," said Ellie, as they hugged goodbye.

On her way home through the dark frosty streets, she again avoided the high street. Most cottages were already dark, although the blue light of a television showed in some windows.

As she passed Miss Worthy's cottage on Chapel Lane, she saw that her sitting room lights were still brightly lit behind the curtains.

It was only nine-thirty. Maybe she should try to talk to her now. Catch her off guard.

Ellie was about to knock at the door, when she realized that she could hear an unexpected sound coming from within: the rapid clickety clack of a manual typewriter.

She listened for a couple of moments, as the sound continued unabated. Miss Worthy was obviously a very good typist. And obviously there was more to her life than church, mushroom hunting, and baking.

Ellie had raised her hand again to knock, when the phone began to ring. The typing stopped, and she heard Miss Worthy speaking into the phone. It wasn't scientific, of course, but listening from outside, she was certain that she'd heard that muffled voice over the phone more than once in the past few days.

Tuesday, November 8

Chapter 16

All night Ellie lay awake wondering how she could get Miss Worthy to admit that she was the mystery caller who'd known all along who Angelo DiGuerro was—and accomplish this before the police came to harass her further. When she finally got up, she felt as if she had a hangover, and her fears about the direction of Mullane's investigation appeared justified when she saw the *Daily Telegraph.*

"WHAT RHYMES WITH MURDER? DEAD MAN WAS POET" said the headline, which, thankfully, was not amusing enough to be on the front page. The article went on to say that a publisher in Rome had identified the man found dead in the Oxfordshire village of Little Beecham on the morning after Halloween. His name was Angelo DiGuerro, but, according to the Oxfordshire police, little more was known than that he'd published a book of poetry.

Detective Inspector Derek Mullane of the Thames Valley Police was quoted as being pleased with this progress, but said the investigation was still in its early days. According to police sources, the American wife of the local vicar, continues to be a "person of interest" although no charges have been brought against her.

This story was illustrated not only by the omnipresent photo of the dead man's face, but also a 10-year-old photo of Ellie and a devastatingly handsome Vito Ruggieri. The photo had been taken at a reception, and she thought Vito looked a little drunk, but there was no mistaking her own expression as anything other than that of a very pretty young woman, besotted with love. The caption read: "Poetic license or rhyme scheme? Mrs. Graham Kent, who found the body of the dead Italian poet, was formerly married to award-winning, Italian-American poet Vito Ruggieri."

Graham came in to get some tea while she was reading this and stood over her shoulder looking at the photo with a glum expression. "You never told me Vito was so good looking," he said.

Ellie closed the newspaper. "I told you he was a rat, which is all I hoped you'd ever need to know about him."

"But obviously, you adored him."

"When I was twenty four. Since then my judgment has improved vastly. Now I adore you." She gave him a hug, and he put his arms around her, resting his chin on her head. "I'd give anything for this not to have happened," she said. "I want our private life back."

"Me too. But somehow we'll just have to cope." Ellie hoped he would kiss her, but he didn't.

Instead they went to their separate studies with two floors of empty house between them. In her room, the bare space on her desk reminded Ellie that her laptop was in police custody, even if she wasn't, and that her whole life was teetering on the edge of an abyss.

For a moment, she considered the option of disappearing. Surely it wasn't too late for her to leave the country? But instead, she took out one of the yellow legal pads she liked to use for her research notes and set to work writing out in longhand everything that had happened in the past week.

When she'd finished the narrative, she made separate pages for each person she knew in Little Beecham and put down anything that seemed even remotely odd or in any way connected to the murder:

Michael-John Parker: Rich, handsome, gay. Moved to obscure village to open a business for what customers? Money. How much does he have? Lives over his shop and spends his free time collecting trash at Beech Hall. Is he looking for something?? Claims to be writing Rutherford history and wants to buy the manor. Why? Is he connected to them? Illegitimate offspring? Working on a claim to the estate? How would I find out??? Is he telling the truth about the book? He has an alibi for the weekend in question. Could he have returned without being seen? What connection could he have with AD?

Jackie Henning: Jackie was using our shed. Probably the person Charlotte saw. Not the killer, but person who broke into the church? Stole AD's wallet? Is there a connection with his death? If yes, the murderer has killed twice in one week. Scary.

Priscilla Worthy: Is she mystery caller? Would mean she knew AD. How? Why? Where? When? Could she have killed him? Could she be covering for murderer? Lost button. Was she visiting AD at Beech Hall? Has she been to Italy? Could she be Cara Mia? What was she typing?

Mystery woman: If not Miss W, who? Why doesn't she come forward? Why call me instead of the police? Is she Cara Mia? The killer?

Charlotte Worthy: Saw someone, but won't say who. Probably Jackie Henning. Did he see her? Is there more to this story? ASK HER AGAIN.

Mrs. Bigelow: Claimed to see AD near church on Sunday. Could she be Cara Mia? Mystery woman? Seems unlikely.

Cara Mia: Loved by the poet, with whom she had a past and a hoped-for future (at least on his part). Lost the book. Careless, frightened, angry, disgusted?

Angelo DiGuerro: Wrote poems about nature and "memories of home." Spent good money to have them published beautifully. Bought English clothes in London, came to Little Beecham by train, had money, but "slept rough." Dedicated a copy of the book to Cara Mia— someone he knew here. Someone wanted him dead.

Ellie read this over twice and tried to figure out what questions she should try to answer first. In her experience, one answer led to other questions, but also other answers.

Then she remembered that she'd printed out a list of B&Bs and campgrounds when she was in Chipping Martin. She rummaged in her purse, and there it was, crumpled at the bottom.

Within five miles of Little Beecham, there were four bed and breakfasts, and when she called them, she learned that they all had vacancies on Sunday, 30 October. She called the campgrounds too, but they were all closed for the season.

So, with money and a choice, why would he have slept outdoors in his new clothes? It didn't make sense, yet he appeared to have known exactly where he was going when she saw him.

Ellie got out a map book and began to draw her own map. AD had arrived at Kingbrook on Sunday at 1 pm. It was a five-mile walk from the station to Little Beecham. That put him in the village around 2:30, when Mrs. Bigelow saw him walking down on the high street wearing his backpack. So where was he between then and 4:30 when Ellie saw him in the woods. At that time, he'd been heading away from the village in the direction of Beech Hall—and there wasn't much else out there except fields and woods.

On Monday he was back in the village having lunch at The Three Lambs. At that time, Mrs. Teaser said he had cash, but no backpack. A number of other people saw him around the village—or claimed they had—but no one reported talking to him except the Teasers. So where was he and with whom? Because by Monday night he was dead in the churchyard with no backpack and no money.

The police had searched for the backpack in the area around the churchyard and found nothing, but so what? It could be under the murderer's bed, buried, burned or scattered in pieces across the countryside. Or, if he stayed at Beech Hall, it might even be still hidden there.

She drew a circle around this idea and tried to remember the room Michael-John had showed her. If there was any place a bulky object like a backpack could be hidden.

By noon, the phone had not rung, and no police had showed up to arrest her. Ellie began to breathe a little easier, but she wished she knew how long it would take them to determine that Angelo DiGuerro had never been in the Vicarage. And when would they return her computer? She was very glad there were no documents on it about her investigation, and she hoped Sgt. Jones would enjoy her article on Jane Austen and the role of gossip in her novels.

She made some cheddar and pickle sandwiches and took them in to Graham's study, where they ate and made a concerted effort to talk about anything but death and murder, but it was heavy going. At last Ellie said, "I feel like I'm allowing myself to appear guilty if I don't go out. I think I'll try to round up some more donations to the coffee morning raffle."

Graham blanched, but all he said was, "If you think that's a good idea."

She knew he worried about how people might treat her, but then he didn't know why she was really going. She told herself deceiving him was a necessity as she changed into her tweed suit, brushed her hair until it lay against her head like a shiny cap, and set off disguised as Mrs. Vicar, determined to see Miss Worthy.

It was a cold day with a frozen fog shrouding the honey-colored stone buildings and leafless trees. As she set off, she observed her surroundings carefully. Out of the grey mist, two women on horseback emerged, the clip-clop of their horses' hooves magnified by the subdued atmosphere, but no shadowy policemen.

Those people who were out on the high street were preoccupied with keeping their noses tucked into their scarves and getting their business done quickly. Through the window framing the bright, warm interior of the village shop, Ellie saw Mrs. Wiggins nod to her, but no one else appeared to notice the murder suspect in their midst.

She kept her own nose down and hurried to Chapel Lane, thinking hard about what she would say to Miss Worthy. She'd start by saying she wanted to discuss the coffee morning, then somehow get around to the topic of the dead man and the mystery woman. She hoped her reaction would reveal if her theory was right.

But when she arrived at Miss Worthy's cottage, no one answered her knock, and there were no sounds from within. Ellie peeked through the crack between the curtains in the front window. The dim interior looked cozy, full of doilies and pillows, framed photos and books, but there was no sign of the owner.

She'd have liked to have a closer look at those photos, but breaking and entering in broad daylight was not among her current skills as a detective so she went to Plan B. The indirect plan of attack. She'd see if Mrs. Bell might shed some light on the mystery.

Mrs. Bell hardly seemed the type to make anonymous phone calls, but she had lived in Little Beecham for decades, and she was unsurprised when Mrs. Bigelow said Louise knew everyone's secrets. She must know her share of village secrets too.

As Ellie walked along the road to Castor House, she thought perhaps she'd paid too little attention to Mrs. Bell, just because she was always so neatly dressed. Her proper façade might be designed to hide all kinds of chaotic emotions.

This idea faded quickly, though, when the immaculate Mrs. Bell answered the door. With only the slightest hint that surprise visits were not welcome, she invited Ellie in and offered her a cup of tea in what she called the drawing room.

While her hostess prepared the tea, Ellie took the opportunity to look around, but there was nothing that you wouldn't find in countless other such rooms. No personal photos, nothing idiosyncratic, not even anything very interesting. Every aspect of the room was tasteful, expensive, and conventional. However, a fire was burning in the fireplace and a half-worked cross-stitch canvas and tumble of colored yarn in a chair pulled close to the hearth made clear what Ellie had interrupted.

When Mrs. Bell returned with the tea tray, Ellie sat down with her teacup balanced on her knee, smiled politely, and plunged in. "I apologize for dropping in without calling first, but I've been a bit worried about a situation that has come up, and I hoped you might be able to advise me about it."

Mrs. Bell took a cautious sip of tea, her face showing that she was torn between pleasure at this acknowledgement of her experience and suspicion regarding what Ellie might be about to say. "I will certainly advise you if I can," she said slowly. "What type of situation are you referring to?"

"There's a woman who's been calling the Vicarage who sounds quite elderly and frightened, but she won't give me her name," said Ellie with all the innocent boldness she could muster.

"Really?" said Mrs. Bell. Nothing in this description alarmed her; in fact, her interest was barely piqued. "Does she say what she's frightened of? You know sometimes elderly people become fearful about things that aren't very likely to happen."

"Well, this woman talks about a real event. In fact she seems to know a great deal about the man who was murdered in the village last week."

"You mean that foreigner?" Mrs. Bell pulled her head back sharply as if she'd smelled something rotten. "But surely, that's a matter for the police? Why is she calling the Vicarage?" Then she blushed and set down her tea cup. "I'm sure you know I don't for a moment believe the stories that have been going around about that unfortunate event."

"Thank you," said Ellie. "I think she calls because the police have dismissed her as a crank. And, frankly, I've worried she might be in danger, and I wondered, since you've lived here so long, whether you might have some idea who it is."

Mrs. Bell shook her head, as she went to the fireplace and picked up the poker. "I'm sure whoever she is she believes what she's telling you," she said, jabbing violently at the burning logs. "But since you've asked for my opinion, Mrs. Kent, I'd urge you to stay as clear as possible of that whole business.

"I think you'll find there are some people in the village with time on their hands who like to associate themselves with any kind of excitement in the news. In time, you'll learn to distinguish those who really need your help from those who don't."

"She didn't sound like that," Ellie persisted.

Mrs. Bell pursed her lips and gave the fire a few more jabs so one of the logs finally collapsed and burst into fresh flames. "I'm sure you must have discussed this with the Vicar as well. What does he say?"

"He agrees with the police. But men don't always..."

"No, they don't, but at the risk of sounding hopelessly old-fashioned, I recommend that you let yourself be guided by the Vicar in all things, Mrs. Kent. That way, I'm sure you will not put a foot wrong." With that, she put away the poker and resettled the fire screen. When she turned back to face her visitor, her eyes drifted to her needlework, and it was clear that the subject was closed.

Ellie left Castor House, sure that she had confirmed Mrs. Bell's opinion that she was not only an inexperienced young woman, but also credulous and lacking in common sense. Still, she'd gotten what she wanted.

Mrs. Bell had consistently expressed distaste regarding the foreigner, and Ellie was sure she was not the caller herself and genuinely did not know the dead man, Cara Mia, or the mystery caller. This was interesting, not only from the point of view of elimination, but also because it meant that, if Miss Worthy was involved, she had not confided in the person who appeared to be her closest friend. Therefore, in whom might she have confided?

The name that floated up out of her memory was Louise.

Unfortunately, Louise had been dead for nearly three years. But wasn't it highly likely that feelings so strong that they led to Angelo DiGuerro's death within little more than a day after his arrival would have had roots in the past? And if in the past, how far in the past?

The sun broke through the fog as she thought of this. Warm golden beams of light burnished the trunks of the trees along the road and jeweled the dew clinging to the hedges and grasses. Ellie thought this must be a sign that she was on the right track and tried to remember if Graham had said he was going to be away this afternoon. If so, this would be a good time to take a look at Louise's diaries.

As she walked back to the village, Ellie called Morag to report on her progress.

"Miss Worthy was out, so I've just visited Mrs. Bell."

"Did you learn anything new?"

"Only that I don't think she knows anything."

"Well, that's something. I've been investigating too. I decided to treat myself to lunch at The Three Lambs, and it proved quite fruitful. Your gorgeous ex- was a big topic of conversation."

"Oh, no. I'm going to have to leave town."

"Not at all. I think your stock went up with the pub crowd. But speaking of leaving town, they were also discussing Michael-John Parker. Did you know he's scarpered? Apparently the police were threatening to search his shop and flat until he got hold of someone who gave him an unimpeachable alibi for the time of the murder. And no one has seen him since."

"Is Whistler gone too? The dog?"

"Yes. Dog. Car. Man."

"That's probably fine then." Ellie was not ready to discuss the idea about the diaries, so all she said was, "I'll try Miss Worthy again later. I just hope she hasn't left town too."

At home though the Mini was in the drive, which meant Graham was at home, and she would not be able to pursue her secret reading mission. On the back doorstep she found a cardboard box wrapped in brown paper addressed to Mrs. Ellie Kent, The Vicarage. She carried it inside and was about to open it when she heard voices coming from the front hall. Graham and two others.

It only took an instant to recognize Emily Rutherford Hughes, who was saying, "I realize this is awkward for you, Vicar, but St. Michael's must not be seen to profit from this kind of notoriety. It simply won't do."

A softer man's voice concurred. "We must put the reputation of the church above personal feelings."

Then Graham said, "I quite agree, but I won't support any decision that implies the Anglican church finds a person guilty who's never been charged with any wrongdoing or tried before a court of law."

"The Parish Council—" began the man.

"The last I heard, the Parish Council did not operate outside the rule of law. Correct me if I'm wrong, Charles," said Graham, sounding more angry than she'd ever heard him.

The man, who Ellie now realized must be Charles Bell, muttered a reply that Ellie could not hear although she'd crept to the kitchen door, which was partly ajar.

"I think you'll find widespread agreement in the parish on this issue, and it will not benefit the church to go against it," said Mrs. Rutherford Hughes.

"If that is the case, then I've failed at my job," said Graham. "Regarding my wife, I will do whatever I can to shield her from false rumors or accusations, no matter who the source is. All things considered, however, I agree that she may be better off withdrawing from the coffee morning committee for this year. You have carried out your purpose, now I think we have nothing more to say to each other today."

Ellie heard them leave and then the door to Graham's study slammed. She admired that he'd restrained himself from slamming the front door behind their backs as well. She filled the kettle for tea and wondered what to do: whether it was better to let him know that she'd overheard the conversation or not.

While she waited for the water to boil, she opened the box and found a note on top of something wrapped in tissue paper:

"My dear Mrs. Kent,

I imagine I'm persona non grata at the Vicarage, thanks to my last gift, but I did not forget that I also promised you the enclosed.

If you can, if you will, please accept my apologies for the way I inadvertently added to your difficulties.

I am off to London to rethink my situation. I also hope to obtain one or two bits of information that may be of use to you.

Your repentant neighbor and friend,
MJP"

The signature was an elegant swirl executed with skill and a very expensive pen.

Ellie pulled away the tissue and saw that cheerful bauble, the Christmas tree music box. As soon as she picked it up and set it on the table, it began tinkling "Joy to the World." Hardly the tune to fit her mood.

She decided it did, however, give her an opening for a conversation with Graham, so she picked it up, went to his door, and knocked before entering.

She expected the medieval manuscript to have come out, but he wasn't even working on that. Instead he was sitting with his chin in his hands, just staring at the empty blotter on his desk.

"Graham," she said, going to him. She set down the tree and put her arms around his shoulders. "I didn't mean to eavesdrop, but I came in while you were talking in the hallway. So you don't need to worry about telling me. I already know how things stand."

He turned in his chair and hugged her, his face against her belly. "Sometimes the gap between what happens and what I believe is right becomes unbearable."

"But you don't really think you've failed, do you?"

"With Emily, yes. She's always been the way she is, and I've had to accept it. I'm very disappointed in Charles, but she's one of his most important clients, so I suppose she expects him to tow the line. As she does me."

"Well, I thought you defended me against the dragon with great bravery, Sir George. I feel safely nestled between you, God, and the Magna Carta, and, believe me, I do not care about the coffee morning committee. It's embarrassing, but I'll live.

"And, by the way, here's a contribution to the raffle. I'll leave it to you to pass it on." Ellie gave the tree a little twist and the tune began tinkling again.

"That's very nice," said Graham. "Where did it come from?"

"The Chestnut Tree."

"Oh, Lord, I don't think this is the right moment to mention donations to the church from Michael-John Parker." Then he looked at his watch and heaved himself to his feet like a man twice his age. "I have to call on the Hennings now and see how they're doing. Jack has arrived, which means the drinking will have begun."

"Have your tea first. You look knackered. As in, unfit for human consumption."

"Do I?"

"Yes, but I'll fix you up in no time," and, with that, she gave him a kiss.

After he'd eaten, showered, and changed into his black suit, Graham left and Ellie took Hector for a short walk. This was no country ramble though. She was eager to use the time alone to look at Louise's diaries, so he had to make do with a quick stroll around the village.

They'd just returned, when the doorbell rang. With some misgivings she went to see who it was, and there stood Detective Inspector Mullane. The day seemed determined to go from bad to worse.

"Oh, it's you," she said. "Let me guess. You're here to arrest me."

"No," he said, with a stolid expression. "I'm here to return your laptop and other things."

"And would that be with an apology for persuading the whole village, if not the whole world, that I'm a murderer?"

"I don't apologize for doing my job. I'd like to come in, though, if I may. I have something to tell you."

"Why do I get the feeling this is a test?" Ellie asked, but she stepped back to let him in, and waited in the hall, with her arms crossed, while he carried in the clothes, computer, and other objects they'd taken for testing.

"Is that everything?"

"We're keeping the book for the time being, more in hopes of identifying this Cara Mia than the author."

"You already know the author."

"Do we now, that's the point, isn't it?"

"What do you mean?"

"We've learned a little bit more about this Angelo DiGuerro since yesterday, and, he may have written those poems, but it turns out he had quite another profession. Con man."

"A con man? What kind of con man?"

"We're still trying to figure that out, but we have confirmed evidence of him living under two other names."

"No kidding?" Ellie had to admit, this was some kind of breakthrough. "What were they?"

"Apparently Angelo DiGuerro was only a, what do you call it, *nom de plume*. No one actually seems to have known him by this name. However, the man he rented a flat from in Rome for the past five years came forward and said the photo looked like his tenant Georgio d'Inglesi who recently left on what he called a holiday in the north. The man assumed he meant northern Italy and never paid much attention to the death in England.

"From other reports, however, we've learned that his real name was Rodolfo Scotti. At least that's the name he lived under in Tuscany for years. He and his wife had a farm near"—he consulted a scrap of paper he pulled out of his pocket—"Fontebuona. The Italian police interviewed some of the locals, and they said the Scottis had no children and didn't go to church or mix with anyone. No one knew where either one of them came from originally, which is unusual in that part of the world. After the wife died, he sold the property and moved away without a word or backward glance. Apparently they all assumed he was already dead, until his photo appeared in the papers."

"That's amazing," said Ellie. "And now I suppose you're hoping I'll reveal how I had an affair with him during the summer my ex-husband and I lived in that region."

Mullane pursed his lips. "If there is a connection, believe me, we'll find it. But at the moment, it would seem that Ralph Teaser pegged this bloke right from the start. He was here for no good purpose."

"So what makes you think I didn't already know all this?"

"We found no evidence of him having been in this house, the church or the shed. It seems most likely someone dumped the body where you found it."

"What a shock. Then what about Cara Mia?"

"We're still checking into that. There were some unidentified prints on the book, in addition to yours, DiGuerro's and Parker's."

"Does this mean I'm no longer suspect number one?"

"Let's put it this way, Mrs. Kent, I wouldn't plan any travel for the moment. We'll be pursuing every avenue necessary to find a solution to this murder."

"I hope you'll be quick about it then," said Ellie, who said goodbye and shut the door.

The news that the dead man had had three different identities totally threw her. Ellie tried to square each of these names with the person she'd seen in the woods and none of them seemed to fit. The surrounding details—English clothes, English woods—confused the picture.

Having a pen name was common enough, but why would he have changed his name when he left Tuscany? Was there some other Cara Mia he was trying to escape? Or was she mixing him up with Vito? She was certainly not the person to argue that men who wrote poetry were better than others, but a con man?

She found herself wishing that Michael-John was around to discuss this with. She was sure he'd have insight into why a man would change his identity so late in life. The reasons didn't have to be criminal. Despite what Ralph Teaser thought, Mullane hadn't told her anything that substantiated that theory. He'd simply morphed from one person to another. At home, people did this all the time. It was one of the freedoms held dear.

Ellie considered calling Morag, but decided she'd rather keep this news to herself for the moment. She picked up her laptop and other things to carry them upstairs, and, when her computer was re-installed in its usual place on her desk, she felt that events were finally beginning to turn back toward normal.

She'd planned to use this time to look at Louise's diaries, but instead she took out the photocopy she'd made of *Memorie del mio paese* and her Italian dictionary and settled herself at her desk in front of the window overlooking the churchyard.

In the circle of light from her lamp, she spread the pages in front of her and began to study them. Her whole career had been focused on prising out information about who writers were from what they wrote, and she was sure these poems must also hold a key to the life of Angelo-Georgio-Rodolfo.

Ellie read each poem quickly, then slowly line by line. She checked unfamiliar words in the dictionary and wrote out each line in English on a sheet of yellow lined paper until she could read the poem in both English and Italian.

By the time she'd translated three poems, she was tired and stiff from concentrating so hard. She also thought fatigue must be making her confused. She was no expert on Tuscan geography, but, when she closed her eyes and pictured the place where she and Vito had lived and the surrounding countryside, it was nothing like Angelo DiGuerro's lyrical evocations of green fields and grey skies.

In fact, they didn't sound like any part of Italy she'd ever seen. They made her think of England. And, even more precisely than that, of the Cotswolds.

She stood up and stretched, squeezing her eyes shut, then sat back down and skimmed several more poems quickly. Perhaps the difference was seasonal. Perhaps this was a different part of the province. But the more she read, the more convinced she became that Angelo DiGuerro's memories of home were memories not of Italy, but of England.

When she stopped fighting the idea that she was wrong, she suddenly realized that the evidence proving she was correct had been in front of her all along. She threw down her pencil and laughed.

Angelo DiGuerro had also called himself Georgio d'Inglesi because that's what he was. English. The name was Italian for George of England. It was so obvious, she couldn't believe she hadn't noticed it immediately.

And George of England's pen name? Angelo diGuerro. Angel of War.

A shiver raised the hair on her arms as she wrote down the names and their translations.

So was Rodolfo Scotti also an Italianization of an English name?

With the same feeling of excitement that fueled her literary research, she wrote down the name and whispered it to herself. Ro-dol-fo Scot-ti.

And then, with a whoop of triumph, she got it.

Randolph Scott. Rodolfo Scotti!

Whoever the dead man really was, over the years he had assumed the names of a great Hollywood hero, England's patron saint and an avenging angel.

Wednesday, November 9

Chapter 17

On Wednesday morning, Ellie woke up just as it was getting light. All night she'd been tossing and turning, thinking about the man who'd written his memories of England in Italian and returned home only to be killed after one night. She had an idea she wanted desperately to check out, but first she had to be the attentive wife, chatting with Graham, as he carefully polished his shoes and put on his black suit with a fresh white collar.

Jackie Henning's funeral was scheduled for that afternoon, and he had to meet with the family again to go over the service and other arrangements. Reading the funeral service for a child was the hardest of all his duties, he said, and the second hardest was coping with families dealing with this kind of devastating blow.

"I guess the only good part is that they have someone like you to help them through it," Ellie said, giving him an extra hug as he was leaving.

Her own first task was facing Mrs. Finch for the first time since the house search, and she paid special care to her preparations—cleaning up the breakfast dishes and making the bed—before getting ready for her private expedition.

When she went back downstairs, she found the housekeeper already at work, mopping the kitchen floor. She used an old-fashioned mop, the kind with long grey strands of cotton that looked like the wig of a drowned woman. Her face was already damp with sweat from the effort, and, at Ellie's entrance, she stopped to lean on the mop handle. She stared, in her usual judgmental way, but said nothing until spoken to.

"Good morning, Mrs. Finch," said Ellie. To herself, she sounded like she was reciting lines. Badly. "Are you feeling better today? I'm sorry that you had to be involved in what happened on Monday. As you have probably heard, nothing came of it."

Mrs. Finch's face squeezed into a sour frown, and Ellie braced herself for the expected tirade about how nothing like that ever happened when Louise was alive. Instead the old lady said fiercely, "I heard. And I told Jim, them police were the only ones surprised by that. It's a terrible thing what they get away with now. Seems like we're all guilty, unless we can prove ourselves innocent! And what kind of a state is that?"

"I don't know," said Ellie, who was surprised but relieved that the woman's anger was not directed at her. "I suppose they believed they had a good reason."

"Well, I hope the Vicar complains to the Council. And the MP," said Mrs. Finch, stabbing the mop into the bucket and swishing it up and down, which made a loud sucking noise. "If they can treat folks like him that way, just think what they'll be doing to the likes of us."

Ellie noticed that she didn't say, "folks like you," but she promised to remind him.

"By the way," said Mrs. Finch, spreading a swath of water across the floor, "There's a package came for you from abroad by special post." She nodded at a thin brown parcel on the table.

Ellie saw the Italian stamps and knew immediately that it was the copy of Angelo DiGuerro's book that she'd ordered on Saturday. She saw the housekeeper watching her furtively and understood that, no matter what she said, she—and no doubt many others—still had suspicions about her. Nothing but a solution to the mystery would change that.

She moved the package to the sideboard, smiled at Mrs. Finch, and, calling to Hector, went out.

It was a cold morning with a weak sun that did little to melt the heavy frost, and Ellie was glad she'd worn wellingtons and a warm coat. She and Hector took the direction away from the village and quickly crossed the countryside. When she reached the hillside overlooking Beech Hall, she clambered down the steep bank and climbed through the fences onto the overgrown drive. The old stones crunched under her feet with a lonely sound, and she thought of all the other people who'd walked along this drive over the centuries. None had had a purpose like hers.

She climbed the ruined staircase, her footsteps setting off small cascades of crumbling marble, and found her way to the room with the view over the valley. There she took her translation of DiGuerro's poems out of the inner pocket of her coat, and unfolded them in front of her on the windowsill.

She gazed at the view, watching the morning's mist slowly lift and reveal the details of that tranquil landscape. Then with a deep breath, she picked up a poem called "Untitled" and began to read aloud, first in Italian, then in English.

To an uninformed reader, it could have been describing many places, but the fact was that point by point it described this very view—the patchwork of fields bordered by hedges and stonewalls and punctuated by trees and clusters of houses, each with its sheltering church tower. Was it too farfetched to believe that the author had been remembering this spot?

She read aloud several other poems and felt an eerie peace come over her as if she were carrying forward the writer's purpose to its natural conclusion. She was reading the love poems to the loved one, and it was not a person, it was a place. This place.

Detective Inspector Mullane would say this was her imagination working overtime. It was not evidence that would stand up in any court, so she put the poems back in her pocket and turned to look for some more substantial clue to the dead man's presence.

She crouched to study the charred remains of the campfire on the floor and poked around, hoping to find what? The missing backpack? Something, anything with

DNA on it? But although she searched every room, she found nothing.

Discouraged, she went back to the window, and looking out at that view, told herself a story. About an old friend who came home, after many years away, and asked Miss Worthy to meet him here. She agreed, and what he told her about his life was so shocking that she twisted off her button in her agitation over what he said. Not only that, she was so upset that she dropped the precious gift he'd given her as she hurried home, and no amount of looking for it later would bring it back because, in the meantime, someone else had picked it up.

When she thought about how Miss Worthy had behaved over the past week, she couldn't believe she was the murderer. She was sure she was the mystery caller, and she was also the one who wanted the dead man buried in Little Beecham. She wanted him to remain close by. She doubted the murderer would like that idea.

So what happened? Perhaps before she could help him or prevent it, this friend repeated his story to someone who was not at all happy to see him back. Someone who was threatened enough to spike his drinks with Valium and drop him off to die alone in the churchyard.

And for reasons known only to Miss Worthy, she'd kept silent to protect both Angelo DiGuerro and his murderer, so that the story both past and present would never come out. As she contemplated this scenario, it felt believable. Right. But how could she ever prove it?

Ellie and Hector were waiting on the doorstep of the library when Charlotte arrived at 1 pm. At the sight of her, the girl looked startled and glanced anxiously over her shoulder.

"Hello, Charlotte. I haven't seen you for awhile," said Ellie, tying Hector's leash to the railing of the front steps.

"My baby caught cold at the bonfire. I've been home taking care of him," said Charlotte. "He's better now," she added, but instead of unlocking the door, she looked up and down the street. "Aunt Pris will be here any minute. I can't open until she comes. She doesn't like me to be alone. It's too dangerous."

"You're not frightened of me, I hope."

"Better safe than sorry, Mrs. Kent. That's what my aunt says."

Ellie couldn't imagine Miss Worthy would be much help when it came to defending Charlotte from a murderer, but all she said was, "Safety in numbers."

Charlotte nodded at this exchange of wisdom, and they both watched Miss Worthy hurrying toward them down the street, her tweed coat flapping in the wind.

"Oh, it's you, Mrs. Kent," she said, trying to slow her breathing. "I—I didn't recognize you in those clothes," she added lamely.

"Yes, it's just me. Nothing to worry about."

Miss Worthy and Charlotte both blushed, and Charlotte hurried up the stairs to open the door. Inside she turned on the lights and then settled herself at the librarian's desk, where she restlessly straightened her papers, pens, and pencils. Miss Worthy stationed herself nearby and pulled a wad of knitting out of her carry-all.

Ellie looked from one to the other and tried not to feel resentful. If she were right, these two, with their innocent blue-eyed stares, were entirely responsible for all of the trouble she and Graham had been through in the past ten days. If they'd only told the truth from the beginning, the whole mystery could have been solved immediately—and Jackie Henning would be out riding his bike today, instead of awaiting his burial.

"Did you want to order some books, Mrs. Kent?" Charlotte asked, bringing Ellie out of her thoughts.

"No, I'd like to see any historical photos of the village that you have in your collection."

Charlotte frowned. "There's not much. People keep saying they're going to do one of those histories, but no one has. Once they got as far as collecting people's photos though. I can let you look at those, if you like." She lumbered out of her chair and went into the office, returning a few minutes later with two archival photo boxes.

"This is it, I'm afraid. A lot of them aren't even marked with dates or anything. Is there something specific you're looking for?"

Ellie saw Miss Worthy glance up from her knitting. "Not really. I'm just curious," she said, taking the boxes. They both watched her as she moved past the rows of bookshelves and sat down at a table out of their sight.

The first box contained a hodgepodge of small color snapshots covering about 40 years of village fetes, school plays, and homes decorated for Christmas. Nothing much had changed over the years—even the clothes and hairdos were remarkably the same. When Ellie came across a photo of Louise and Graham with baby Isabelle, she paused to study their happy, untroubled faces. Graham didn't look like that today, with the sleepless shadows under his eyes.

Well, there was no news in that. Wasn't that why she was doing this? To get this business cleared up and return to normal? She closed that box and opened the other one.

The second box contained black-and-white photos that went back to the war years and earlier, so she looked through them more slowly. They documented the same social events—but it was interesting to see the old shops, the farm horses pulling hay wagons and flocks of sheep coming down the high street.

Finally she was rewarded with a postcard shot of Beech Hall before it burned. She pulled out the magnifying glass that she'd tucked in her purse and studied this photo closely. She didn't know what she hoped to see, but all she learned was what she'd already known—it had been a lovely old manor and the shock of its destruction must have been terrible.

She felt her heartbeat quicken when she discovered a photo of the staff in their uniforms lined up in front in the house, and she peered at each face for a long time, but she could see no traces of any person now living—or recently dead. Unfortunately, there was not a single Rutherford family photo in the box and none of the inside of the house either. The omission seemed striking. Unbelievable, actually.

She returned the boxes to Charlotte, smiled politely, and said: "Thanks, that was exactly what I needed to know."

"Really?" asked Charlotte, and Ellie was pleased to see a flash of anxiety in the girl's face. She fingered the lid of the top box as if she couldn't wait to see what was so interesting, while Miss Worthy bent over her knitting, concentrating furiously.

"Well, goodbye. I've got to go and get ready for the funeral," said Ellie. "Oh, by the way, Miss Worthy, I've turned all my raffle information over Graham. I'm sure he'll pass it on to the committee soon."

Miss Worthy looked up, open-mouthed, but before she could say a word, Ellie went out the door.

Outside, she collected Hector and hurried home to change for Jackie Henning's funeral. No doubt it was petty and childish to tease those two, but she couldn't help herself. Her capacity to be the nice, unflappable vicar's wife was wearing very thin. Of course, if she had solid evidence of what had happened, she would not need to play such games.

By the time she'd put on her black suit—what she used to call her 'New York armor'—and slipped into a pew next to Morag, the church was already crowded. Everyone had turned out to say goodbye to the ne'er-do-well boy, including the police. DI Mullane, dressed in a navy suit with a traditional black tie, sat at the back.

Morag raised an eyebrow, as if to ask if there was any news, and Ellie mouthed, "Later," because the organist had begun to play.

The neighborly rustling and chatting ended as Phyllis and Jack Henning and their children filed in with an assortment of other red-haired relatives and sat down in the front pews, followed by Graham. When the music stopped, there was complete silence until he spoke and brought them all back to life.

Ellie was a little awed by the way Graham's presence exuded comfort and order. Whatever his private worries were, when he spoke in church, his voice drew the congregation together like cold men and women warming their hands at a fire; and they listened with rapt attention as he read the funeral service, led them in prayers, and spoke about the gift of life and the inevitability of death.

Ellie had once told him she couldn't imagine standing up there and representing God—being the channel and mouthpiece for such an unpredictable and capricious power—–and he said he could do it because he didn't see it that way. "Life is always unpredictable, and God helps us get through it. In that way, I believe God is constant. That's how I can have faith."

"I'm not sure I'll ever get that," Ellie said, worried that he would be angry, but he only smiled.

"It's a dynamic process. Different every day," he said, and she had to admit that she was glad to know that, even for him, there was no such thing as perfect faith.

The service for Jackie included the usual eulogies: the games master at the village school talked about his enthusiasm for football; and Phyllis's father, dressed in a 40-year-old black suit, talked in a choked voice about how Jackie was a good lad who'd always helped him with his bit of garden and might have become a good farmer. Then all the children, led by Sarah, filed up and stood together at the front of the church. Sarah, looking pale but composed, announced that they had written a letter to Jackie and that she was going to read it for all of them.

"Dear Jackie," she began, "We are very sorry that you have died and left our family. We will always remember you. Especially your hard pinches, your honk-honk laugh, the way you hogged the remote, the ghost stories you told us, and the times you got us into trouble by taking us on what you called smashing adventures. We will also remember you whenever we eat chocolate cake, crisps, or wiggly worms. Thank you for being our brother, which you will always be forever, even though you are gone. Love, Sarah, Donny, Mike, and Lucy."

By the time they sat down, practically everyone in the congregation was reaching for tissues. Then came the closing words, and they stood to sing "There is a green hill far away", their combined voices giving them a unity and strength they did not possess in ordinary life.

Finally, they processed into the damp and chilly churchyard for the interment. The strong smell of freshly turned earth, which Ellie associated with a different kind of planting, gave the whole burial a new and vivid meaning. Phyllis fainted at the sight of her son's coffin being lowered into the ground, and the children cried, but somehow they all got through it, and a boy who'd been full of life a week before with no thought of leaving this earth, was now a part of it.

The reception was in the village hall—the only room big enough—and the police had had to push their desks and equipment against the wall to make room. The village ladies had made a huge spread of sandwiches and cakes, so the subdued crowd who arrived from the churchyard cold and dispirited gradually revived.

Ellie wasn't hungry, but she picked at a plate of food, while she watched the crowd. Sometimes she was aware that she was the one being watched and noticed eyes skitter away from her as if looking at her might be dangerous. She told herself she didn't care; she was on the job. She needed to test her hypothesis against other possibilities, before she could be certain.

For example, there was Mrs. Bigelow, who was swathed from head to toe in drooping black knit, and hungrily consuming cake. Ellie would have liked to cast her as a murderer. She had a mysterious past and was certainly self-righteous enough to sit in judgment on her fellow man. She looked strong enough to drag Angelo DiGuerro across the road from her house and into the churchyard. She was also mean enough to leave him there to die.

"Well?" said Morag coming up to her with a cup of coffee and a plate of Victoria sponge. "You look deep in thought. What's this news you referred to? Mrs. Bigelow has been telling everyone she's sure Jackie was murdered and that Mullane's coming to the funeral proves it."

"Really, and here I was considering her as a suspect. Does she look like a Cara Mia to you?"

"She does, actually. Very operatic. Unfortunately, if Jackie was murdered, she's out of the running. She doesn't drive. In fact, that would eliminate quite a few of the older women as suspects," said Morag.

"Conversely, you could say it narrows the field," said Ellie, who'd just spotted Miss Worthy and Charlotte's parents at one of the tables around the perimeter of the room. Dressed in layers of black, Miss Worthy looked pale and ill, as if the afternoon—or a bad conscience—was wearing on her. An untouched plate of food sat in front of her.

"Are you suggesting you know who did it?"

"I have some ideas, but no proof," and despite Morag's cajoling, she didn't tell her any more.

When the heat and noise of the crowd became uncomfortable, Ellie went outside to get some fresh air and noticed a small figure huddled on a bench in the adjacent schoolyard. She recognized the red hair immediately and realized that it was Donny Henning. He glanced up as she approached him and then looked away.

"Hello, Donny. Would you like company or would you prefer to be alone?"

He hesitated, then shoved over a little, and Ellie sat down. At eleven, Donny was still thin and child-like, lost in a cheap black suit that was two sizes too big for him. Ellie hoped he wouldn't have very many occasions to wear it before he outgrew it.

He continued a glum appraisal of his new black shoes, until she finally said, "I thought your letter to Jackie was very nice."

Donny shrugged, an attempt at adolescent indifference, but a tear dropped onto his trousers, and he rubbed it away quickly.

"It's all right to be sad when someone dies, you know."

Donny sniffed. "I'm not sad," he insisted, even though the tears fell faster. "All that rubbish was Sarah's idea, not mine. I only stood there because Mum and Dad said we all had to."

"So you and Jackie weren't close?"

"Never," he said vehemently. "I hated him. I wished he'd disappear and now he has." Donny started sobbing, and Ellie put her arm around him. His fragile pride gone, he let himself be held, his hot face pressed against her. As he cried, she felt ashamed that she'd almost begun thinking about death as a puzzle to be solved, as remote from real life as a research project in literature.

She stroked the boy's back and said, "Everyone hates the people they love sometimes. You and Jackie might not have liked each other now, but you might still have been friends when you got older."

"No, we wouldn't. Not ever. When I saw all the money he had, I thought he really was going to run away this time, and I was glad. I never knew he was dead."

Ellie felt her heart slow down at his words and very quietly asked, "All what money, Donny?"

"Jackie had a whole wad of money in a sock. I saw him counting it, and I was going to steal it back. I thought he'd pinched it from Mum, but then I realized she never had that much money in her life."

"How do you think he got it then?"

"Jackie was always on the lookout for what he could steal. He said it's the only way kids like us get what we need." He looked up at her and reddened with embarrassment. "I guess I shouldn't be saying that to you."

"You can say anything you want to me. I'm not anybody."

He sniffed again. "Anyways, I never took it, and I dint really care what he did, except he killed Scrubber, and I won't ever forgive him for that."

A little shiver went up Ellie's spine. "Scrubber? Who was that?"

"He was my hamster, and I loved him. And Jackie took him and put him outdoors, and I couldn't find him, even though I searched and searched. Mum said it was just a prank. He didn't mean anything by it, but I don't believe it. He liked to hurt animals, just to show he could."

"That must have been terrible for you."

"Worse for Scrubber. He ended up dead."

"Yes. You're right about that." Neither one of them added—"And so did Jackie"—but they were probably both thinking it because Donny began sobbing all over again.

Ellie stayed with him until the arm around him felt nearly frozen, but at least he was all cried out. The only sound was the rattle of the beech leaves falling around them and the distant murmur of voices—and even laughter—from the hall.

Ellie bent down to see his face. "So Donny, did you ever tell the police about that money Jackie had?"

"No, Mum was that upset already I thought she'd gone crazy, and there's no way of knowing where he got it from."

Ellie was not so sure about that. If it was the money that Angelo DiGuerro had in his wallet, it would have his fingerprints on it. "It's still in the sock then?"

Donny nodded.

"Will you do me a favor and make sure it's in a safe place? Then when your Mum is feeling better we can figure out what to do with it."

"OK," said Donny. Slumped beside her, he looked like a doll that's had all the stuffing pulled out of it.

"You must be getting cold. Wouldn't you like to go in and have some hot tea and cake?"

"No," he said, "I don't want anything to eat. I'm going to take some of Jackie's flowers and put them on Scrubber's grave."

"Does he have a grave?"

"No, but I have a place where I pretend he is, so he knows I haven't forgotten him."

"I'm sure he does know," said Ellie, who immediately regretted stepping out onto such theologically thin ice. Donny seemed to agree, though, because he got up and said goodbye.

When Donny had trudged off, Ellie went back inside the hall, where the last people were still eating and talking, while some of the women had begun to clear up. She offered to help, but Mrs. Teaser declined. "You go along, Mrs. Kent. The Vicar was wondering where you'd got to," she said, as if Ellie must have been up to no good.

She went home, but neither Graham nor Hector was there. *They must have gone for a walk*, she thought, and wished she could have joined them. As usual, Graham's mobile phone was sitting on the kitchen table, so there was no way to locate him.

As she changed into her jeans and a sweater, she thought about Donny and Jackie, Miss Worthy, Charlotte and proof. She listened to the silence in the house and felt only a tiny pang of guilt when she opened the door to Isabelle's room and began hunting in her closet for the carton marked 'Datebooks.' This invasion was not nosiness, it was for a good purpose, and she was sure Isabelle would approve. Even Louise would approve.

She found the box at the very back, behind Isabelle's prodigious collection of shoes. It was heavy and she was sweating by the time she'd dragged it out into the middle of the floor.

Inside she found annual datebooks that noted meetings and appointments, and underneath them, diaries. She resisted the urge to look at the early diaries that she was sure would describe Louise's happy and trouble-free first years as vicar's wife and searched through the pile to find the most recent one instead.

This was a blue leather diary, and she opened it eagerly only to find page after page of neat entries about the garden, Isabelle at school, and the sermons Graham had preached. She felt a surge of disappointment and then anger at herself. Why had she ever imagined that the oh-so-discreet Louise would record people's secrets in her diary? She did not even write about her own.

Nevertheless, she reminded herself that a good researcher is alert and patient. She watches for connections and patterns and avoids pre-conceived ideas that will skew her findings.

So she set the diary aside, found the datebook for the same year, and was slowly turning the pages of dentist appointments, oil changes, and committee meetings, when a picture postcard fell out. This she picked up eagerly and tried to keep her excitement in check, when she saw where it was from: the Coliseum in Rome. Italy.

Ellie turned the card over and read the message. A small spiky handwriting said that the writer was having a marvelous time seeing the sights, which she described in as much detail as could be fitted in the small message space. At the bottom, there was a P.S. Some wonderful news to tell you when I get back. The signature was P.W. The postmark showed that the card had been mailed five years ago.

Ellie sat for a long time holding the postcard. She didn't want to let her desire for a breakthrough overwhelm the facts, but P.W. could certain be Priscilla Worthy, and the date coincided with the time Angelo DiGuerro was living there.

Could the wonderful news have been that they had met in Rome? Accidently or on purpose?

Carefully she set aside the postcard and routed out the diary for that year. The postcard had been sent in March, so she turned to Louise's entries for March and April.

She found nothing of interest in the diary, but, in the datebook, under April 18, there was an entry that said, "Tea in Ox with PW," and then two weeks later: Remembrance Day!

She stared at the entry about tea. It could mean that Louise had a friend from Oxford named PW, who went to Rome on a holiday. It could also mean that Louise had gone 20 miles to have tea with Miss Worthy—far from the Vicarage and the village. It was hard to imagine why two women who lived only a five-minute walk apart would need to travel so far unless they had something very private to discuss. Some wonderful news, for example. It was a slender thread, but did the fact that Louise had saved the postcard signal its importance? She made a quick search and found no other letters or cards in the box.

And was it important that the postcard was stuck into the datebook for the wrong year? Ellie paged through the last entries of the final datebook and found that Louise had met with PW four times in the last two weeks of her life. What could have been going on that caused such urgent attention?

And what did "Remembrance Day" in April mean? Those words were everywhere this week, but she had a feeling she'd also seen them in another context. What was it?

She stood up and stretched, and she was surprised to realize that night had fallen. Wherever Graham and Hector had gone off to, they should be home any minute. As she rolled her shoulders and stretched her back, she scanned the bookshelf by Isabelle's bed, and there, right in front of her, was the answer to her question: *Remembrance Day* by Ramona Blaisdell Scott.

Eagerly she pulled the book out and opened it. On the flyleaf, there was a handwritten dedication: For Louise, with affection and gratitude, PW

The spiky writing matched the handwriting on the postcard and the copyright date matched. Undoubtedly this was what Louise was referring to in her datebook, but why was this gift so important that it merited a mention?

Ellie studied the book and suddenly felt very close to Louise. As if she were whispering in her ear. If only she could understand what she wanted her to know!

On the same shelf, she found a first edition of *No Regrets*, also by the elusive Ms. Scott and autographed in the same unmistakable handwriting. Clearly, PW and Louise had shared an enthusiasm for these books. Or was it something more?

Suddenly Ellie recalled the books on display in Chipping Martin—the rare ones signed by the author, and she burst out laughing.

She would have to verify it, of course, but she was certain that the signature she'd seen there was written by the same hand, and that therefore the shy, dowdy Miss Priscilla Worthy must also be Ramona Blaisdell Scott, the mysterious best-selling author.

And, in another flash, she realized that there was a further connection: that this author, this woman in a Cotswold village, had taken virtually the same alias as the unknown man who turned up in a Tuscan village calling himself Rodolfo Scotti.

As fast as she could, Ellie repacked the box and stowed it back in Isabelle's closet, keeping out only the diary, datebook and postcard that were part of her evidence. These she took with the novels up to her study and hid them in a carton of her own books.

Who was she hiding them from? She didn't know, but it felt necessary, as if she were safeguarding her new knowledge. The identity not only of Ramona Blaisdell Scott, but also, she thought, of Cara Mia.

She looked at the clock and wondered again where Graham could possibly be. Then she hurried downstairs, scribbled him a note, grabbed her coat, and went out. She was now absolutely certain that Miss Worthy had known all along who the dead man was—and most likely why he died and who killed him. She intended to waste no more time in confronting her about it.

Ellie hurried down the quiet, dark high street and turned left into Chapel Lane, so named for a former Methodist chapel that had now been converted into a home. Miss Worthy's thatched roofed cottage was at the end of the lane, surrounded by a low stone wall and a small garden.

There were no lights on in the sitting room, but an upstairs window was lit up, so Ellie rang the bell and waited anxiously on the doorstep. When no one answered, she rang again.

It was early, but she wondered if Miss Worthy might have already gone up to bed. She had not looked well after the funeral—and Ellie could imagine why, if her silence had in any way contributed to Jackie's death.

She tried to peek into the downstairs window. The curtains were not drawn, but it was too dark to see much. She went around to the back of the cottage and stood on her tiptoes to peer into the kitchen. A lamp was still lit there, but the room was empty.

She pulled an old wooden garden chair over to the side of the house and then, with a quick glance around, stood on it, so she could have a better look into the sitting room. The room was shadowy and dim, but the light from the kitchen partially illuminated the hall.

She was about to give up, when she noticed something that looked wrong. She stared, trying to make out what it was. A pair of shoes discarded in the middle of the hall.

Or rather a shoe. Or rather not just a shoe. A foot.

Ellie began to shiver as the meaning of this struck her.

It was no time to worry about breaking and entering. She hurried around the cottage and tried the back door. It was locked, but she hoped Miss Worthy was not very inventive about where she hid her spare key, and she wasn't. It hung behind a window shutter, within easy reach of the door.

Ellie unlocked the door and ran through to the front of the cottage. There she found Priscilla Worthy in a heap at the bottom of her stairs. At the top, Ellie saw a rumpled rug that appeared to explain how she had fallen.

One leg and foot—what she had seen from the window—were bent at an awkward angle. Underneath her head, there was a pool of blood. With shaking knees, she knelt down beside the old lady and checked her breathing. She was still alive, but her pulse was faint and irregular.

In the sitting room, Ellie found a couple of lap blankets to cover her, then she picked up her heavy old telephone receiver and dialed the emergency service.

When she at last reached an ambulance dispatcher, she stuttered her way through giving directions, the phone number, and other information.

"We'll be there as soon as possible," said dispatcher, but she didn't say, "Don't worry," and she didn't define soon.

Ellie went back to check Miss Worthy, then tried the Vicarage, but Graham was still not home. Where was he? She tried to remember if he'd told her where he was going after the funeral.

As she stood listening to the ringing phone in the empty Vicarage, she stared at the framed photographs arrayed on the top shelf of the bookcase: a girl with ribbons in her hair who was surely Priscilla; two dark-haired boys, wearing capes and brandishing homemade swords; and a group of children at play in front of the ruins of Beech Hall. In this one, Priscilla and one of the boys were looking at each other and laughing as if they had just played the best joke in the world on everyone.

Angelo, she thought, but then she heard the whoop-whoop of the ambulance siren and rushed to open the front door. The crew clambered past her with a gurney and immediately took charge of Miss Worthy, much to Ellie's relief.

"Will she be all right?" she asked, as they assessed her.

"Can't tell you, luv," said the paramedic as he and his partner carefully moved the unconscious woman onto the gurney. "What happened?"

"I don't really know. I just came by to see her and spotted her on the floor from the window. It looks like she might have slipped on that little rug at the top of the stairs," said Ellie.

He clucked and shook his head. "I don't know why these old girls are so attached to scatter rugs. I mean the name says it all, don't it? And they don't usually do so well after this kind of fall. Just so you know."

The possibility that Miss Worthy might actually die made Ellie so dizzy that she had to sit down. She watched the two men lift the gurney and carry it out of the front door, where several neighbors had now gathered, drawn out of their homes by the arrival of the ambulance.

"Is she dead?" asked a boy, and his mother shushed him.

"What happened?" they asked, peering in at Ellie sitting on the steps above the pool of blood. She could almost hear their brains whirring.

"She had a fall," said Ellie, as she squeezed past them to ask the ambulance crew where they were taking her.

"Kingbrook Regional," said the driver. "It's the closest." Then he turned on the engine and the siren and pulled away from the curb.

"You're the vicar's new wife, aren't you?" asked an elderly woman with a blanket around her shoulders and thick glasses. Her hand snapped around Ellie's wrist like a handcuff.

"Yes, I'm Ellie Kent. Are you a friend of Miss Worthy's?"

"I've lived next door to her for 30 years, but I can't say as we're friends. Chalk and cheese we are. Always have been. Still, we manage. Have you called her niece?"

"No," said Ellie. "To be honest, I only thought about getting the ambulance."

The old lady bobbed her head. "Better do it now. She won't take kindly to being the last one to hear about this."

"I will, thanks," said Ellie, as she tried to politely release her arm.

"Better get that blood up too. If it stains the floor there'll be no re-selling that place."

"Thank you for your suggestions," she repeated, jerking her arm away to hurry back inside.

She dropped a kitchen towel over the blood and was still looking for Mildred Worthy's phone number when the doorbell rang again. She expected it would be some other neighbor, so she was taken aback to see Detective Inspector Mullane waiting on the doorstep.

"Mrs. Kent," he said. "What a surprise."

"What do you mean? What are you doing here?"

"We are notified in certain situations when the emergency services are called out. Not that I expected to find you here, but you do have a way of being everywhere there's trouble in this village, so this time I'm going to have to make it official and ask you to come with me."

Ellie's mouth dropped open, but she didn't bother to ask what for.

Chapter 18

It wasn't like they were giving her a choice. A woman police constable came forward to take Ellie by the elbow, and two other policemen entered Miss Worthy's cottage to investigate the scene. The neighbors gawped with ill-concealed excitement as the vicar's wife was led down the path and Mullane opened the door of the waiting police car. She resisted the urge to hide her face as she climbed into the back seat with the woman PC next to her. The car door shut and locked with a harsh-sounding click.

No one said a word all the way to Chipping Martin, but it didn't matter. Ellie's heart was pounding so loud it took the place of conversation. By the time they reached the police station, she thought she'd gotten a grip on her panic, but when she had to get out of the car, she found her knees shaking so much that she could barely stand. However, the police officers didn't appear to notice and led her into the station as if this were something that happened to her every day.

The woman PC took her coat and purse, read her her rights, and then left her with a cup of weak tea in an interview room. This was about as bleak and dispiriting a place as Ellie could imagine, with almost colorless walls, no windows, and the barest of furnishings. If it was meant to create a blank screen against which hapless prisoners would project their fears and guilty thoughts, it was pretty effective, but in her case it only served to make her mad. As a result, when Mullane and Jones entered the room, she was ready for them.

The minute they were seated opposite her, she went on the offensive. "I demand to know why I'm here. If I'm being charged with something, I want my lawyer to be present. If not, I want to be taken home right now."

DI Mullane leaned back in his chair and said, "You aren't being charged yet, Mrs. Kent, but we felt it necessary to talk to you in a more formal setting in hopes that you would be inspired to tell us the truth. The whole truth."

Ellie stared back at him and said nothing.

"For example," he said, letting the chair fall back onto four legs, "we'd like to know why you were at Miss Worthy's cottage this evening and what happened there."

"I went by to talk to her about the Christmas coffee morning. We're both on the committee," said Ellie.

"So for this you visited her at six thirty pm?"

Ellie shrugged. "I've tried to catch up with her a couple of times this week. My husband was out, and I was at loose ends after the funeral. I thought she'd be home."

Mullane looked skeptical. "So what happened?"

"I rang the bell and no one answered, although there were some lights on. I looked in the window and saw what looked like her foot. Obviously something was very wrong. So I found the key and went in. I found her lying unconscious at the foot of the stairs."

"If no one answered the door, why didn't you just go home?"

"It's a good thing I didn't!"

"True enough. So then what did you do?"

"I checked to see if she was breathing, then I called for an ambulance, and I tried to reach my husband, but I couldn't."

Mullane was doodling on a piece of paper. He looked up. "Is that it?"

"Yes, Inspector, that's it. Except for an explanation of why *you* were there."

"As I said, we were alerted about the ambulance call."

"And a Chief Inspector has nothing else to do but chase ambulances?"

"At the moment, anything that happens in Little Beecham receives our close attention. Two people have died under highly suspicious circumstances in less than two weeks, and now a third has suffered a near-fatal accident. You seem to have been the first on the scene in two of these, shall we say, unfortunate incidents."

"That's purely coincidence," Ellie claimed, "and you have no evidence that it's not. I've told you what you wanted to know, and since you seem totally bent on destroying my reputation, my marriage, and my ability to do my job in the most public way possible, I can assure you I do not feel very inclined to help with yours. So I'd like to go home now."

"Not quite yet, Mrs. Kent. There's more to be covered in our little talk, and we're not just dependent on your good will here. The law requires it, and both obstruction and withholding evidence are crimes.

"So I'd like you to tell me now everything you know and even what you think you know about these events in your village. If you don't, I won't hesitate to charge you. Do you understand? You could go to prison. Is that what you want?"

"No."

"Then you'd better start talking."

Ellie stared at the man who'd been hounding her for ten days and thought about how close she was to figuring out the real story herself. But she also thought about Graham and Isabelle and her parents and what they'd want her to do. Even though she felt as alone as she ever had in her life, she would not bear the consequences of what she did now alone.

She took a sip of her tea, more to summon up her dignity and courage than because she was thirsty.

"The truth is, I don't *know* anything. I can tell you what I think I know: Angelo DiGuerro, Georgio d'Inglesi, Rodolfo Scotti—whatever you want to call him—was not an Italian. He was English, and based on my translation of the poems he wrote, I believe he was from this area."

Mullane and Jones looked suitably surprised, as she continued. "If you translate the names he used into English, they create a sort of pattern. Rodolfo Scotti...Randolph Scott. He was a famous actor who starred in Hollywood Westerns in the 1930s—and in war movies during the 40s. My guess is that, whatever happened back when he took that name, he was trying to think of himself in heroic terms. Later, when he moved to Rome, he became Georgio d'Inglesi...George of England. The patron saint of England. I think this was when he first started planning to coming back. He broke his ties with his long-standing identity in Tuscany and obtained new papers. A new identity.

"Finally, he took the pen name of Angelo DiGuerro. The Angel of War. I don't think he saw himself as an avenger, more that he was an innocent victim or maybe even a spirit returning from the war. No matter what, he certainly always saw himself in larger than life terms and not really bound by the same rules as ordinary people. That's probably what got him killed."

"Very interesting," said Mullane. He crossed his arms and leaned back in his chair again. "Maybe we should have an English professor advise us on all our cases."

"So I'm here as an advisor now, not a suspect."

He dropped the chair legs back onto the floor.

"What about this Cara Mia?" he said, not answering her question.

"I think she's someone who knew him in his youth. Maybe a girlfriend from before the war. But aside from assuming that she must be local, I have no idea who she was."

"You think she killed him because he came back?"

"I have no idea."

"Now that I don't believe. You seem very good at spinning out a story. Tell me the story about Cara Mia."

Ellie shrugged. She did not want to give away Miss Worthy, who had enough trouble at the moment as it was.

"For what it's worth, and it's not worth much, I think someone felt deeply betrayed by his return after so many years. That might have been Cara Mia, but it might have been someone else. Who knows what other relationships he might have had?"

"If she didn't kill him, why hasn't she come forward?"

"Come on, Inspector. That's easy. I can think of three reasons, right off the top of my head." She ticked them off on her fingers: "One: she's protecting him from his true story coming out. Two: she's protecting herself from involvement in whatever that reveals. And three: she's protecting the person whom she knows or suspects killed him."

"Well done. And who fits these categories?"

"I don't know."

"So you claim. And you also claim you're not worried about Miss Worthy's sudden fall down the stairs in her own home?"

Ellie flinched. "Are you saying you think Miss Worthy's fall wasn't an accident?"

Mullane looked at her steadily.

"You think I pushed her down the stairs?"

"You're still in the frame, Mrs. Kent."

"But why? And, if that were true, why would I call the ambulance? To say nothing of the fact that I've just explained how far back this story really goes. How could someone who never heard of any of these people a couple of months ago have a motive for killing them?"

"You're a good storyteller. How about this one? Angelo whoever-he-was really was a con man who knew too much about your past. You helped him out of this world, but you were seen by two witnesses: the boy Jackie Henning, who mysteriously died a few days later, and the girl Charlotte Worthy. She's under protection, by the way. But the girl told that foolish old aunt of hers, so now she's a threat too."

"I've never met an English professor with such exciting secrets."

"One thing I've learned from my years on the force is that everyone has secrets. And the most innocent looking often have the most surprising ones."

At that moment, there was a knock on the door, and Mullane stepped out of the room.

Ellie contemplated her cold tea and wondered how she was ever going to get clear of all this. She'd tried to solve the mystery herself without much headway, and she was deathly tired. At the moment, all she wanted was to go home and sleep. Let Mullane chase the murderer. She just wanted to be left alone.

When he came back in, his manner had changed. "All right, Mrs. Kent. We'll take you home now," he said.

"Why? What's happened?"

"We've interviewed the neighbors, and several people observed you arrive at the cottage. The forensic team and the doctors agree that Miss Worthy fell at least an hour before that. Not that we won't continue our investigation, but we have no basis for charging you with anything today."

"Thanks for nothing," said Ellie, standing up, and she didn't say another word all the way back to Little Beecham. The only good thing about the whole situation was that it was dark. She made the police officer drop her off outside the village, so she could return home as she had left, on foot.

It was now after 9 o'clock, and she was surprised to find Hector sleeping peacefully in his basket, but no sign of Graham. For once, though, he'd remembered his mobile, so she rang the number.

"Ellie," he said, "where have you been?"

"It's a long story. Where have you been?"

"I had to go with the Hennings after the funeral. Jack had got drunk, and he was threatening to kill Phyllis. Lord, it took hours to quiet them all down. Then I got the call about Priscilla Worthy being in the hospital. I'm just heading home from there now."

"How is she?"

"Not well. She's conscious now, but delirious. She keeps talking about Louise and then you and saying how frightened she is."

"She does sound confused."

"But, Ellie, there's one thing that's clear. Over and over, she keeps saying, 'I can't believe she pushed me.'"

"She *pushed* me? Does she say who?"

"No. Do you have any idea?"

"No, but I wish I did," and she tried to believe that she only imagined the worry in his voice.

Thursday, November 10

Chapter 19

Ellie knew that secrets led to trouble in marriage, but she kept thinking of what an old friend used to say: tell people things on a need-to-know basis. That was different from keeping a secret. Maybe.

Anyway, that was her excuse for not telling Graham that she knew all about Miss Worthy's fall; had, in fact, been the one who called the ambulance; and had also spent the evening at the police station while he was at the hospital. By the time he arrived home, she was in bed with the light off, and he'd assumed she was asleep.

She also told herself she was doing Graham a favor. He was distraught enough over everything that had happened and had to deal with a day-long meeting in Oxford that day. In the evening, when he came home and they could talk quietly together, it would be a much better time for such revelations.

"I thought I'd call in on the Hennings today. See if they need any help," she said, as they hurried through breakfast.

"Good idea," he said, munching toast with marmite and gulping down his tea.

"Will your meeting really last all day?"

"Not quite, but then there's a run through for tomorrow's ceremony."

"Oh, right. Remembrance Day," she said. "Well, if you're too busy, I could also stop by to see how Miss Worthy is." She tried to keep her tone light—speaking as the responsible vicar's wife, not the detective in hot pursuit of clues.

"Brilliant," he said, swallowing the last of his tea as he stood up. "You know, I really think she must have been hallucinating when she said that about being pushed. They had her on heavy medication."

"That would be a relief," said Ellie wholeheartedly.

"Indeed it would." He leaned over to kiss her as he pulled on his coat. "I'm not taking the car, but I've got to run over to the church now to talk to Jim Finch before my ride comes. He's starting back at work today."

Then he was off, leaving that peculiar vacuum in the house, but Ellie had a busy day ahead too, and she was glad to have the car. There was a special errand she wanted to do in Chipping Martin before she went to the Hennings.

It was a sunny day, and she drove along with the window open, for once feeling that she might eventually become comfortable driving on the right. She was able to transact her business in town quickly and was heading back along the B road singing along to an old Beatles song when she saw a string of police cars parked by the side of the road.

Abruptly her spirit slid back into that dark place where good humor and a normal everyday life seemed impossible. She slowed to a crawl to pass them on the single-track road and, from the corner of her eye, saw several officers poking through the grass and hedges, while two others took measurements on the road. In light of Miss Worthy's fall, she thought they must be taking another look at Jackie's accident.

She turned off the radio, and arrived at the Hennings' cottage feeling subdued. The curtains were all closed, but she could hear the television blaring inside, so there was no doubt the family was at home.

Sarah answered the door, dressed in a shirt and jeans that looked as though she'd been wearing them for several days. "Hullo, Mrs. Kent," she said, leaning against the doorframe. "Have you come to see Mum?" Her voice was wistful.

"Yes, but all of you, really," said Ellie. She glanced into the lounge, where Donny and Mike were fighting, tumbling across the floor. A lamp wobbled as their feet banged against a side table and a pile of magazines slid off it. Lucy sat huddled in one corner of the sofa, still in her pajamas, sucking her thumb. "Is Lucy sick?"

"No. Her clothes are dirty, and she won't wear them. Mum's been too low to go to the launderette."

"I see," said Ellie, looking around at the disarray in the house, which had been spotless a few days ago.

"Dad's left. He went crazy after the funeral. Jackie was always his favorite."

"Well, this is a very hard time for all of you, isn't it? But I'm sure he'll come back."

Sarah's face looked tight with the effort not to cry. "Hey, you lot," she said to her brothers, "can't you see Mrs. Kent is here? Why don't you knock off that fighting?"

The three children turned to look at Ellie and immediately focused on the packages she held in her arms.

"I've brought you all a treat," she said, "and Donny, remember who we talked about the other day?" Donny flushed, and the other children stared at him. "I know Scrubber can't ever be replaced, but I thought this little guy might be welcome."

"Scrubber?" said Lucy, perking up. "Has Scrubber come back?" The sudden hope in her face was heartbreaking, as she ran over to see what Ellie had brought.

"No, stupid," said Mike. "He's dead. He's not ever coming back."

Donny paled as Ellie held out a box with holes in it. Through the cardboard, they could all hear the tiny scrabbling of claws.

All the children gathered around as Donny took the box. He opened it carefully as if it were something magic, and inside they saw a golden hamster who looked up at them with bright black eyes. They were silent for a moment.

"He looks like Scrubber," said Lucy. "Really he does!"

"No, he doesn't," said Donny. "But he's brilliant. Absolutely brilliant!"

"I brought some food and things for him, in case you didn't have them any more," said Ellie, handing him a bag of supplies. "And cake for everyone else," she said, presenting Sarah with the last box.

Donny's face turned almost as red as his hair as he muttered thank you and then stumped up the stairs with his new pet and disappeared.

Sarah took the cake to the kitchen, and Mike flopped down in front of the TV, while Lucy clung to the newel post of the staircase, looking lost.

"Are you going to cheer up Mum, Mrs. Kent?" she asked. "She's been ever so sad. We all have, but she won't even get out of bed."

"I'll do my best," said Ellie, then she swept the little girl into a hug. Lucy clung so hard that she added, "Would you like to go up with me?" but she shook her head into the folds of Ellie's skirt.

"All right. I'll be down in a few minutes, and then we'll make lunch. Now tell me where your Mum's room is." Lucy pointed to a closed door at the top of the stairs.

Ellie went up and knocked, calling out softly, "Phyllis, it's Ellie Kent. May I come in?" She heard only a soft rustling, but took this for permission to enter the darkened room, where Phyllis lay in a tangled bed. Her clothes from the funeral yesterday had been flung over a chair and the air was stale.

Ellie opened the blinds to let in some light, and Phyllis stirred. "Mrs. Kent?" she said wearily.

"Hello, Phyllis. I came by to see if you and the children needed anything."

"That's nice of you. I'm afraid I haven't been able to. I just can't." She turned her face into the pillows.

"The children and I are going to make some lunch. Do you think you could come down?"

"No," she said, starting to sob. "I can't look at them. I know they all think I failed them."

Ellie sat down on the edge of the bed and put her hand on her shoulder. "You didn't fail anyone. What happened was terrible and unpredictable—like a hurricane, but now it's over, and you all have to work together to recover. I really think you might start to feel better if you got up and ate a hot meal."

"No. I can't face it. I've heard all the noise. I can imagine what it looks like down there."

"How about a bath then?"

Phyllis looked doubtful, but Ellie didn't wait for an answer. She started the water running, and Phyllis allowed her to help her get in. Despite being no older than Ellie, she felt as frail and unsteady as a pile of twigs.

Once she was in the tub, Ellie stripped her bed and made it up with sheets she found in the closet. There were some big laundry bags, and she went through the bedrooms stuffing them with clothes.

By the time Phyllis came out, pink and damp, but slightly revived, Ellie had tidied up her room. She flushed with embarrassment and began to cry again. "I'm so ashamed to have anyone see us in such a state."

"Please don't be, your family has had a terrible loss, and you need help. Some day it will be your turn to help someone else. Me. Another neighbor."

When she'd tucked Phyllis back in bed, Ellie went down to see what the girls were doing. Sarah was washing dishes, and Lucy was setting the table. The kettle rattled with boiling water.

"This looks nice," said Ellie. "Now, what do you think we have to eat?"

"There's all kinds of mucky casseroles," said Sarah. "The boys say they won't eat them."

"Really? Then we'll have to find something else."

Together they rummaged through the pantry and refrigerator until they found eggs, canned beans, and bread. Ellie showed Lucy how to make scrambled eggs, while Sarah put the beans on to heat and made toast.

"Mike," she said, going to the lounge. "Lunch is going to be ready in ten minutes. Why don't you pick up all those magazines and things off the floor and straighten the furniture out while you wait."

He glared at her for a moment, but then he got up. Elle was amazed, but she'd always been surprised when her students did what she said too.

"OK, everyone. Wash faces and hands, brush teeth, comb hair. When you get back, lunch will be on the table."

The children looked baffled for a moment, but then they disappeared. Ellie heard the sounds of water running and some sharp squabbles. A few minutes later they returned, looking considerably better.

"Sarah," she said, "you carry this tray up to your mother. Mike, you help serve everyone else."

Eventually, they all sat down to eat the food, which, if not delicious, was at least hot and filling. Afterwards Ellie said, "Now, you boys are going to clean up the kitchen and pick up your room, while Sarah and Lucy and I go do the laundry. Lucy, put some clothes on. Anything will do."

The boys looked surprised, but they didn't say anything. The girls brightened at the prospect of going out.

Once they'd loaded all of the laundry into Graham's Mini, there was barely room for the three of them, but they managed to squeeze in. Ellie took them to the launderette in Chipping Martin to start the wash, and then to shop for groceries.

By the time the clothes were in the dryer, Lucy had fallen asleep with her head in Ellie's lap. Sarah stared thoughtfully at the clothes rolling around in the dryer. She still looked wan, but there was a little more color in her cheeks.

After watching her for a while, Ellie said: "Sarah, may I ask you a question?"

The girl turned to Ellie and nodded. Her face had lost some of its baby roundness in the past week and her eyes had a new depth.

"Was Jackie a good bike rider?"

"Oh, sure; he was brilliant. He learned all kinds of tricks, and he always won when he and his mates went racing. Why, Mrs. Kent?"

"I just wondered."

"Is it because they say he rode straight off the road?" Ellie nodded. "The police asked Mum and Dad about that. They asked if he could have been racing, and they said no. But that's because they never did know anything when it came to Jackie."

"So you think it might have been a race that went wrong, and the other boys got scared when they saw...what happened to him?"

"It might've been," said Sarah, and Ellie hated the knowledge she saw in her face. That friends could do that.

"But it might not. Was there anyone who disliked Jackie?"

Sarah shrugged. "Jackie got up a lot of noses. He thought the village was shite, and he didn't care who knew it."

"But he was just a boy. Everyone knows that's part of growing up. To look down on where you're from."

"I guess. Only Jackie won't be doing any growing up now, will he, Mrs. Kent?"

Fortunately Ellie did not need to answer. The driers, one by one, had begun to slow to a halt. They woke Lucy to help pull out the clothes, and Sarah and Ellie folded, while Lucy sorted them into piles, according to whom they belonged.

When Ellie handed Lucy a green shirt with several pockets and zippers, the little girl turned pale. "That's Jackie's shirt," she said, as it slipped from her hands and fell to the floor.

Ellie bent to pick the shirt up. "I'm sorry, girls," she said. "I didn't know. I just stuffed all the clothes that were around into the laundry bags."

"Jackie wore that shirt the day before he died," Sarah said. "It was his favorite. He only wore it for special."

"Well, let's make a separate pile of anything that's Jackie's, and then your mum can decide what to do with them. Maybe you'd each like to keep something that was his."

Lucy brightened. "I'd like to have his Nirvana t-shirt."

"I see it," said Ellie, pulling the t-shirt out of the mound of clothes.

Lucy looked at it with a kind of awe and held it against her chest. "Can I put it on now?"

"Of course," said Ellie, helping her pull the big shirt over her clothes.

The sight of her sister wearing a t-shirt of Jackie's seemed to bring his death home to Sarah, and she suddenly lost her temper. "Lucy, you're supposed to be sorting. Not playing dress up like a baby."

Lucy's face trembled as she tried—and failed—to think of a come back.

"Hey, now; go easy on each other," said Ellie. "Let's finish up so we can go home and have cake."

She was pairing up socks, when she noticed that one of them was balled up in a lump. Something was inside. It didn't occur to Ellie that it was the money Donny had told her about until she pulled it out of the sock.

The two girls stared at the wad of damp 20-pound notes, and all Ellie could think of was that Donny had forgotten what she said about putting it somewhere safe.

"What's that?" said Lucy.

"I don't know," said Ellie. "Looks like someone's savings. Maybe your dad left this behind by mistake." She smiled brightly, but Sarah's expression showed she was not fooled.

"Dad never keeps money in a sock," said Lucy.

"Oh, what do you know about Dad?" said Sarah. "We hardly ever even see him."

"Well, why don't I put this away for safekeeping now, and I'll ask your mother about it when she's feeling better. Does that sound all right?" asked Ellie, quickly tucking the money into her purse.

"I think that was Jackie's sock," said Lucy stubbornly.

"It was not, you little berk," said Sarah. "And don't say a word to anyone about this."

"I will if I want to," said Lucy.

"You won't if you care about Mum at all!"

Lucy's eyes widened, then she flounced off to a chair and refused to help any more.

No one said anything more about the money until they returned to the Hennings, unloaded everything and filled up with cake and tea. Then, just before she left, Ellie drew Sarah aside and said, "I think we both know that money was Jackie's."

Sarah nodded solemnly.

"Do you know how he got it?"

"No," she said. "Do you think that's why he died, Mrs. Kent? Because of that money?"

"I don't know, but I'm going to take it to the police. Hopefully, they can find out. In the meantime, please don't say anything to anyone and try to persuade Lucy not to either."

"All right," Sarah promised and thanked her for all her help.

When she got home, Ellie carefully smoothed out the 15 £20 notes and put them into an envelope. Did fingerprints wash off in the laundry? She had no idea, but, if they didn't, it might be possible to trace the recent history of Jackie's stash. She put the envelope in Louise's desk, then set out again for Kingbrook Hospital.

The obvious sources of the money were either Angelo DiGuerro—as she still thought of the dead man—or the murderer. Jackie apparently was capable of stealing, but blackmailing an adult would take a lot more nerve. Unless the murderer was incredibly lucky and Jackie just happened to have a fatal bicycle accident, he or she had reacted by running him off the road to his death. And then pushed Miss Worthy down the stairs too?

As she drove along the peaceful country roads, Ellie told herself a new story: about a girl and a boy who both loved Randolph Scott and playacting and secret lives and each other and how they'd been separated by the war, and after many years they'd plotted their reunion. But everything had gone terribly wrong because—for someone else—the boy's reappearance had been such an impossible threat that he had to die.

And Miss Worthy, who was surely the girl of this story, knew the murderer's identity so she constituted a risk and had to die too. "I can't believe she pushed me," she'd told Graham. But why did she not protect herself by revealing who it was? As long as she said nothing, the murderer was free to try again!

With that thought, Ellie stepped harder on the accelerator as if every minute counted. As if she alone could prevent another death. She pulled into the hospital car park and ran into the lobby, where she breathlessly asked the receptionist for Miss Worthy's room number, then took the stairs by twos to avoid waiting for the elevator. But when she arrived on Miss Worthy's floor, she found the usual hushed atmosphere that made her footsteps sound loud and intrusive as she searched the halls for the right room.

One looked the same as the other until she spotted a familiar figure sitting in a chair outside one of the closed doors. DS Jones.

"Sergeant," said Ellie, feeling her face flush, "what are you doing here?"

"DI Mullane has put Priscilla Worthy under police protection until she can explain how she came to fall," he said. "No visitors are allowed, except for immediate family."

"But the vicar asked me to visit. He's not able to come today, and Miss Worthy is expecting him."

Jones pursed his lips and shrugged. "Sorry. Those are my orders. I'll tell her you came."

Ellie had to admit that the police were undoubtedly better equipped to protect Miss Worthy than she was, but she didn't want to leave either. She was still debating what to do, when Charlotte came around the corner, carrying a tray with a soda and sandwiches.

"Mrs. Kent!" said the girl. "What are you doing here?"

"Graham promised your aunt he'd come back today, but he has a meeting, so I said I'd come instead."

"Aunt Pris is asleep. There's no point in going in now."

"OK then, I'll keep you company while you have your tea, and maybe she'll be awake a bit later."

Charlotte looked as if Ellie's company was the last thing she wanted, but she didn't know how to get out of it, so she stumped after Ellie down to a waiting area that smelled of bygone cigarettes, sweat and anxiety.

"How is Miss Worthy today?" asked Ellie, settling herself in a sagging armchair.

Charlotte shrugged, her mouth full of ham sandwich. "She's been asleep the whole time I've been here," she said, after she'd swallowed. "I have to stay though, because Mum doesn't want her left alone. Not for a minute. She was here all night."

"They're very close, aren't they...your mum and your great aunt."

Charlotte nodded as she unwrapped her second sandwich, chicken and bacon on whole meal bread. "Aunt Pris is Dad's aunt, not Mum's, but she stood up for them when they wanted to get married, and no one else did. Mum's father was a barrister, and he thought the Worthys weren't posh enough for their daughter. But Aunt Pris told them love was more important, and people should marry from the heart not the head."

"That sounds like your Ramona Blaisdell Scott," said Ellie, watching her reaction closely.

Charlotte kept on eating without a pause. "It does, doesn't it."

"Did your aunt ever love someone?"

"I think so. Yonks ago, but whenever I've asked her, didn't she want to get married, she says something weird like she has love in her life. I don't know how," she said, sucking up the last of her soda through a straw. "I've never seen any evidence of it."

"There's more than one kind of love."

Charlotte scowled. "Even I know bonking and love are not the same thing by a long chalk." She balled up the remains of her tea and stuffed it in the trash. "I'd better get back," she said.

Ellie followed her, thinking about what she'd said, but her attention shifted and her heart jerked suddenly when they reached Miss Worthy's corridor, and she saw that the chair outside the door was empty. Sergeant Jones was not at his post.

As if there were not a moment to lose, she sped past Charlotte and threw open the door to Miss Worthy's room. When she saw a tall, dark figure bending over the bed, a shock ran through her body, and she shouted: "Stop!" before she could even take in what was going on.

Charlotte burst in, colliding with Ellie, as the figure turned from the bed and Ellie saw the cold eyes and gaunt white face of Emily Rutherford Hughes.

"Mrs. Kent, kindly do not use that tone of voice when speaking to me. I was merely straightening Priscilla's pillows and do not expect to be chastised. Least of all by you."

Charlotte gawped at both of them, but Ellie hurried around the bed for a closer look at Miss Worthy, who slept on, her quiet breathing a sharp contrast to her badly bruised and swollen face. She took a deep breath to slow her own beating heart, but it was harder to slow her thoughts.

Maybe she'd over-reacted, but something about the sight of Mrs. Rutherford Hughes like a predatory bird with its prey shook her deeply. It was almost as if she had seen it before.

She was quick enough to realize she should not let on what she was thinking. "I'm sorry if I sounded rude," she said, falling back on her blundering American reputation. "I was just so surprised. There's supposed to be a policeman on duty outside to be sure no one except family comes in. That's why it was a shock to see you here."

"Considering I've known Priscilla all my life, I should think I'm as close as any family member could be, and closer than many," she said with a scornful look at Charlotte. "Regardless, in those circumstances I can't see why you're here, Mrs. Kent."

"I—" Ellie started to explain, but the door pushed open and Sergeant Jones rushed in, saying: "What's going on here?"

"Mrs. Rutherford Hughes came to visit," said Ellie. "Since you were not at your post, she couldn't know that she wasn't supposed to disturb Miss Worthy."

Jones turned red and mumbled something about needing to go to the gents. "I was only gone for a tick, but what she says is true, madam. I'm sorry but you'll all have to leave, except for the girl. Those are my strict orders."

Mrs. Rutherford Hughes glared, but she drew herself up and stalked toward the door. "In that case, perhaps you should take more care to fulfill them," she said.

He dipped his head humbly, and she swooped out. His gaze then fixed on Ellie. "You too, please, Mrs. Kent," he said.

"Of course, but I hope from now on you won't leave your post unless Charlotte or someone else is here."

Charlotte still looked goggle-eyed. "Blimey, Mrs. Rutherford Hughes is aunty's oldest friend. There was no need to tear into her like that."

Ellie squeezed out a smile. "Perhaps you're right. I'll telephone later to see how Miss Worthy is doing. Charlotte, if you get a chance to pass on any news, that would be great. The Vicar will want to know."

Then she left the room and took the stairs down to the car park, hoping that she would not run into Emily Rutherford Hughes again.

She could still feel the adrenaline in her system when she reached the car. The image of that dark figure bending over the bed made her shudder, and she locked the car doors as if that could help shut it out. The feeling that she'd seen that scene before lingered despite the fact that she had never been to Kingbrook Hospital in her life. Finally, she took out her mobile phone and punched in a number. It was just an idea, but maybe it would help her put the incident behind her.

The phone rang and rang, and the answering message had reached "Cheerio!" when at the last moment, the call was picked up.

"Hi Isabelle. Is that you? It's Ellie." The loud background chatter made it clear that Isabelle was in a pub.

"Hi, Ellie, what's up?" Ellie had never called her before.

"I'm sorry to bother you, but I have a question to ask you. About the day your mother died."

"Oh. Really?" said the girl, her voice darkening. "What is it?"

"I know someone stopped your father in the hall when you were on your way to visit her, but I've never heard who it was. Do you remember?"

There was no hesitation. The answer came straight away, although Isabelle could have no idea of the impact it would have.

"Of course, I remember. It was Mrs. Rutherford Hughes. She'd been there visiting someone. I'm not sure who. And, of course, she had to take the opportunity to bend Dad's ear about some parish matter. She never misses a chance like that. So I just went on, you know. And, well, you know what happened."

"Yes," said Ellie, trying to keep her voice calm. "OK, well. Thanks. There's just one other thing. Did you bring anything to your mother when you visited earlier that day?"

"Just the post. I always brought her the post. She was never much of one for e-mail, and that day she got a thick letter from Italy. It's funny, I just remembered that."

Ellie's heart jumped so hard she was sure Isabelle must have heard it, because her tone completely changed when she said: "What's going on, Ellie? Has something happened? Is Dad all right?"

"He's fine. There's nothing to worry about. It was just...something I was wondering about. Please forget it."

"If you promise Dad's OK, I will. I've got to run now, anyway. My lecture starts in five minutes."

They rang off, but Ellie had no time to think about what she'd just learned because the phone began to ring. She looked at the readout and saw that it was Michael-John Parker.

"I thought you'd disappeared in a puff of smoke," said Ellie, when she answered.

"The devil himself? No. It's not like that, but I do thank you for taking my call. You have every right to be mad, and I've been beavering away here in London to make amends, so will you hear me out?"

"You mean you've learned something? About our mystery?"

"Yes. You see, I placed an ad for my Rutherford project a while back, asking for information about the family, and on Tuesday I received my first reply. I could have telephoned, but what with the bad smell in my flat from the police presence and everything else going on, I thought it would be a good time to get away for a while.

"My correspondent turned out to be an elderly woman who worked on the Society pages of *The Times* in the 1940s and 50s. I invited her to tea at Claridge's and, my Lord, that old lady ate like a horse! However, the pay off was worth it.

"She remembered the Rutherfords not only because both brothers were killed in the same battle, but also because she'd once been asked to print an engagement announcement for George Rutherford, and then the family canceled it. She remembered the incident because she recently read a book where the same thing happened."

"Don't tell me. Who was the author of the book?"

"The author of the book? Why do you want to know that? I would've thought you'd want to know the name of the girl he was going to marry."

"I do. But I think we both know that, already, don't we?"

"Yes. We do. Cara Mia."

"Exactly. Miss Priscilla Worthy. And I'll bet you anything that the book was by Ramona Blaisdell Scott."

"Mrs. Kent, your powers amaze me, but I'm crushed. Does this mean my offering is completely useless? I am unforgiven?"

"Not at all. I mean, it's very helpful, and I guess you are. There are only a couple of pieces of the puzzle left to fit in, and I think I know how to do it."

"You mean you know who the murderer is?"

"Yes," said Ellie, "I believe I do," and then she hung up before he could ask her who she thought it was.

Until she had confirmation—some tangible proof—she could not imagine telling anyone her new theory about what happened. She was sure, if she could find this proof anywhere, it would be in Miss Worthy's cottage, and she drove there directly from the hospital.

When she pulled up in front of the cottage on Chapel Lane, she took her time getting out of the car, making a show of being completely at ease. Unlike the last time she was here, when she left in the police car. She hoped she'd see a neighbor she could wave to, but the street gave the appearance of being deserted. No one was in sight and not a curtain twitched. No matter.

Ellie walked around to the back of the house, removed the spare key, lifted the police tape, and opened the door. Inside the silence was eerie, and everywhere there were signs of a normal day brutally interrupted. A half-drunk cup of tea in the sitting room had been dusted for fingerprints, and there were other signs of the crime scene investigators. The same knitting Miss Worthy had brought to the library lay on the sofa, and Ellie thought it was ironic that she worked so hard to protect Charlotte and gave so little thought to her own safety.

In the sitting room there was no sign of her leading any other life than that of a village spinster. She went upstairs, carefully stepping over the still-tangled rug, and found the two bedrooms were consistent with this. The furnishings were old, but not antiques, and everything looked a bit shabby with a lifetime of use. Miss Worthy had a nice brass bed, but otherwise the most interesting thing in her bedroom was a row of photographs on the top of a bookcase crammed with murder mysteries and romances. None by Ramona Blaisdell Scott. Ellie studied the photos and was a bit surprised that there were none of the dark-haired boy she'd seen in the sitting room

The other was a guest room cum store room. She poked around amongst the boxes of old books, metal cookie tins, magazines with recipes and helpful hints, leftover balls of knitting wool and more well-thumbed mysteries. Nothing suggested that the woman who lived there was one of Britain's most successful and popular novelists.

She went back downstairs to the sitting room. The sound of Miss Worthy typing had come from here, but there was no typewriter or computer in evidence now. She studied the room carefully without seeing any hiding places. Then she spotted a door in the panels at the base of the bookcase that was almost completely hidden by a high wing-backed armchair.

She pulled aside the heavy chair, opened the door, and there it was. A green Smith-Corona manual typewriter exactly like the one she remembered her father using when she was growing up. There could, of course, be an everyday reason for Miss Worthy to own a typewriter, but Ellie's excitement grew when she lifted out the machine and discovered it was sitting on a cardboard box marked in pencil: *Desertion.*

She sat back on her heels and laughed. She'd found it. She had proof.

She pulled the box out and opened it. Inside she found the neatly stacked typescript copies and printer's proofs for Ramona Blaisdell Scott's latest book, *Love and Desertion.* She couldn't have been more tickled if she'd opened a cupboard and found the missing letters of Jane Austen.

She had to crouch way down to reach the back of the cupboard, but they were all in there. The manuscripts and proofs of every one of Ramona Blaisdell Scott's best-selling books, each in its own box. She pulled them out one by one, then worked her fingers blindly along the wall to be sure there was nothing else.

Naturally, it was just at the moment when she had started to think the dirt, dust and uncomfortable position justified her giving up, that her fingers brushed against another box. One much smaller than the others. She scrabbled at it until she could edge it away from the wall, and she was able to get it out.

When she had it on the floor in front of her, Ellie sat up, eased her back against the armchair and brushed the dust off her face with the back of her sleeve. She took a few deep breaths to slow her excited breathing, then pulled the box onto her lap. It was heavy.

This box was altogether different from the others—the kind of flat green box used for storing important documents—-and she was sure she knew what it must contain. Like a surgeon who opens a patient's chest knows that inside there will be a beating heart and must still feel awe at the sight, she lifted the lid on Miss Worthy's greatest secret.

The neatly arranged letters went back 70 years. The earliest ones, written in a boyish hand, were addressed to "R.S." and signed "Yours ever, R.S.". These detailed wild adventures in the Highlands and on other trips away from home. As Ellie read them, she could hear the voice of the caped boy, the sword-swinging adventurer, and cowboy.

By the late 1930s, the letters began to take on a different tone. These were love letters, not from an uninhibited boy but from a young man, who was increasingly frustrated by his family, society, and the demands placed on him by the prospect of a new world war. The last of these letters described the desperate misery, fatigue and fear of life as a soldier. It did not say where he was writing from.

Then there was a gap of some 60 years before the letters began again. Five years ago. They all said the same thing. How happy he was to be in communication again, but how tired he was of living in exile. How much he just wanted to come home. Why couldn't they finally have what they wanted? Who could stop them?

These appeals obviously did not receive the response he was hoping for because they continued until he had upped the ante three years ago. That's when he confessed he'd written to the vicar's wife to enlist her support.

Ellie felt all the hairs on her arms rise as she read these words and looked at the postmark on the envelope. It was only a few days before Louise died.

Ellie put everything back as she had found it and drove home in a daze. She'd learned so much that day that she needed time and space to assimilate it. Before she said a word to anyone, she needed to put the pieces together and see if they really formed the pattern she thought she saw.

She was glad she arrived at the Vicarage ahead of Graham and could lay the table for tea and take Hector out for a quick run before he returned. Somehow she managed to give an account of her day and listen to what he said about his meeting.

But after the dishes were done, and they'd taken up their usual places in the sitting room, Graham said: "You're very subdued tonight, Ellie. Is anything wrong?"

"No," she said, feeling only a slight pang over lying to him yet again. She looked away from his curious, compassionate eyes, and focused on the crackling fire. "It was just such a long day. So difficult talking to Phyllis—and the kids too. Listening to them struggle to come to grips with what happened. It must be a very hard part of your job."

As she remembered Lucy's face when she thought Scrubber had miraculously returned, her eyes filled with tears, and Graham came over to the sofa and put his arms around her. She leaned into the warmth of his body and waited for his words of comfort and experience, but all he said was: "It is," and then he kissed her.

"Maybe what we should do is go to bed," he added. "Sleep is a great aid to faith."

"You mean we should 'knit up the raveled sleeve of care'?"

"Exactly," he said, standing up and offering her his hand.

"OK, but I just need a few minutes."

His eyes were questioning, but he left her. Hector looked up from his bed by the fire, uncertain what to do, then jumped onto the sofa beside Ellie. She kissed his bristly nose and held him close as she gave in to the thoughts that had been troubling her even more than what she told Graham.

About Louise, who'd been kind and eager to help and totally unaware of the danger she was in. About Graham and Isabelle and the terrible loss they suffered. And about the news she was about to bring them, which was worse than they ever could have imagined.

With tears streaming down her face, she went to the mantel and picked up one of Louise's little pots. The glaze reflected the glow from the fire. Her own face.

Graham had told her that *why* was the question that got you nowhere. But it was human nature to want to answer it, wasn't it? Didn't they really want to know what happened? she asked Louise.

I'm sure they do, she told herself. *And now they will.*

Friday, November 11 (Remembrance Day)

Chapter 20

In the morning, Ellie took Hector out for an early walk. It was a clear, cold day—the kind of weather that made you feel your head ought to be equally clear, but hers was still a muddle. She sat for a long time on the hill overlooking Beech Hall, until her pants were wet through and even the dog became bored and yipped to move on.

She believed she knew what had happened, and even the why and the who, but the how still eluded her. She also could not decide whether to call DI Mullane and tell him what she'd learned or wait until she could present him with the whole story. Assuming she figured out what the whole story was.

Back at the Vicarage, she found Jim Finch busy raking the churchyard, and he'd created several small mountains of trash and leaves that he was piling into the garden cart. When Ellie greeted him and asked how he was, he scowled and said, "In twenty years I've never seen such a mess in this churchyard. Must be all the nosy folk come round to see the spot where that chap died."

"The flowers are nice though," said Ellie, surveying the many bouquets that had cropped up over the past few days.

"Aye, Mrs. Rutherford Hughes isn't the only one who remembers her dead, for all she has the biggest wreaths every year."

He pointed to the memorial stone for Henry and George Rutherford, which was adorned today with a wreath of red poppies. Ellie walked over and looked at the inscription: Sacred to the memory of Henry and George Rutherford, who died serving their country at Anzio, 1944.

She traced the word Anzio with her gloved fingers, but aloud she just said: "I never noticed this before, but I've always liked the window dedicated to them."

Jim nodded, leaning on his rake and his expression softened. "Yes, many's the day I've sat and remembered my own brother looking at that window. So I guess we have to thank her for that for all she's so unpleasant. This morning she gave me a blistering about her gate being left unlocked. As if I opened it!"

"Her gate?"

"Aye, that gate over there leads into her property. Not that anyone uses it any more."

He pointed to a small metal gate in the stone wall edging the churchyard. Ellie had never noticed that before either.

"You mean that wood belongs to Mrs. Rutherford Hughes?"

"Aye, the Hughes family owns all that property from here to the B road. Years ago, she used the path to come to church, but she can't manage it now. It's easier to come round by the road."

"But there's still a path?"

"Not so's you'd notice. I take my wheelbarrow through and pick up kindling for her, so that keeps it open a bit."

Ellie squinted through the trees and realized, now that the leaves were nearly all down, that you could actually see Mrs. Rutherford Hughes's house from the churchyard. She turned to Jim and smiled politely. "Well, see you later, I guess," she said and hoped her expression did not show the exultation she felt. The last piece of her puzzle had just dropped into place with a satisfying little snap.

She hurried into the house, where Graham was already dressed for the Remembrance Day ceremony in the village. "Where have you been all morning?" he asked, but he was too distracted to listen to her answer and went on to ask her to bring the car, because he'd put two boxes of hymnbooks on the back seat.

She said she would and went upstairs to put on her black suit. As she attached a red poppy pin to her lapel, she looked at herself in the mirror and thought her first Remembrance

Day was definitely going to be one to remember. On her way out, she blew a kiss to Louise's pots and whispered "Wish me luck."

Driving down the high street, she could hear the unmistakable whine and groan of a bagpipe, and a small crowd had already gathered. "Green" was rather an overstatement for the island of grass opposite the school, which was created by the split in the road where the B road to Chipping Martin went off in one direction and the lane continued in the other. It was barely big enough for the flagpole and war memorial it contained, but this morning, it was a hub of activity with people milling around and talking quietly.

Ellie parked and carried the boxes of hymnals over to a bench by the war memorial. For a small village, Little Beecham had lost quite a few men in the World Wars. The memorial stone listed 14 who died in World War I and six from World War II. Many of the family names were familiar even to a newcomer, and the dates brought home the fact that two successive generations of young men had gone to war to keep Europe free. Nearly a century later, the moment when the Armistice ending World War I was signed—the 11th hour of the 11th day of the 11th month—brought Great Britain to a standstill.

The bagpipe whined again and Ellie saw the piper was Andrew MacInnes, who played the pipe and tabor for the Beecham Morris. Today he was dressed in his tartans, and Graham went over to talk to him as he intermittently blew a few warm-up notes. Mr. Bell, John Tiddington, and a handful of other men had put on their military uniforms for the occasion. They looked stiff and uncomfortable, but proud.

Michael-John had returned from London and was standing outside his shop to watch, while Whistler ran around the green excitedly with several other dogs. A couple of men lounged in the doorway of The Three Lambs with their morning pints.

Mr. and Mrs. Bell had taken seats on the bench, while Mrs. Bigelow stood alone, wearing a voluminous red cape.

Ellie looked around for Mrs. Rutherford Hughes and saw her coming down the high street at a stately pace, dressed entirely in black.

Then the school doors opened, and all the children, their navy blazers brightened by the poppies they wore, filed out and lined up by the flagpole. Morag followed with the teachers, her former colleagues, and waved to Ellie cheerily. More shopkeepers came to their doors with expectant looks.

At 10:45, the loud voice of bagpipes split the air, and people fell silent as Andrew played a mournful tune. Graham read a prayer, his coat blowing in the cold wind that had sprung up, and the children led the singing of the patriotic hymn, "Jerusalem," while the crowd joined in singing with hearty conviction.

When Seamus MacDonald stepped up to the microphone to recite Rupert Brooke's poem "The Soldier," the hush before he spoke sent prickles up Ellie's arms. He looked the quintessential English schoolboy, pink-cheeked and fair skinned, with a mop of thick dark hair, and his delivery was both devastatingly direct and innocent:

"If I should die, think only this of me:
That there's some corner of a foreign field
That is forever England. There shall be
In that rich earth a richer dust concealed;
A dust whom England bore, shaped, made aware,
Gave, once, her flowers to love, her ways to roam,
A body of England's, breathing English air,
Washed by the rivers, blest by suns of home.

And think, this heart, all evil shed away,
A pulse in the eternal mind, no less
Gives somewhere back the thoughts by England given;
Her sights and sounds; dreams happy as her day;
And laughter, learnt of friends; and gentleness,
In hearts at peace, under an English heaven."

In the hush that followed, Mrs. Rutherford Hughes, her face white and drawn, carried a poppy wreath forward to lay it at the foot of the memorial. As she bent down, she suddenly swayed and appeared to be about to faint. Mrs. Bell gave a little cry of alarm, but Graham caught the old lady under the elbow and prevented her from falling. A murmur of sympathy went through the crowd as Graham helped her to a seat next to the Bells. Then John Tiddington played "The Last Post" on a bugle.

A deeper silence fell as the church bell began to toll 11 o'clock. A car passing through the village stopped in the middle of the road. Even the dogs and birds fell silent.

For two minutes, the village stood still. Remembering.

Trees swayed, leaves rattled down, but no one else moved.

Then it was over. The children began to chatter again and were ushered back to school; car engines revved up; and adults moved off to resume their usual activities.

Ellie was gathering up the hymnbooks, when Graham said, "Ellie, would you mind taking Emily home in the car? She's not well enough to walk."

"Not at all, I'd be glad to," she replied, surprised at the cool calmness of her own voice.

Mrs. Rutherford Hughes looked ashen and the claw-like hand that grasped Ellie's arm shook, as she and Graham helped her to the car. When he'd closed the door on her and waved them off, Ellie drove with care, but she couldn't help stealing glances at the woman beside her. A woman she was certain had murdered three people and nearly killed another––all to save her own pride.

At the moment though, she looked near death herself, as if she'd shrunk since their last encounter at the hospital. Not that Ellie felt sympathy for her. She had shown no sympathy and deserved none in return. So what should she do? Say? How could she make the most of this opportunity to confront her?

She pulled into the circular drive in front of the imposing three-story stone Hughes House with a pounding heart, and she prayed—really did pray—for guidance. Yet the formidable foe she faced in her mind was leaning against the passenger door, eyes closed and mouth hanging slightly open. She seemed unaware that the car had stopped.

Ellie went around to help her out of the car and up the broad stone steps to the door. The old lady did not even seem to notice when Ellie took her purse, found her keys, and led her into a high-ceilinged entrance hall.

She'd never been invited to this house before, but the first thing she noticed was that it was cold, as if no one had turned on the heat for quite awhile. The hall was sparely furnished, but the mahogany Queen Anne hall table with its tall hurricane lamps was lovely. She guessed the drawing room would be on the right and pushed open the door into another room made shadowy by the closed draperies.

Ellie settled her charge in a tall wingback armchair in front of the fireplace, then lit the fire, which had been laid, but the hearth was dusty from lack of use. Even the sudden flare of light and warmth failed to draw a response from Mrs. Rutherford Hughes. In fact, the bright fire only served to highlight her extreme pallor.

Ellie put a lap blanket over her legs then looked around for the liquor supply and poured her some sherry. The hand that reached for the glass shook so much that Ellie had to hold it to her lips.

"Perhaps hot tea would be better," she said and went off to find the kitchen.

This room was clean too with no sign of recent cooking or eating, and all the tools and appliances were so old it looked like a museum of the war years. It reminded Ellie that Beech Hall had made her think of Miss Havisham, the Dickens character whose life stopped when she was jilted on her wedding day.

She managed to light the stove and make a pot of tea, but by the time she brought it out to the drawing room, Mrs. Rutherford Hughes was asleep, her breathing rough and uneven.

Ellie regarded her silently and wondered what to do next. She looked so old and frail. It was hard to imagine waking her and saying, "I know what you've done."

Instead she turned to study the photos on the mantel. One showed Emily and her husband John Hughes on their wedding day, but all the rest were older family photos. The very pictures she'd been hoping to find at the library. There were the two dark-haired, dark-eyed Rutherford boys with long legs and knobby knees sitting with their little blonde half-sister in front of a towering Christmas tree in what must have been the drawing room of Beech Hall. There were the children in their school uniforms, riding first ponies and then horses. The difference in their looks grew more accentuated as they became older. Emily became a long-faced, tall and awkward girl, while they turned into handsome young men. The last photo showed her looking adoringly at them, dashing in their Army uniforms. This was inscribed 'To our darling Emily' with signatures in two separate hands, one of which Ellie was certain she had seen before.

Perhaps this was the last time she saw them, and their loss certainly was a tragedy, but many people had suffered during the war. They had lost their families and homes, their livelihoods and their hopes for the future without resorting to murder.

When a sharp voice suddenly broke the silence, saying, "What are you doing here?" she turned to see that Mrs. Rutherford Hughes had awakened, still pale, but with fully alert cold, hard eyes.

"I brought you home from the Remembrance Day ceremony, Mrs. Rutherford Hughes. You became ill, don't you remember?" Ellie said mildly.

The old lady faltered for an instant, then said. "Yes, of course. That MacDonald boy's reading upset me. My brother sent me that poem in a letter right before he died."

"Which brother was that?" Ellie asked.

"George. George was the one who loved poetry."

Indeed, thought Ellie. "It must be very painful for you to remember them," she said, picking up the signed photo from the mantel.

"I don't remember. I never forget. Not for a day."

"I can see that, and I doubt anyone in Little Beecham could forget that Henry and George Rutherford were killed in the war."

"I've devoted my life to that," she said, closing her eyes again, but her expression was tight-lipped and smug, and that gave Ellie the courage to go on.

"It must have been a tremendous shock to discover that George was alive all these years and never let you know."

"What are you saying?" The old lady's eyes snapped open, and she struggled to straighten herself up in her chair.

"Your brother George. He was here. I saw him in the woods and two days later I found his body in the churchyard."

"That man was an Italian tramp."

"He wasn't a tramp, and he wasn't Italian, although he lived in Italy for most of his life. He was George Rutherford, and I can prove it."

If she was surprised, it only served to renew Mrs. Rutherford Hughes's strength. "My brothers died in 1944 in the battle of Anzio," she said, "and I have the papers to prove *that*, so you won't exonerate yourself from that man's death by trying to drag me and my family into it."

"I'm not at all involved in his death. It's you and Priscilla Worthy who are at the center of that mystery, and you've both gone to great lengths to prevent anyone from learning the truth.

"She's been very loyal to you—except for not letting you know about George—but then, their relationship was always their little secret, wasn't it? And she didn't want his reputation ruined any more than you did. You know she might have persuaded him to leave again, but you couldn't count on that, could you?"

"I have no idea what you're talking about." With great effort, Mrs. Rutherford Hughes stood and made her way over to the mahogany side table with its decanters of sherry and whisky. She poured herself a glass of whisky, which she drank with impressive speed.

"So you deny that George was here? That he sat in this very room and told you he was going to come back and marry Miss Worthy the way he wanted to years ago? How, now that she had money, they were going to restore Beech Hall just the way you all planned?"

Mrs. Rutherford Hughes poured herself more whisky, then in her steeliest voice, said: "That is the most absurd story I've ever heard. I had you down as silly, but I never imagined you were such a wild fantasist.

"If, as you claim, my brother George had not died in the war, he would know perfectly well that he could never return to England, and there would be no happy ever after, no matter how much he or I or anyone else longed for it. And I would say, that *if* that were the case, it would be more than enough reason for suicide."

Ellie tried not to gulp visibly. There was no denying this sounded believable. Possibly even more believable than her theory that this old woman in her proper black suit and sturdy heels was a murderer. She faltered, and she could see that Mrs. Rutherford Hughes knew she had won her point.

"I think you need a drink, Mrs. Kent," she said, holding up the decanter of whisky with a satisfied look.

"No, thank you," said Ellie, who suddenly saw that her gloating was a sign that she was right. "I agree that might have been what happened. And that is probably how you intended it to look, but in that case, why was Jackie Henning blackmailing you? And why did you pay him?"

"Blackmailing me? That vicious brat? How did you fit him into your bizarre tale?"

"He was in the churchyard that night, and I think he saw George come staggering through the gate from your property. After you poisoned him."

"You *think*!" Mrs. Rutherford Hughes snorted and re-filled her whisky glass.

"I know what I'm talking about. I've read George's letters. And furthermore I believe that you've known that he was alive for more than three years. Ever since he wrote to Louise and asked for her help."

"Louise! Louise Kent! What on earth has she to do with any of this?"

"That's when it all started. I couldn't put the pieces all together until that day at the hospital. You claimed you were straightening Miss Worthy's pillows, but you weren't. You were going to smother her, just like you smothered Louise to keep George's existence a secret.

"But this time you failed. Miss Worthy is not dead. In fact she's awake and can now tell the police who she meant when she said, 'I can't believe she pushed me'. If you never harmed anyone, why would you need to do that?"

Mrs. Rutherford Hughes poured herself yet another drink and leaned against the drinks table with her arms folded. "Louise died from an infection. Everyone knows that."

"No one knows why she died. Graham wouldn't let them do a post-mortem, but Isabelle remembers. You were the last person in her room, and the letter from Italy—from George— —that she brought to the hospital that afternoon, disappeared."

"A coincidence. And if you're counting on Priscilla Worthy to back you up, I'm afraid you'll be very disappointed. A dafter woman never lived.

"Everything you've said is based on suppositions and fantasies, and if you repeat them to anyone, anyone at all, you will be the one entirely discredited, Mrs. Kent, not me. Now I want you to leave, and furthermore I never want to see you in this house again."

"You won't," said Ellie recklessly. Although the smoke from her burning bridges was getting thicker by the minute. "And maybe you're right. Maybe Miss Worthy will go to any lengths to keep your family secrets, but there is plenty of hard evidence that George Rutherford was a deserter and that will definitely come out. I'll see to that."

Moving swiftly back to the mantel, Ellie grabbed the signed photo of Emily and her brothers.

"Put that back! How dare you touch my things!" cried Mrs. Rutherford Hughes and lunged at her with surprising speed.

Ellie made for the front hall, but the old woman got ahold of her jacket and frantically tried to take the photo away from her. As they struggled, they bumped into the hall table and the hurricane lamps crashed to the floor in a spray of broken glass.

Mrs. Rutherford Hughes jumped back in surprise, giving Ellie the opportunity reach the front door, but, as she fumbled with old-fashioned fittings, the old woman caught her around the neck from behind and began to try to choke her. Her bony fingers dug in as Ellie gasped and struggled to pull them away with one hand and open the door with the other. Unable to do either, she threw herself backward, causing them both to fall to the glass-strewn floor.

Just then the door opened, and there stood Graham, his eyes wide with shock at the sight of Ellie and Mrs. Rutherford Hughes grappling with each other with bleeding hands.

"Ellie! My God! What is going on?"

She dropped her grip and said: "Graham! I—," but she broke off when she saw his expression change from shock to confirmation of the fact that she was, after all, capable of murder.

She let go of Mrs. Rutherford Hughes and got to her feet, as he rushed to help the woman, brushing off shards of glass that clung to her black suit.

"Are you injured, Emily? Should I call an ambulance?" he asked solicitously.

Mrs. Rutherford Hughes shook her head disdainfully, and Ellie had to admit she admired how quickly she regained the upper hand.

Ellie was shattered, but also angry. "You've got this all wrong, Graham," as he took Emily by the elbow to help her back into the drawing room. "No matter what you think of me, that woman is the one who's behind everything that's happened." She waved the photo at him. "Here's your dead man. George Rutherford. Never dead at all. Until last week, when Emily killed him to keep the truth from getting out. And she killed the others too."

Graham looked from Ellie to Mrs. Rutherford Hughes, who looked dangerously pale again.

"The others? I think the best thing would be for you to leave, Ellie. Now."

"Why? Are you part of the Rutherford secret-keeping team too? Because if you are, you should know the cost. You should ask her what really happened to Louise."

At that, Graham turned white himself. "Please, just go," he repeated, and the coldness in his face broke Ellie's heart, but she did what he asked.

Chapter 21

She took the path that ran from the house to the churchyard—the same one George had used on his last stumbling walk. It was overgrown and she slipped on the wet leaves as she ran. Sharp bare branches snapped in her face, but they didn't hurt at all compared to the stinging thoughts in her head. The searing memory of Graham's face when he opened the door and saw her grappling on the floor with Mrs. Rutherford Hughes. The principal benefactor of the church. She would never forget it, and neither would he.

Back at the Vicarage, she didn't know what to do. Every room felt alien, not like any place where she'd lived or could live. Even up in her study, her own things that she'd brought from California looked like they belonged to someone else. The links between before and now were broken because the link was Graham, and, in the end, no matter what vows they'd taken, he had not trusted her. He had asked her to go.

These words sounded in her ears with a finality that did not leave any opening for discussion. In a daze, she left her study and went downstairs to pack. If he wanted her to go, she would go. In fact, she couldn't imagine staying.

It wasn't her fault that she didn't fit in and probably never would. She had tried, and, these past few days, all she'd been trying to do was set things right so they could go forward, but none of that mattered.

She took off the black suit she'd worn for the Remembrance Day ceremony—back when she was the vicar's wife—and pulled on her old familiar black jeans and sweater. Unfortunately they felt like they belonged to someone else too.

She didn't know where she should go, and tears fell onto the clothes she piled into a duffel bag. She couldn't return to California and have everyone say, "I told you so." Maybe she'd go to New York instead. Maybe she could start over again there.

When she'd finished packing, she set her bag in the hall and called a taxi.

"Be there in twenty minutes, luv," the dispatcher said, and Ellie wondered how she would bear the wait. Hector looked up at her from his basket with sad eyes, and she bent down to pet him. The phone rang, but she didn't answer. Her mobile rang too, so she switched it off.

When the Vicarage became unbearable, she decided to go over to the church and say goodbye to St Michael's.

The clear, sunny morning had turned dark, and the sky was heavy with clouds. A wind wet with the rain to come rattled the leaves still clinging to the trees. She crossed the churchyard, unlocked the door, and entered the dim, comforting silence. With no sun behind it, the peace window was dark, as if a curtain had been drawn over it.

Ellie stood in front of the window, today with its posy of poppies, and felt the last missing piece of the story fall into place: that it must have been George after all, who climbed in through the window to see for himself his sister's tribute to the lie that he had lived with so long. George, who dashed the vase of flowers to the floor, and climbed out the window.

And then, in that mood of confidence and defiance, he'd gone to surprise his sister on Halloween night. Of all nights to choose. To be the dead who walked. For he could not have known that she already knew he was alive. Had already killed one person to prevent the news from coming out.

No doubt he counted on being welcomed. This was the sister who'd remembered him with posies all these years. The sister whom he'd always been able to manipulate. Who thought the world of him. Miss Worthy must have tried to warn him, but he wouldn't listen. So whatever George's hopes for the future might have been, in the end he'd paid the penalty for his desertion.

"When the judge takes his place, what is hidden will be revealed, nothing will remain unavenged." That's what the requiem mass said. So where did the peace of God come into the picture? Where was forgiveness?

She was glad these questions were not hers to answer, but she was sure no one on earth would forgive Emily Rutherford Hughes for taking three lives to preserve her image of her brave and loyal brothers.

She sat down in one of the old wooden pews, and she continued to sit there as dark afternoon turned into night. She forgot about the taxi, which must have come and gone. She would either have to walk to the train station in Kingbrook or ask Morag to put her up for the night. But at the moment she couldn't worry about that. She was too tired to move. Too tired for anything.

Then suddenly, the lights in the church came on, and she heard a voice say:

"Ellie? Thank God. I've been looking all over for you. The last place I expected to find you was here."

She turned and saw Graham hurrying toward her down the aisle, his wet raincoat showering drops in all directions.

"Are you all right?" he asked. "You're not injured? My God, the things I've been imagining. I've been worried sick."

Ellie shrugged. "I'm fine," she said. "I just needed a little rest before I go."

"What do you mean go?" he said, slipping into the pew beside her. He looked surprised that she pulled away from his attempt to embrace her.

"I saw your face, Graham, and you told me to leave. I don't think there's any going back from that."

"What are you talking about?"

"You don't trust me. You thought I was trying to kill Mrs. Rutherford Hughes."

"Are you mad? I've been frantic. To walk in and see my own wife fighting for her life with a woman I've known and respected for years!" He shook his head. "I don't know what you saw in my face, but all I wanted at that moment was for you to be away from there and safe. Please, Ellie, you can't believe I thought anything other than that. It will break my heart."

A sigh escaped her as she realized that he was telling the truth, that she'd been wrong, and her pent-up tears had just started to come when the church door screeched open and banged against the wall.

"She's here? You found her?" said DI Mullane striding down the aisle. His face was flushed and sweaty despite his streaming raincoat.

"Yes, I found her, and, thank God, she's all right," said Graham.

"She wasn't poisoned then."

"No, it seems not."

The relief in Mullane's face made him look almost human. Ellie quickly brushed away her tears.

"What's going on?" she asked, looking from one man to the other. "What do you mean I wasn't poisoned?"

DI Mullane sat down heavily in the pew behind them. "He means, Mrs. Kent, that we all thought you were well on your way to becoming murder victim number four. You can imagine how your husband here felt finding out in the span of a few minutes not only that his first wife had been murdered, but also that his second wife might be dying as we floundered about the woods looking for you."

"But how?"

"The whisky, Ellie," said Graham. "There were two glasses. We thought you'd had some too."

"But I didn't. Mrs. Rutherford Hughes drank it all. Wait a minute, you mean it was poisoned? Like before?"

"Exactly," said Mullane. "Exactly like before," he repeated as if this were a confession that he now knew once and for all that Ellie was innocent."

"So what happened to her? Is she all right?"

"She's dead, and it was dreadful. At first, she tried to blame you, but in the end she told me everything."

"You mean she confessed to the murders? And you think she would have killed me too?"

"Yes," he said. She began to shake as this information sank in, and Graham tightened his grip on her. "Ellie, when you've lost one wife unexpectedly, you realize how thin the line between life and death can be. It's hard to get over the fear that it could happen again. When I couldn't find you I was so afraid, I was completely beside myself."

"That's a fact," said Mullane. "My officers have been searching that Hughes property inch by inch. Speaking of which, I'd better let them know there's no need to continue." He stood up, but he hesitated before leaving.

"I have to say this, Mrs. Kent. I know you wanted to prove yourself and show me you were right and innocent when I didn't believe you, but you risked your life needlessly to do it. I hope in the future you'll be more careful."

Ellie flared up, "If I hadn't confronted her, she never would have confessed to anything. She even had me half-convinced George actually did kill himself. It was only because of the blackmail money that I knew she was lying."

"What blackmail money?" Graham and Mullane asked simultaneously.

"The money the Henning girls and I found in Jackie's sock when we were doing the laundry. Three hundred pounds. I've been meaning to turn it over to you, there's just been no time."

"Well, there's no real need now. I suggest you give it to Father Kent here and let him decide what to do with it."

"You mean there's no case now. Won't it all come out anyway?"

"I don't suppose it will be possible to keep such a story quiet, but, as far as the police are concerned, the case will be closed. Now, I really must go and let my officers know they can go home to their tea."

"We should do that too," said Graham, when Mullane had left, and they were alone again in the church. Ellie stood up to go, but Graham first slipped to his knees and bowed his head. She watched for a moment, knowing she was witnessing a very private conversation, then knelt down too and bowed her head, feeling deep within—what was it called?—the peace of God which passes all understanding.

Later, as they walked back to the Vicarage through the churchyard, Graham took Ellie's hand. The rain had stopped although the trees dripped heavily and wet grass caught at their ankles, but Ellie barely noticed anything except the warmth of his palm against hers.

"You know," he said, "when I finally stopped searching the woods and came home, I saw your bag in the hall. At first I was so relieved, because you must be alive, and then the meaning of it hit me, and it was almost worse. Please tell me that you're not going to leave me. I couldn't bear it if you did."

"I don't want to leave. I just feel I've made such a mess of things. I'll always have this added baggage now, and I'm farther than ever from being your Mrs. Vicar."

Graham was silent long enough for Ellie to wonder if he agreed, but then he said, "I didn't marry you to hire a Mrs. Vicar, Ellie. I married you because I want to spend my life with you. And, as far as baggage is concerned, you have lifted the heaviest baggage I've ever carried in my life—and at great risk to yourself."

"What do you mean?"

"You found out what happened to Louise. Without you, Isabelle and I would have had to go on thinking that her death was one of those quirks of fate that we must accept, no matter how unacceptable they seem to us. You have no idea how immeasurably grateful I am for that.

"Coming second is hard—for both of us. I've realized that over these past weeks. I mean I'm no prize-winning, sought-after poet, after all. Just a village vicar."

Ellie laughed. "Believe me, being nothing like Vito is one of your highest qualifications in my mind."

"Then you'll forgive me for ever giving you a moment's doubt? We can start again?"

"Yes, we can start again," said Ellie, "and I'm turning both cheeks to be kissed."

"Likewise I'm sure," said Graham, and, under the dripping trees, surrounded by the witnessing dead, they sealed their agreement.

Saturday, November 12

Chapter 22

The next morning Ellie and Graham went together to Kingbrook Hospital to visit Miss Worthy. Despite her bandaged head and the cast on her leg, relief had brought color and even youth back into her face.

"I'm terribly sorry for what you went through, Mrs. Kent," she said to Ellie, "and I'll have that boy on my conscience for the rest of my life. If I'd spoken up right away, he could never have got into trouble like that. But when something so devastating happens, you try to save what's left, don't you?

"It was such a miracle to have George back, after all those years, and then suddenly he was dead again. I don't understand why loving someone should have such awful consequences for so many people. We never dreamed that could happen."

"But did he really imagine he could come back and live here in Little Beecham?" asked Ellie.

She shook her head sadly. "He did. His life was nearing its end, and he wanted to come home. I have money now, you see, and he imagined that, at long last, we could carry out our old childhood dream of fixing up Beech Hall and living there."

"Emily would have had some mixed feelings about that, I expect," said Graham, and Miss Worthy nodded.

"I tried to point out the obstacles, but he couldn't see them any more. He'd waited so long to come back from the war."

"Did he ever tell you what really happened at Anzio?" asked Ellie.

"Yes, he told me everything. About Henry's death. About coming to in a field full of broken and dead bodies. How he knew he couldn't go on. He put his identity tags on a dead soldier whose body was in so many pieces that it could never be identified otherwise and ran for his life. It was an impulse, but once he'd done it there was no going back. And, in some ways, he was very equipped to do what he did.

"He spoke Italian, you see. George was always good at languages, and he was also a skilled hunter. He hoped to pass for an Italian, but he couldn't be caught by either side as long as the war was on, so he lived rough in the mountains."

"That was more than a year," said Graham. "It must have been hard to be on his own for so long."

"It was, but then the war ended. It was a very chaotic time, and at first he hoped he'd be able to figure out a way to come back to England, but the best he could do was to blend in with the thousands of other dislocated people. He found work in a vineyard in Tuscany, where he told them his name was Rodolfo Scotti. They needed help badly, so they didn't ask too many questions."

"Eventually he married a local woman, who had a very remote farm. He never told her who he really was. Can you imagine? All those years? When she died, he sold up and left for Rome. He hoped he could begin again and have a different kind of life. He changed his identity again to be sure no one connected him with Rodolfo Scotti, but he said he felt like a ghost, wandering the streets there.

"It was pure coincidence that we met. I'd always wanted to go to Italy, and finally I did. After all, if you have a bit of money, you should do the things you would enjoy, don't you think?

"None of us ever imagined that George was not dead, although, over the years, there were many times when I glimpsed someone who reminded me of him. Who gave me one of those heart-stopping moments of hope.

"But this was different. I was in St Peter's, walking around, somewhat in a daze, you know. It's all so much, the beauty of it. But then I caught sight of a man, also just standing there, looking up. I saw his profile first, but even before he turned and looked towards me, even before I could form the words in my mind, I knew it was George, and all the beauty around me vanished. The face I had longed to see, all those years, meant more to me than anything else ever could. He knew me at the same moment."

Ellie and Graham glanced at each other, reminded of when they met. How their lives had turned in a new direction from that hour.

The light went out in Miss Worthy's face, though, as she clutched Graham's hand. "At that moment, I was sure God was compensating us for our long years of loneliness. Why else had we found each other again? And yet it all turned out so badly! I just don't understand it."

Ellie hoped Graham wouldn't say, "God moves in mysterious ways his wonders to perform," and he didn't. He simply shook his head.

"I don't know," he said. "But it's not your fault that Emily or George reacted the way they did, and I doubt you could have prevented either one of them from pursuing what they wanted."

"I suppose you're right," said Miss Worthy. Tears leaked out of the corners of her eyes. "When we were young, George and I were so close. Real soul mates, in many ways, but he was always a Rutherford, and I was always a Worthy. I suppose that's why we were happiest when we assumed other identities.

"That week in Rome, we spent every minute together, and I was ready to move there in an instant. But George wouldn't have it. He loved me, but even more than he wanted to be with me, he wanted to come home.

"We agreed that I would tell no one but Louise," explained Miss Worthy. "She was the one person I had told about my writing, and I knew she would never say a word. I don't know how Emily found out, and I never imagined there was a link between Louise's death and our situation."

"I think George wrote to Louise himself. Isabelle said she received a letter from Italy that last day," said Ellie.

"I remember that," said Graham, a queer look coming over his face. "She was slitting it open to read it when we left her that afternoon. So perhaps Louise said something to Emily when she came to visit. Or Emily saw the letter by the bed." He shook his head. "However it happened, Emily seized the opportunity to make sure the information didn't go any further."

"It's hard to believe she could do such a thing. And to take such a risk! How did she know that you hadn't already read the letter yourself?"

"Graham would never read someone else's mail," said Ellie. "She must have counted on that."

"I'm not sure she thought at all," said Graham.

"And poor George was just dreaming of his homecoming all this time, never knowing how she would feel about it. Compared to Emily, he was really a simple soul. He did the wrong thing, when he was young and badly shocked, but he wasn't a bad person. Not like they'll be saying now."

"Well, he's past worrying about that now, isn't he?" said Graham.

"Speaking of home, I have something that belongs to you," said Ellie, taking a small package out of her purse.

Miss Worthy took it with shaking hands and tore off the paper. Blotches of color appeared in her cheeks, and her eyes filled again as she saw what it was: *Memoire del mio paese* by Angelo DiGuerro. When she turned to the page where it was inscribed to Cara Mia, tears streamed down her face.

"I was so frantic that day," she said. "I never expected George to show up out of the blue like that, although he talked about it often enough. And then when he arrived, I tried to convince myself that a short visit could do no harm, but he didn't see it that way. From the moment he set foot in England—once he had actually seen Beech Hall, the village, and the old familiar scenes, he said would never ever leave again. I tried to show him how impossible that was, but he didn't care.

"He insisted on going to see Emily and telling her everything. He didn't understand what it had been like for her all these years. I had told him about the window, the memorial. All the rituals Emily had created out of her brothers being dead.

"But I don't think he ever could really take it in. It was a bit like waking up in your coffin. You've been declared dead and buried, even though you're not.

"I also knew the shock of seeing him would be terrible for Emily. The anger she would feel over the years lost to grief and the blow to her pride would be unendurable."

They all fell silent, contemplating the high cost of what Mrs. Rutherford Hughes could not endure.

"Well," said Ellie, the first to stir herself. "Thank you for filling us in. We should let you rest now. But first, do you read Italian, Miss Worthy?"

"Oh, my no. I've never been good at languages."

"Then let me give you this so that you can enjoy your book." She handed the old woman a neat copy of her translation of the poems.

"Thank you, my dear. And speaking of books," she pointed to her bedside table where a copy of *Love and Desertion* lay. "It's not much of a thank you for what you did. But all of us who loved Louise do thank you."

Ellie blushed. "Thank you," she said, taking the book. "I'm delighted to have it. Now you get better soon. You have to recover in time for the coffee morning."

"Oh, dear, do you really think we should have it this year?"

"I think it's what the village needs, don't you? To get back to normal as soon as possible?"

"I do. In fact, if you do not think it would be too presumptuous, I thought of something to add to your raffle. Some books signed by Ramona Blaisdell Scott. In person."

"Oh, Miss Worthy, are you sure you really want to do that?"

"Yes, my dear, I think the time for disguises has come to an end at last."

Epilogue

Chapter 23

In the weeks that followed, the village did slowly return to normal. Emily Rutherford Hughes was buried quietly in her family's vault, and, when her will was read, it turned out that she'd left all of her assets to a trust for St. Michael's.

Graham was both pleased and dismayed by this windfall. "There's no question the funds are a great boon for St. Michael's, but I'm afraid we'll be known forever as the church funded by a murderer."

His concerns did seem justified by the increased number of visitors who came to see the peace window and the memorial stone to the Rutherford brothers. Mrs. Bigelow finally got tired of watching and kept her front curtains drawn shut.

When Michael-John Parker came to tea at the Vicarage and made his proposal to take Beech Hall off the church's hands, Graham and Ellie sat up late, deliberating what to do.

The next day, Ellie went to The Chestnut Tree and told him, "We decided on 'dust unto dust,' I'm afraid. We think it's what the family would have wanted."

Michael-John smiled ruefully. "All right then. As long as I can continue to visit. Pick up the rubbish. I've almost finished my family history, which, as it turns out, has a sensational ending."

"I'll look forward to reading it," she said.

Plans for the Christmas coffee morning on the first Saturday in December went forward, but first they had one more funeral to attend.

It was Miss Worthy who planned the service, and it was her choice to hold it at Beech Hall rather than at the church. "This was the home he wanted to return to for all those years," she told the small gathering of family and friends. She stood before them in a dignified black dress, wearing a corsage that Ellie had bought for her.

Graham read the funeral service, and Ellie recited one of the Angelo DiGuerro poems in Italian and English. Then Seamus recited "The Soldier" again, his hair blowing in the wintry breeze.

When he finished, Miss Worthy stood at the empty window frame overlooking the frozen frosty fields that glinted in the morning sun. She opened a small wooden box and invited them each to scatter a few of the ashes.

Charlotte was nearly overcome by the romantic stature her great-aunt had achieved and stood by her, clutching Dolphin, with an awed expression. Even Whistler looked solemn as he and Michael-John observed this final Rutherford family ceremony.

When they had all taken a turn, Priscilla Worthy lifted the box and scattered the remaining ashes. They glittered as the wind took them. She watched silently as they disappeared, then said:

"Rest well now, my dear, under our English heaven."

About the Author

Alice K. Boatwright is the author of the Ellie Kent mysteries, which debuted with *Under an English Heaven* and continue with the sequel, *What Child Is This? Under an English Heaven* was awarded the 2016 Mystery and Mayhem Grand Prize for Best Mystery from the Chanticleer International Book Awards. Boatwright is also the author of *Collateral Damage*, an award-winning collection of novellas about the long-term impact of the Vietnam War. She lived in Oxfordshire and Paris for 10 years before returning to the U.S., where she now lives in the Pacific Northwest.

For the latest news about the Ellie Kent mysteries, visit http://alicekboatwright.com and sign up for a newsletter at http://eepurl.com/cER4Cj

Photo: Maria Aragon

What Child Is This?
Read an excerpt from the sequel to *Under an English Heaven.*

Tuesday, December 22
Winter Solstice

Chapter 1

All we want for Christmas is our Anthea. The MISSING posters were tacked to every telephone pole on the high street of Little Beecham. The message in bold red type created a plaintive contrast to the evergreen swags and fairy lights that decorated the honey-colored limestone cottages and shops of the Cotswold village.

Ellie Kent could only imagine the need that had driven someone to hang them on a day like this when the temperature had been dropping steadily from raw to bitter cold. And now it was snowing. The swirling flakes that made the village look like an enchanted snow globe were quickly puckering the signs. There were more shoppers about than usual, but they hurried past without a glance, heads bent against the storm, eager to be home for their tea. It was only three o'clock, but the turn toward dusk had begun.

Ellie tightened her grip on her own packages and leaned in for a closer look at the photo of a slim, dark-haired young woman. It showed her laughing, with her arms spread wide as if to embrace the world and her future. A student at Oxford, the poster said.

Name: Anthea Davies
Age: 20
Last seen: 1st October in Oxford

She studied the face and felt an uncomfortable twinge of recognition. Anthea Davies looked a lot like she had at that age.

All we want for Christmas is our Anthea. Please help.
The number was local.

But there was really nothing she could do to help, Ellie told herself, as she walked quickly away. She had only moved to Little Beecham from San Francisco in the autumn and still had trouble navigating the winding lanes from there to anywhere. She was more likely to get lost herself than to find a missing person.

Still. She couldn't help wondering what had happened to Anthea, whose joyful confidence had taken her down some wrong road. That was another thing Ellie recognized.

As she approached The Vicarage, a rambling brick Georgian house that stood at the end of the high street next to the church, she turned her focus back to the challenge she had already taken on: what she had come to think of as the 40 days of Christmas.

When she was younger, she had always enjoyed Christmas, but, since the end of her first marriage (admittedly, a major wrong road), she had limited her holiday celebrations to the obligatory party for the English Department at the university where she taught, Chinese food with friends on Christmas Eve, and Christmas Day with her parents where they ate turkey and exchanged books.

She had fantasized about someday spending this time of year in the place she'd studied for so long, imagining an idyllic season of frosty winds and candlelit Christmas trees, roasting chestnuts and pink-cheeked carolers, flaming puddings and the appearance of a ghost or three. Now she was here—and it was even snowing—but she was not on a vacation. Four months ago she had married Graham Kent, the vicar of Little Beecham's Church of St. Michael and All Angels, and that meant she was in for what she jokingly called "the full English" when it came to Christmas. Today was day 25, starting from the church's annual Christmas coffee morning, with 15 days to go until the three kings would arrive in Bethlehem, and the season would be over.

Today at least she could cross off one big item on her to-do list. She had settled on her family gifts, which she purchased after endless rumination at the village antique shop, The Chestnut Tree. Her friend Michael-John Parker owned the shop, and he had congratulated her roundly on her final choices: an antique rosewood fife with brass fittings for Graham and delicate gold Victorian earrings for his daughter—her new stepdaughter—Isabelle.

"Now I hope you'll begin to relax and enjoy yourself," said Michael-John, as he handed her a gift bag embossed with a spreading chestnut tree. "You should be excited. I'm sure the Kent family Christmas will be just like one of those Leech illustrations of Dickens that we all love so much."

"I am excited," said Ellie. "I'm just having trouble seeing myself as part of the picture, instead of looking at it."

"Put on your paper crown, say 'Please pass the bread sauce', and you'll fit in perfectly."

"Bread sauce?" said Ellie. "Isn't that an oxymoron?"

He laughed. "Oh, you do have a lot to learn," he said, and wished her luck.

She thanked him for his help and for the luck, both of which she surely needed. Even Graham, who appeared to love Christmas unreservedly, had looked tired that morning, hunched over his typewriter, banging out yet another sermon conveying the world-changing importance of one long-ago birth to people addled with more immediate expectations—both good and bad.

All we want for Christmas is our Anthea. Please help.

The electric candles in The Vicarage windows were already lit, a welcome sight twinkling through the blue dusk and falling snow. Ellie crossed the snowy yard to the back door, as always a little amazed that this 18th century Georgian house was where she now lived.

The kitchen was so toasty from the day's baking that Hector, their rough-coated Jack Russell, barely opened his eyes to greet her then promptly went back to sleep in his basket by the Aga. Mrs. Finch, The Vicarage's longtime housekeeper, had left for the day, but on the farmhouse table that doubled as a worktop, a new batch of her mini mince pies was cooling on racks. Ellie had begun the season eating these traditional pastries with gusto, but by now the smell alone gave her heartburn. She stowed her gifts at the back of the china cupboard and went to find Graham.

When they'd met at her parents' home in Berkeley nearly a year ago, Ellie hadn't known Graham was a vicar. She had dropped by to see how her mother was faring after some minor surgery and found her on the patio drinking iced tea and carrying on a lively discussion about the subject–object dichotomy with Ellie's philosophy professor father and an attractive Englishman. A widower, it turned out, a few years older than Ellie, but with a lanky body, gingery hair, and lively blue eyes that gave him an aura of boyishness.

Of course she joined in the discussion of whether the subjective realm of perception and belief is separate from the world of events and objects—and ended up staying for dinner. Of course she rode back to San Francisco on the BART train with the Englishman, who happened to be renting a room not far from where she lived while he was in the Bay Area on sabbatical. Of course, she saw him again, the very next day. She had been certain from the first moment that this was not a wrong road taken, but who ever knew where a new road would lead?

The door to the study where Graham worked and conducted parish business was closed, but she could hear the clatter of typewriter keys, which meant he was alone. Ellie went back to the kitchen and put together a tray for tea then returned, saying, "Room service," as she opened the door.

He pulled a piece of paper out of the typewriter with a flourish, turned to her, and smiled. Dressed in old corduroys, denim shirt, and a sweater with patched elbows, he was what she thought of as "her Graham," not the priest in Holy Orders whose closest ties were beyond her comprehension.

"Just what I need," he said, helping himself to a McVitie's digestive biscuit coated with dark chocolate.

"Biscuits, tea, or me?" asked Ellie, as she handed him a mug and settled into the chair beside his desk.

"You, of course. But the tea and biscuits are brilliant too."

A mountain of crumpled paper had been consigned to the wastebasket, and three neat piles of pages were lined up on the desk. How he could write on a typewriter was beyond her comprehension too.

He yawned, stretched his full length, and took off his tortoiseshell glasses. "I'm always amazed when I finish. Until I get there, it seems like I never will," he said, coming back to upright.

"I know what you mean. So what did you decide to say about the virgin mother and her little babe?"

"I can't tell you," he said, with a twinkle in his eyes. "It would spoil the surprise."

"You mean I'll have to come to church to find out?"

He nodded. "All three times."

"It's the magic number," she said and leaned over to give him a kiss.

The snow was still falling at five o'clock when Graham set off to meet the members of Beecham Morris, the Morris dance side he belonged to. As part of a longstanding tradition, they were performing a medieval mummers' play at several pubs in the area that evening. This was called a Christmas play, but it was really about the Winter Solstice: the death of the old year and the birth of the new.

Ellie had never given much thought to the Solstice before, but in a place where the shortest day offered only seven hours, 49 minutes, and 45 seconds of light, she could see why you'd want to celebrate the fact that the next day would be one second longer. According to Graham, the date of Christmas had been arbitrarily set in December to piggyback on the hope generated by this seasonal change.

He was playing Saint George this year and, before he left, he put on his costume with its tin knight's helmet and demonstrated his sword-fighting moves for Ellie and Hector, swinging and thrusting at an imaginary dragon. Ellie was impressed—she hadn't known he was on the fencing team when he was at Oxford—but Hector was beside himself, barking and leaping until he collapsed, exhausted with pleasure.

When she was alone, she tidied up the kitchen and then sat idly watching the snow beat against the window and transform the landscape of church, churchyard, and the woods beyond. She had been warned not to expect a white

Christmas. The "snow on snow, snow on snow" described in one of her favorite carols was hardly more true for Oxfordshire than it was for Bethlehem, and a cold, dismal rain was far more likely. Still, this storm showed no signs of stopping, so maybe she was going to be lucky. Her first English Christmas would include all the special effects.

As she drank a cup of chamomile tea, her thoughts drifted and eddied from memories of Christmases past to the face of Anthea Davies, who might or might not fulfill her parents' wish by turning up for the holiday. Who might or might not turn up anywhere ever again.

Ellie had run away once, when she was 16—even younger than Anthea. At the time she'd thought of it as a highly romantic adventure—a lark—and a chance to show she was not a child any longer. She had never even considered the impact on her parents until she saw the look on her father's face when he found her three days later in a motel with the boy she loved. It was years before he could say out loud how terrified he'd been that he would never see her again, and 20 years on, Ellie knew her mother hadn't entirely forgiven her for not being the girl she thought she was.

Three months was a lot longer than three days though. She checked the clock and decided she had time to see what was online about Anthea Davies' disappearance before she had to get to the pub for the mummers' play. She went up to her study on the third floor, which was her little bit of home filled with the things she had brought from California. Moving aside a pile of books on Jane Austen that she had been using to research a book idea, she set down her mug of tea, opened her laptop, and entered the words: Anthea Davies Oxford.

There had been a flurry of coverage in the Oxford and local papers with stories illustrated by the same photo as appeared on the poster. This had apparently been taken in Oxford, and Anthea had emailed it to her parents on the first of October with a brief message saying she would see them soon, but that was the last time they heard from her.

She had spent the summer in London, working as an intern at the Joffrey Museum of British History, and had left her job and lodging there as scheduled at the end of September. Her parents expected her to visit before the start of the Michelmas term and then join the other students, with whom she shared a flat in Oxford, but she had never arrived at either place.

Arthur and Frances Davies of Pidlington reported her missing on October 7th, and the police had launched an investigation. Although there was evidence, in addition to the photo, that confirmed she was in Oxford on the first of the month, no trace of her had been found since. Detective Inspector Derek Mullane of the Thames Valley Constabulary said the police were doing everything they could to locate Miss Davies, and members of the public were urged to call if they had any information. But the story petered out fairly quickly. You could only report that there was no new information so often. No wonder her parents were desperate.

Ellie checked the places she knew students went online, but Anthea Davies was apparently not a fan of social media. The only thing she found was a Facebook page that offered the minimum of public information and a photo that appeared to be Anthea with her back to the camera and only a suggestion of her face looking over her shoulder. On October 18th, a Melanie Thomas had posted: "PM me," but if there had been a reply, it was not visible. Ellie looked at Melanie's page and learned that she was also an undergraduate at Oxford but all of her other information was private.

The village of Pidlington, where the Davies family lived, was about 10 miles southwest of Little Beecham. So why had posters about Anthea's disappearance been put up in their village? Did she have connections here? And why were they put up now, so long after she had last been heard from?

Perhaps her parents were blanketing the area, hoping to stir up some fresh information. Losing a daughter was not, after all, something you could easily come to accept and choose to move on. Also it was Christmas: the season when your happiness and all of your relationships come under a microscope that defines your life. How well it is—or isn't—going.

All we want for Christmas is our Anthea. Please help.

She put her computer on sleep and then pawed through a Plexiglas box that held business cards and other scraps of paper until she found the one she wanted. On the front it said Detective Inspector Derek Mullane with the seal of the Thames Valley Constabulary. On the back, his mobile phone number was written in his awkward sloping hand.

The snow was still coming down quickly when Ellie walked to The Three Lambs on the high street. There were few streetlights in the village, but the golden squares of the lamp-lit windows illuminated the way and reminded her of the old-fashioned Advent calendar Graham had put on the mantel in the sitting room. Her boots squeaked, and she tipped her face to feel the icy flakes kiss her cheeks. There was something wonderful about snow that made it seem like all should be right in the world, even though you knew it wasn't.

The Lambs was surprisingly crowded for a Tuesday night. Dark and low-ceilinged, Little Beecham's only pub prided itself on not giving in to new marketing ploys, such as white tablecloths and posh food, and mainly catered to the locals as a place for a quiet pint, a bag of crisps, and a good gossip. Ellie recognized a few faces—Mrs. Wiggins from the village shop and Mrs. Tiddington, the butcher's wife—but she also received looks that made it clear that she was recognized as an incomer, despite wearing an ancient Barbour parka she'd found in the coat closet, jeans, and wellingtons.

She was standing uncertainly with her pint of Hooky Bitter, looking for a place to sit, when a familiar voice called "Over here, Guv!" and she saw her friend Morag MacDonald's son Seamus waving to her. Relieved, she waved back and made her way through the jostling crowd to where he and his mother were sitting.

Like herself a former teacher, Morag was the first friend Ellie had made in the village, and 14-year-old Seamus had become a good friend too. With their dark curly hair, fair skin, and pink cheeks, the two were as unmistakably related as a pair of twins.

"Wow," she said, as she slid into a chair at their small corner table. "I had no idea a mummers' play would draw a standing-room-only crowd in Little Beecham."

Morag laughed and patted her hand. "I hate to disillusion you, but I expect the weather has more to do with it than the mummers. We wanted to go to the cinema, but the roads were so rubbish, we turned back."

"I think it was fate that we've met. The game is afoot, you know," Seamus said, taking a damp copy of the MISSING poster out of his pocket. "Have you seen this?"

"I have," said Ellie, not quite liking the eager look on Seamus's face. His ambition was to be a private detective, and he thought there was no reason to wait until he grew up to pursue this career.

"Don't you think we should help? I mean, they're asking everyone, aren't they?"

"Seamus, what are you talking about—the game is afoot?" said Morag, taking the flyer. She frowned. "This does not look like a game to me. And since when do you call Ellie 'Guv'? Have you both joined the police force?"

Seamus glared at his mother. "We did solve a murder together, you know. Better than the police," he claimed, and this was more or less true. Soon after she arrived in Little Beecham, Ellie had found a dead man in the churchyard and had ended up trying to discover what happened if only to fend off the suggestion that she was responsible for the death herself. Seamus and his network of friends had proved a valuable asset in finding the truth.

"But, Seamus, that was different. I was forced to become involved by the circumstances. I had to clear my name. This really isn't any of my business."

"So you don't want to help?" he asked, and Ellie was glad that Morag did not give her time to answer.

"Whether *you* want to help or not, you are not going off looking for missing girls," she said. "I am taking you to your dad's parents tomorrow so you can celebrate Christmas with them. Remember?"

The boy scowled and shrank back in his chair with his arms crossed. "And you'll spend all the time I'm gone with Crispix, I suppose."

"Crispix?" asked Ellie, pleased to find the subject changing.

"He's not a cereal. His name is Crispin," said Morag. For Ellie, she added, "He's a former colleague from Shepherd's Hill School, and I've been seeing him a bit."

This was news. In the past Morag had claimed she was off men forever since her divorce from Seamus's father.

"You mean Crispin—like in *Henry the Fifth*? St. Crispin's Crispian?" Ellie asked.

"Yes. And he's really a very nice man, even though Seamus can't abide him."

"I just hope I won't have to abide with him, that's all. You hardly know him, and he already acts like he's moved in with us."

"Seamus, you sound jealous," said Ellie, teasing, and the boy's face flared pink.

"I am not. I'd just sooner be here doing something useful than off at my gran's playing darts with my cousins. I already launched my inquiries this afternoon."

"Meaning what?" asked Ellie, but before he could reply, the pub lights flashed twice and, across the crowded room, chattering voices died down.

Then John Tiddington, local butcher and leader of Beecham Morris, strode through the front door dressed as Father Christmas with a dramatic flourish of blowing snow. "Here come I, old Father Christmas!" he bellowed, "Welcome or welcome not, I hope old Father Christmas will ne'er be forgot!"

A few girls giggled, and someone shouted, "Welcome not!" But he was quickly drowned out by a chorus of "Welcome!" and the crowd tightened up to make room for the mummers who danced in dressed as Saint George, the Turkish Knight, Princess Sabra, the Doctor, the Fool, and the

Dragon. A musician playing a pipe and tabor brought up the rear.

A few people turned away to watch sports on a silent TV hanging behind the bar, but most were prepared to ooh-and-ah in exchange for the novelty of having a green dragon and a lot of sword fighting enliven an evening at the pub.

The story, with its mish-mash of characters from the Crusades to mythology, didn't make much sense to Ellie. Nonetheless, the singsong speeches and cheerful music, the worn felt costumes, and slapstick action charmed her completely.

Graham threw himself into his role as Saint George, getting loud cheers as he rescued the Princess, killed the Knight, and slayed the Dragon, though at the cost of his own life. There was a hush when they all lay still on the floor, until the Doctor's silly incantations brought them back from the dead. Then the audience clapped and stamped their feet as the mummers, with clashing swords and jingling bells, came together for the closing sword dance.

Did the crowd gathered at The Three Lambs know—or care—that for centuries this story had represented the return of light and life? The triumph of faith over fear? Probably not. But when Father Christmas circulated among them, saying, "Come throw in your money and think it no wrong," they dug into their pockets to give to the poor anyway.

Ellie put a five-pound note in the basket, thinking how perverse it was that every person who wished her "Happy Christmas" reminded her sharply that she was in a foreign country, while this medieval play made her feel that she had at last found her way to where she belonged in the world. How did that work? Which was the true truth? She had no idea.

Nevertheless, when it was all over, and her grimy, sweaty Saint George came through the crowd to claim her, she felt proud and happy. They had a pint with the other mummers and their friends, then there was a rush of good nights and good wishes.

"I'll let you know what I find out," said Seamus, as Morag urged him toward the door with a goodbye wave to Ellie and Graham.

"Find out about what?" asked Graham, when he and Ellie had stepped out into the snow. It glittered in the lights from the pub, and the fresh, cold air was a relief after the stifling atmosphere inside.

"He's all gung-ho to help to find that missing girl."

"What missing girl?" asked Graham.

"Never mind about that now," said Ellie, putting her arm through his. "Let's take a walk in the snow before bed," and they did. But later, she found it hard not to mind and lay awake for a long time thinking of that plea:

All we want for Christmas is our Anthea. Please help.

If you enjoyed this excerpt, you can purchase the entire book at your favorite online retailer.

CPSIA information can be obtained
at www.ICGtesting.com
Printed in the USA
LVOW10s1623250518
578520LV00001B/274/P

JUL 2 3 2018

9 781939 816368